The Weir House

EVE BRAYLE, brought up to a life of luxury, finds herself suddenly penniless and faced with the alternative of discovering a job without any training or marrying Phillip Shawn, whom she does not love but to whom she has inadvertently become indebted.

Out of the blue comes Lewis Belamie with an extraordinary proposition; he offers her the 'job' of posing as his fiancée for a week to enable him to qualify for a fortune which he hopes to inherit.

When she goes to the Weir House, she finds the whole course of her life changed by the man she meets, and the blithe spirit of adventure with which she had set out gives way to deeper and more vulnerable feelings.

In *The Weir House* Netta Muskett's admirers will find all her familiar qualities of warmth, excitement and feeling.

NETTA MUSKETT

The Weir House

The Valentine Romance Club

THE VALENTINE ROMANCE CLUB
178–202 Great Portland Street, London, W.1

First published by
Hutchinson & Co. (Publishers) Ltd., 1962
This edition 1963

This book has been set in Baskerville type
face. It has been printed in Great Britain by
The Anchor Press, Ltd., in Tiptree, Essex, on
Antique Wove paper.

I

IT WAS oppressively hot in the little top flat with the sun pouring in at the one inadequate dormer window and beating down through the roof and the low ceiling. Half a century ago it would have been called what it was, an attic, and considered quite suitable for the poor little servants who toiled unceasingly between it and the basement kitchen and need not be thought of as human beings at all, but now, with a tiny kitchen and even smaller bathroom, it was called a 'flat' and charged for accordingly and people like Marcia thought themselves very lucky to have it.

But even Marcia, used to the vagaries of the English climate, was sweltering in its heat today, and Eve, who had never spent as much as six months consecutively in her native land, thought longingly of mountain tops and of tree-shaded beaches where soft-footed native servants ministered to one's every need, of ice clinking against glass. . . .

She had cast aside even her briefs and bra, for there was nobody there but Marcia, and certainly no soft-footed servants with cold drinks. She turned over and lay face downwards on the old couch, her hands cupping her small, pointed chin, studying her reflection in the mirror fastened to the wall. It was a charming reflection but it gave her little pleasure. In the greater part of twenty-two years she had become too well used to it, the mop of silky hair of pale, silvery gold, the warm grey of eyes in which sadness still lingered, the generous-lipped mouth made for love and laughter but which at this moment drooped a little. With what? Not discontent, for in spite of what had happened to her, she was not a discontented person.

5

Dissatisfied then? Yes, perhaps that; dissatisfied not with life but with herself, with her inability to take it in her two hands and cope with it.

Marcia cast a loving, thoughtful look at her from behind her thick-lensed glasses, an anxious look as if she shared her thoughts.

'A penny for them,' she said, for it was some time since Eve had spoken, that in itself noteworthy.

'I was taking stock of myself, wondering what my market value is.'

Marcia, who was thirty-five, squarish and plain, smiled. Now and then, particularly since Eve had come to live with her, she envied girls who looked like that but for the most part had come to accept her place in the world, a working world in which her good brain had had to make up for everything else she had missed. Still, no woman in her right senses would have preferred brains to looking like Eve if she had any choice.

'And what conclusion have you come to?' she asked, biting off the cotton with her strong white teeth. She was darning towels.

'That I haven't got any real value,' said Eve with a sigh. 'What good am I? I'm passably good-looking, but it ends there. I've never learned to be anything but decorative. I can speak several languages but couldn't write any of them grammatically. I can't even spell my own language, can't use a typewriter, couldn't possibly learn shorthand and you know what I can do with the grocery bill! I can add up six items and get six different answers, and when you just run a casual eye over it you get a seventh one which is always right! So we come back to the original question, what use am I?'

Marcia's smile deepened. Eve's face wore that expression she had come to know so well, part angry with frustration, part laughing at herself for her inadequacies. Why, when you looked like Eve and had such a gay, courageous spirit, had you to be any 'use' in the world? Things like shorthand and typewriting and book-keeping could surely be left to the Marcias of the world. But wisely when Eve was in this mood, she did not say so.

6

'We shall find something for you to do, dear,' she said, starting on another towel. 'That photography business wasn't a good idea, was it?'

Eve made a grimace.

'You're telling me! How was I to know that all that filthy beast wanted was to get me dressed in less and less so that he could paw me about? I soon packed him up, but what do I do next? Yes, I know what that look in your eye means and what's on the tip of your tongue so you may as well say it. It's Phillip,' and she flung herself restlessly about on the couch. Evidently Phillip was not a palatable thought.

Marcia said nothing. She did not want Eve, or anyone else, to know how she herself thought about Phillip Shawn. That would have to lie buried in her heart for ever.

'I'm sorry about Phillip,' went on Eve reflectively after that little pause. 'He's got most things, hasn't he? He's not really old, and he's good-looking and he's rich and he's in love with me. If I could bring myself to marry him, it would solve all my problems, but – oh Marcia, I just can't think of him like that. Perhaps I've known him too long, nearly all my life in fact, more – more like darling Daddy.'

She was schooling herself by slow and painful degrees to speak of her beloved dead.

Richard Brayle and his only child had been very close. After his wife had died in giving birth to Eve, he had lived for two things only, his daughter and making money. He was a gambler with the Midas touch and had interests all over the world and since he could never bear to be parted from Eve, he had trailed her about with him. Nurses and governesses had gone with them until he decided that with the smattering of education she had learned all that she needed to know, and he had dispensed with them, leaving the two of them in perfect comradeship. She knew every capital city in the world but had never had a home nor felt the lack of one, and since none of the men who had fallen in love with her or with her father's money could ever stand up to the comparison with him, she had never minded the broken friendships nor wanted to turn them into romances.

Phillip Shawn had been the one stable thing in her life, her father's friend though a good many years younger and his business manager when he needed one. It was through Phillip that she met his cousin, Marcia. The Brayles were in Bermuda when he paid one of his periodic visits to them and when Richard learned that he had a cousin recovering from a serious illness, he at once cabled her the money to fly out to them. That had been so typical of him, casual, kindly, generous even to a complete stranger, and when the inevitable crash came, Marcia was quick to offer the bereaved, bewildered girl a home which she knew was unsuitable and could be only temporary. The flat in a London attic was a far cry from the luxury in which Eve had spent the first twenty-two years of her life.

It was in Rome that Richard Brayle was killed in a car crash. He was alone in the car and the accident did not involve anyone else, but, carefully planned and staged though it had been, he had slipped up on one essential and after considerable investigation and argument, it was decided that it was not accidental and the company with which he was heavily insured, refused to pay. His last gamble, with his life as the stake, had failed and Eve was left with nothing, not even a home.

Her father had so far prepared for his death as to have asked Phillip Shawn to come to Rome so that he was actually on his way there at the time of the car crash and arrived in time to deal with the many matters involved, including his discovery, long anticipated, that Richard Brayle was in financial difficulties.

Too crushed and heart-broken by grief to be told the full truth, Eve accepted gratefully Marcia's offer of a temporary home, but Phillip had enjoined on his cousin that she was not to know for the present her actual circumstances.

'She'll have to know some time, Phillip,' said Marcia, but she already knew what he was going to say and the last faint hope which she had held in her heart for so long died.

'I'm hoping that she will marry me, though I must leave her a little while before I ask her. Her father knew and approved and I think that was in his mind when he asked me to go to Rome. Of course, I could not put you to the expense of keeping

8

her, and Eve would not anticipate any such thing, so I will make an arrangement with the bank to cover any cheques she may draw for the time being.'

It was by sheer chance that Eve discovered the position, and she was shocked and appalled. She had had to know something of the position, but not that she was without any money at all. Slightly but not unduly alarmed by an evasive reply to an enquiry as to her bank balance, she had rung up her father's brokers, with whom she had been on friendly terms for years, and told them blithely to 'sell something' and the truth had come out that there was nothing to sell.

Poor Phillip had born the brunt of the discovery.

'You mean that you've been financing me, *keeping* me, all this time?' she raged. 'Even paying Marcia for me? Covering all the cheques I've been gaily paying under the impression that it was my own money? You've put me in a degrading position! What right had you to do this to me?'

'I hoped you would give me the right, Eve. I love you and want to marry you. I think you must know that.'

'So you intended to buy me?' she spat at him. 'To put me in such a position that I should have to marry you?'

'Eve dear, no. Nothing like that. Do believe me. I thought – hoped – that you might come to care for me enough. Your father hoped it too. He – he knew I should look after you, whatever happened.'

'So he was in it too? When he knew I should have nothing? Didn't he know me well enough to know I could never do that?'

That was bitter indeed and there was little which Phillip could find to say which could alleviate the bitterness.

'He thought, as I did, darling, that you would be able to care for me. There was no one else, was there?'

'No, and there won't be. Have I got to find a man to keep me? Is that all I'm good for? I can work. I'll find myself a job as thousands of other girls have to do. And somehow I'll pay you back every penny you've spent on me if it takes me the rest of my life!'

'Eve, at least not that,' he pleaded with her. 'I realise now that I made a bad mistake in not telling you at the beginning how matters stood, but we hoped to get the insurance money so that you'd have had that at least.'

She brushed that aside contemptuously.

'The fact remains that I have been living on you, and I'm not going to do it any longer.'

'I wish you would marry me, Eve. I love you with all my heart,' he said so earnestly that in spite of her anger, some of the resentment died and she knew she was being unfair and ungrateful to him. After all, what would have become of her without him and Marcia?

'I'm sorry, Phillip. I believe you do love me or you would not have done what you have, but I don't feel in the least that way about you and I don't think I ever shall.'

'You won't break with me altogether? We can still be friends?'

She made a little gesture of hopeless impotence. What was she to do? At the moment she could not manage without him.

'I can't very well help myself, can I? Not until I can find myself a job. But what on earth can I do? I don't know anything.'

'I could perhaps find you a job—' he began.

'No, Phillip, thank you. I know what that would mean. You'd skate round amongst your friends and I'd still be living on your charity. I'll find something myself.'

'Well, talk it over with Marcia. She may be able to suggest something,' he said unhopefully.

That had been a month ago, but so far they had not been able to find anything she could do. Since she had a working knowledge of several languages, she thought she might be an air hostess but found herself crowded out by girls who had the better standard of education required by the air lines. Hers, in spite of the governesses and tutors, had been haphazard and she had certainly passed no examinations. She had tried being a model for clothes and for photographic advertising, but they had been casual jobs which had not lasted. She had been taken on at one of the big West End shops as a sales girl, but one day had been enough to show her that she had no aptitude for dealing with difficult customers and she had not gone back for a second day.

She had 'forgiven' Phillip for what he had done, but she drew no more cheques on her non-existent banking account and had ruthlessly sold what little jewellery she had in order to pay her share of the housekeeping expenses of the little flat, and had insisted on giving Phillip the rest. She had, in fact, little jewellery of any value, for her father had kept in safe custody for her the few good pieces she had, and those had gone in the final attempt to rescue himself before the end came.

It was a day in June when all London was sweltering in the sudden heat which had confounded all the weather experts and set minds longingly on holidays, in Eve's case unavailingly. Marcia's was not due until the end of August, and though she had begged in vain for Eve to go with her, saying that she could quite well afford to pay for two, Eve was adamant. It did not, however, prevent her from thinking of the sea, ice-cold, with cool grey rocks and no need to worry, at least for the moment, about ways and means. Still, she was not going to let Marcia pay for it; nor had she for one moment changed her mind about marrying Phillip, though he still hoped she would.

He was taking her out to dinner tonight, which had meant that she could go without her lunch, and she heard his voice in the hall when Marcia let him in.

She cast a last critical glance at herself in the mirror. She had never worn mourning for her father, but she was in black tonight because it was thin and cool and also because it so well became her fair skin and her silvery gold hair and eyes of dark, warm grey. She neither needed nor wore much make-up, but tonight, in a mood of defiance, she had used a vivid lipstick on the generous mouth which had found so much to laugh at in her short life, so much fun, so much careless gaiety.

Just now there was not much to laugh at, but she smiled determinedly back at the face in the mirror and turned to go into the sitting-room.

Phillip Shawn's eyes warmed with love.

He was of medium height, had thick brown hair just touched with grey, and looked exactly what he was, a steady, successful business man who could meet anyone on his own terms and go into any company sure of his acceptance. He was shrewd, clever, kind – but oh, how dull! thought Eve. If ever she had thoughts of spending the rest of her life with him, the first sight of him always dispelled those thoughts.

'You look lovely,' he said, and Marcia, hearing his tone and seeing the look in his eyes, felt the sword-thrust in her heart.

Eve accepted the tribute of voice and eyes with a careless smile.

'Where are we going?' she asked.

'I thought you might like that new place, the Ecarté.'

She gave a shrug. One place with Phillip as her escort was as good as another. If only he wouldn't keep talking about marriage!

But of course he did.

It was when she spoke of the need to get herself a job, though by so doing she had walked straight into it.

He leaned across the table and touched the hand which had been toying with her wine glass.

'Darling, you know there's absolutely no need for you to do any such thing,' he said. 'If only you would marry me —'

She was between anger and distress. She hated to hurt any-one, and she owed so much to Phillip in other ways than mere money.

'Dear Phillip, I know how you feel about me, but I couldn't,' she said. 'I like you enormously, but only as a friend, and if I every marry, I should want a lot more than that.'

'Isn't friendship and liking enough for a start? At least let me go on taking care of you.'

'How can I, when I know I shan't feel any more? It sounds beastly to say it, but isn't it better to be honest? Please believe me and accept it, Phillip. I – I think I'll go and powder my nose and when I come back, we'll change the subject,' and she rose precipitately from the table and made her escape.

She spent as long as she could in the powder room, acutely distressed for him. Why on earth could she not take the easiest way out and marry him? Yet she knew she could not. No man had ever reached the inner fastness of her heart, but she knew that some day, somewhere, she would meet a man who would. Where would they be then, she and Phillip and this unknown man?

At last she knew she must go back to him but hoped he would not still be looking at her with the eyes of a faithful spaniel.

Then, making her way along the narrow corridor which would take her back to him she stopped at the sound of her name.

'Miss Brayle! It is, isn't it?'

She looked at the speaker blankly for a moment and then recognition of him dawned.

'Why – you're Mr Belamie, aren't you?'

'Yes. We met in Cairo.'

He was a thin young man with a slight stoop, and he wore thick, wide-rimmed glasses through which he continued to stare at her in a disconcerting fashion.

She remembered the occasion and laughed reminiscently.

'Wandering round the pyramids,' she said. 'I'd gone on horseback but you had a camel you were distinctly nervous of! I remember that it reminded me of a haughty and supercilious old lady in the way it looked at you!' and she laughed again.

He responded with a nervous smile, but for some reason he seemed to want to linger.

'You – you're with friends?' he asked.

'With one friend, yes,' she said, and it suddenly occurred to her that if she could annex him for a few minutes it would help her over the difficulty of joining Phillip again.

'You have friends here as well?' she asked.

'Er – yes. I came with my brother and his fiancée but I can't see them anywhere. They're probably dancing.'

'Take me back to my escort, will you? He's Phillip Shawn. I don't suppose you know him, by any chance?'

'No, I'm afraid I don't, but of course I shall be – er – delighted – er—'

He followed her as she threaded her way between the dancers and back to the table where Philip was watching for her rather anxiously, made the two men known to each other and kept Mr Belamie talking for a few moments, after which he surprised her by asking her to dance.

'That is, if you don't mind, Mr – er – Shawn?' he added.

'Phillip won't mind,' she said airily, and the next moment she was drifting away in his rather loose and clumsy hold.

Almost immediately, he greatly surprised her.

'Can I see you again?' he asked. 'Will you meet me somewhere? Tomorrow?'

She stifled a gasp of astonishment. It was the last thing she had expected.

'Well—' she began uncertainly, thinking his manner strange, its urgency desperate.

'You're not engaged to him – or anything, are you?'

'To Phillip? No, he's just an old friend. A friend of my father's, actually. My father – died, six months ago.'

Why, she wondered, was she telling him that?

'Yes, I – read about it in the papers. I didn't know we should meet again, of course. I – I remember you.'

Men usually did remember her, of course, though she seldom remembered them. She wondered if he thought she was well off and wanted to borrow from her, or introduce to her notice some scheme of his own. It did not seem the ordinary attraction that held him and she was intrigued.

'Yes?' she asked encouragingly.

'Will you meet me? Tomorrow? Or soon? Anywhere you like.'

'Why?' she asked, and the question did not seem superfluous.

'Somewhere where we can talk. Will you?'

The urgency in his voice was growing and though she could not imagine danger mixed up with this young man, she would not mind a little danger. Life was infinitely dull at the moment.

'All right,' she agreed after a moment's hesitation. 'Where do you suggest?'

'Are you living in London?'

'For the moment, yes. I'm staying with a friend in Baron's Court.'

'Could you meet me – I mean – how about lunch somewhere?'

Lunch? She was not sure about that and there was something furtive about him. It might be better to meet somewhere in the open, so that she could escape from whatever it was without having to flee from a table and cause a scene.

'Let's meet in the Park and decide about lunch then. Say twelve o'clock. The Park's a bit of a mess now with all the alterations, so how about the gate in Knightsbridge near Hyde Park Hotel? You know the one I mean?'

'Yes. I'll meet you there. At twelve? You will come?'

'Yes, I'll come – though I'm usually late! That's one reason why I can't keep a job.'

'A job? You don't mean you have to *work*?'

He was startled, but not displeased, so it could not be money he was after. She had thought it as well to let him know she hadn't any.

'Oh yes,' she said, feeling blithe. 'I'm unemployed at the moment, though, which is why I can meet you tomorrow.'

'But – but—' he stammered.

'When my father died, there wasn't any. I haven't settled yet on what I'm going to do for a living. I'm just browsing round amongst the things I might do. You haven't any ideas, I suppose? No nice easy job up your sleeve, say from eleven till one, two hours for lunch and finish at four?' and she shot him a provocative glance from grey eyes under long lashes. She didn't in the least want him, but then neither did he want her, not in that way. What on earth could he want?

'I'm afraid not,' he said in a stilted tone and she laughed and, as the music finished, went back to Phillip, dismissing this strange young man with an airy nod.

Though she had told Marcia not to wait up for her, she saw the light under her door as she went to the flat.

She knocked softly at the door and opened it. Marcia was reading.

'Darling, you shouldn't have stayed awake for me, though I'm glad you did. I've had the most amusing experience,' said Eve, perching on the end of the bed and lighting a cigarette.

Marcia did not mind the smell of cigarettes in her bedroom. She smoked like a chimney herself. 'Have one of these,' she said, offering her packet. 'Phillip bought them for me. I've made up my mind that I can't afford them now.'

Marcia smiled.

'I expect there'll always be someone who can,' she said. 'Tell me what was so amusing. Not Phillip?'

Eve gurgled. She made no secret of the fact that she always found Phillip rather heavy going.

'No, another man, an almost strange man though I've met him once before, in Cairo. I'm going to meet him tomorrow,' and she told Marcia all about it, embellishing the story with her own gay and somewhat outrageous choice of words. 'He's rather like a large, anxious rabbit in spectacles, but he didn't have even a nibble at me. Wonder what on earth he wants?'

Marcia frowned anxiously.

'You're not going, are you, Eve? A man you've – well – almost picked up?'

'Of course I'm going, but don't worry. We're meeting quite respectably in the Park at twelve o'clock in the morning, and I don't see what can happen there! Or anywhere with an anxious rabbit, specially one in spectacles! Come on, darling. Laugh!'

Unwillingly Marcia smiled.

'I hope you'll have changed your mind by the morning,' she said.

'Oh, but I shan't. Get home as early as you can so that I can tell you all about it. I only hope I shall wake in time. You might set your alarm for eleven before you go and put it near me.'

'Perhaps he wants to marry you?'

'No, he's not that sort, nor the sort that wants to sleep with me either. That's what makes it so intriguing. I shouldn't think he's ever slept with a girl in his life. I don't think he knows what to do. I doubt if he's even got what it takes! Well, good night, darling. I think I'll wear the Dior suit,' and she danced away, her feet already light with the promise of adventure.

Marcia sighed, but since she had to be at work by nine in the morning, put out the light and went to sleep in her orderly fashion.

When the alarm woke Eve at eleven o'clock, the adventure did not seem nearly so attractive, but she struggled out of bed by half-past, had a bath, dressed in her leisurely fashion in the Dior suit which was still not paid for and finally arrived at the rendezvous half an hour late.

Lewis Belamie was there, pacing up and down and looking more like a rabbit than ever.

'Am I late?' she asked airily.

'Very. I thought you weren't coming,' he said ungraciously, but obviously relieved to find that she had. 'Shall we sit down, or do you want to go to lunch yet?'

What a very peculiar young man! she thought, but his very peculiarity was intriguing, so she walked to the two chairs he indicated and sat down expectantly, her eyes bright with mischievous anticipation.

She was surprised when he began immediately to talk about his grandmother! She did not know what had induced her to accept such an unexpected invitation, nor why, since he showed no indication that he was attracted to her, he should even have asked her to meet him, but it could not be to talk about his grandmother!

But it was. With many 'er's' and stumblings and much embarrassment, he told her a garbled tale of a rich old woman who lived in a remote part of Cornwall, who was very old and likely to die at any moment, and who had commanded the presence of her expectant sole heirs, Lewis and his brother with their fiancées. At this point, he gave her a discomfitted, appealing look which she could not understand.

'Have you got a fiancée?' she asked him.

'No. Victor is engaged, but I've never had much interest in girls, and it's imperative that I – I should be engaged to – to a suitable girl.'

Eve was intrigued and astonished. Her lip trembled with laughter.

'Mr Belamie, are you asking me to marry you? You can't be. Why, we don't even know each other!'

17

'But – but I thought that – if you wouldn't mind – I mean, she is likely to die very soon and – there is this big estate, and all the money—'

'But you've got to produce evidence that you are going to get married to someone suitable and you've fixed on me?' and she burst out laughing. 'It's too fantastic and absurd! You might even have to marry me!'

He did not join in her laughter. He was evidently a very serious young man.

'There's no danger of that. My grandmother will not live long enough. All she wants to do is to make sure that Victor and I are going to be married before she makes her final Will and if I am not engaged, she is likely to leave the house and everything else to Victor instead of to both of us jointly. I assure you that I should not have to marry you, Miss Brayle.'

She laughed again, but wryly.

'Well, I've had a good many proposals in my life but never one couched in quite those terms! I can see what you hope to get out of it, but what about me? Why should I pretend to be engaged to you? I don't know that it would even be fun!'

'I – er – you said last night that you – you had been left badly off and would have to get a job,' he stammered.

'And you're offering me one? For how long and what would it involve?'

She was actually toying with this extraordinary idea!

'Only a week or two, possibly only a few days, but you would have to come with me to the Weir House. It's on the Cornish coast, a place called South Cawer, very isolated and she keeps it up in a sort of feudal style, owns most of the village as well. I – I'd – er – recompense you, of course.'

'Pay me, you mean?' asked Eve in her forthright style, and she was remembering how desperately she needed money at this moment and that without a job, she had no means of even paying Marcia for her keep, let alone pay Phillip what she still owed him. And she even owed for the very clothes she was wearing!

He looked relieved by her forthrightness, brightening considerably.

'I thought perhaps – a hundred pounds,' he muttered. 'And your expenses, of course, return fare and nothing to pay meantime. If you would – could – consider it—'

'It's the most fantastic proposition to make, but – well, I won't deny that I'm in a hole at the moment and a hundred pounds and a holiday on the Cornish coast, even if it's only a few days, is very attractive.'

'Then you will?' he asked with desperate urgency.

'I don't know. I've got to think about it. Don't rush me. What about this brother? Is his engagement a put-up job as well?'

'Oh no, he's really engaged to Myrtle Mellor.'

'If they got married, it might spike your guns!' said Eve, who could not take this proposition seriously, though it was evident that he did.

'I don't think so. My grandmother does not even like Myrtle, but a girl like you – I mean – you're attractive and all that.'

She could restrain her mirth no longer and laughed until she cried, and mopped her eyes delicately with the edge of her lace handkerchief and had to look in her little mirror to make sure the very light application of mascara had not smudged her cheeks. He watched her unsmilingly. He did not quite like her attitude.

'She must be very rich!' she said when she could speak.

'Nobody knows how rich, except probably Pawnsford, her solicitor. The house is enormous and the pictures and the antiques alone must be worth hundreds of thousands, to say nothing of the estate, the farm, the village and everything else.'

He sounded awed and impressed. Money evidently meant a great deal to him.

'Victor thinks she's too old to be still in her right mind,' he added, 'but her solicitor says she's quite capable of making a Will.'

'What about your parents?' asked Eve. 'Aren't they still alive?'

'No. My father was killed in the war and my mother died ten years ago, so my brother and I are her natural heirs, but she is just as likely to leave it to the nation, or to charity if – if we displeased her at the last moment. She is determined that we shall get married. She paid for our education and put us into jobs. Victor's a stock-broker and I'm a research chemist working for I.L.A.'

'You've both got good jobs. Why do you need her money?' asked Eve practically.

He stared at her, shocked.

'But all that money, to be just squandered?'

'You couldn't call it squandered to leave it to charity, though I agree with you that it might be if left to the nation unless she's left specific instructions. Even millions could disappear in the maw of the Chancellor! But what would you do with it if you got it?'

'I'd use a lot of it on atomic research,' he said promptly.

'So as to blow us all up more quickly and surely? You might as well let the Chancellor have it.'

'There is such a thing as atomic research for peaceful uses,' he said loftily.

'I suppose so, though there doesn't seem much sign of that yet, does there? They said once that atomic energy could take the *Queen Mary* across to New York for fourpence, but now it seems that even if it were used instead of ordinary domestic electricity, it would cost more than we pay now, so where's the sense?'

'Oh well,' he said with a touch of acerbity, 'we don't want to go into that. The thing is, will you do it?'

'Will anyone else know? Victor, for instance?'

'Certainly not. No one else will know that we're not really engaged.'

'Can I have a day to think it over? It's such a fantastic and absurd idea, you know.'

'Well – till tomorrow? Because if you won't, I shall have to look for somebody else,' he said so dejectedly that she laughed again.

'You really are the most extraordinary person! The most extraordinary family, in fact! Why don't you find a girl you like and ask her to be engaged to you properly, and marry her?'

He looked as if a bad smell had passed under his nose.

'Marry? Me? I'm afraid I take no interest in women,' he said stiffly.

'Won't you find it rather difficult, if your aversion to them is known, as it probably is, to produce a fiancée suddenly? Won't your dislike of me be too obvious?' shooting a merry, mischievous glance at him sideways.

'Er – well – of course I should not let it appear and – er – I do not actually dislike you,' looking almost surprised at the discovery.

'Thank you. That's a starting point, anyway, if we are to have a starting point. Oh, I haven't agreed yet, you know. Let me know how I can get hold of you and I'll tell you tomorrow.'

He gave her an address.

'You know the name, don't you? Belamie, Lewis Belamie,' he added anxiously.

She wrote the address in a little gold-mounted book which she took from her handbag and then rose.

'Till tomorrow then,' she said brightly. 'I'll write tonight so that you'll get it in the morning,' and she walked away.

Even if he were disposed to ask her to lunch with him, she did not want to. She wanted time to think over the extraordinary proposition. She could not call it a 'proposal'!

She did not want to go back to the airless little flat; London's streets smelt of hot tar, petrol and perspiring humanity and the shops would be worse; amused at herself, she spent the afternoon in the National Gallery, where at least it was cool and quiet. Here, undoubtedly, were vast stores of potential wealth, wealth far greater than anything which the grandmother could possess, and she speculated idly on what these pictures were worth, even asked one of the attendants about it, but laughed when she saw him regarding her rather strangely.

'Don't worry,' she said. 'I'm not proposing to steal any of them. I don't even like them much, and what on earth would I do with anything like that?' pointing to a vast Rubens.

When she got back to the flat, Marcia was already home and relieved to see her.

'I've had such fun,' she said, throwing off her hat and the

thin silk coat that matched her dress and gurgling like a child who has been up to mischief and might be found out; and she told Marcia the whole story.

Marcia was alarmed and appalled.

'You're not going to do it, Eve?'

'I might. I can't make up my mind. It would be rather fun, you know. I went into the A.A. and found out where this place, South Cawer, is and it isn't really a place at all. It took even them ages to find it, but it's right on the coast and it must be heavenly there now. Think of the Cornish coast in this sweltering heat! Cool sand and rocks and a cold, cold sea to wallow in! And it's only for a week, Lewis says.'

'Is that his name?'

'Yes. Lewis Belamie. Anything more unromantic you could not imagine, and I should be so unutterably safe as his fiancée! He did admit that he doesn't actually *dislike* me, but he hastened to assure me that he has no interest in girls and never intends to marry one!'

'You can't possibly mean to do it?'

But Marcia saw that it was definitely a possibility and that her own arguments were helping her to make up her mind.

'If I do go, you won't tell anybody? Not Phillip or anybody?' asked Eve.

'I really ought to.'

'Why? He's not my guardian or anything. I haven't given him the right to disapprove of anything I do.'

'I know, but—'

'But nothing,' said Eve and went into the kitchen to prepare the salad she found there. After a few minutes Marcia followed her, but did not refer to the subject again. She could do no good and was afraid of doing more harm. No one had ever crossed Eve, and she had done whatever her father had wanted to do simply because it was what she wanted to do as well.

Long after both of them had presumably gone to bed, Eve stole noiselessly down the stairs to post her letter.

2

Eve turned up for the train only a few minutes before it was due to leave.

Lewis Belamie was pacing the platform, not taking his eyes off the entrance, restless, anxious and angry. Was she going to let him down in spite of her letter saying she would come? He had let her know the time of the train well beforehand and told her he would get her ticket.

When he saw her at last, his brow cleared a little, though he was still angry.

'Fancy leaving it so late!' he said. 'I thought you weren't coming. The train's just about to go and it's packed and probably your seat's been taken by now. For heaven's sake come on!'

He seized her arm and rushed her to the compartment in which he had tried to keep two seats by putting his small case and his newspaper on them, but when they reached it, there was barely room for them to squash into the corner, and no room at all for Eve's larger case. It had to stand in the already crowded corridor.

She was not used to travelling anything but first class and she looked round her, not so much in disgust as with the feeling that two of the people at present standing in the corridor could have seats if they moved into the first class, where she had caught sight of a good many empty places.

She got up, edged her way over people's legs and luggage and along the corridor and then came back.

'There's plenty of room further along,' she said.

'In the first class.'

'Well?'

She saw that he was hesitating, but after all, with all he had at stake, why be so mean? Brought up by a wealthy grandmother, he couldn't be all that poor.

'Bring my case, will you?' she asked coolly and offered their seats to a mother with two small children. 'We can pay the extra fare if necessary,' she said to him as they went. 'Can't you afford to travel first class – *darling*?'

He coloured angrily.

'Of course I can, but I don't think it's necessary. I never do.'

'Well, you're doing it for once, aren't you? After all, it's the first time you've travelled with your fiancée, isn't it?' and with a mocking little smile at him she opened the door of an almost empty carriage and settled herself into a corner seat.

It was a dull journey and very hot. They had lunch in the restaurant car, the usual unimaginative meal on the train, and it was almost a relief when they had to change and wait half an hour for the slow train which, he told her, would take them as far as Helston where they were to be met. The railway did not go to South Cawer, but he had sent a telegram to his grandmother, who would send the car for them.

They had not been able to have much conversation so far, but now she asked him to tell her about South Cawer and the house. He told her without enthusiasm and clearly had something on his mind which was at last able to break through. He produced a small box from his pocket and gave it to her.

'You'd better put this on,' he said. 'If it doesn't fit, you can put a bit of cotton or something round it.'

She opened the box and stared in astonishment. It contained a diamond marquise ring of exquisite workmanship and obvious value.

'Good heavens! I didn't expect this!' she gasped.

'You've got to have a ring and I can always sell it again afterwards. It's second-hand so I didn't have to pay purchase tax. It's a good one, of course. My grandmother knows the value of jewellery and would expect it.'

Eve giggled.

'Oh, Lewis, how funny of you! Aren't you afraid you might not get it back?' and she slipped it on her engagement finger and turned her hand about to catch the light.

He shrugged his shoulders.

'If you want it, keep it, of course,' he said, and just then their train came in.

So that was the way she had got engaged for the first time! Well, well.

They had the compartment, second class this time, to themselves and Eve, with a mischievous grin, slipped her hand through the crook of his arm, feeling his instant withdrawal.

'What's the idea?' he asked suspiciously.

'Don't you think we ought to get used to being, or appearing to be, a little more interested in each other? Now that we're engaged?'

He gave her an uncomfortable look which she rightly interpreted as alarm. Good heavens, was the girl going to hold him to it?

'I see no reason for it when we're alone, he said, making an effort to remove his arm, but she held on tightly.

'Isn't it better to begin whilst there are no onlookers? We may make a mess of it. You will, anyway. I've had more experience.'

He left his arm where it was. It would be too undignified to struggle.

'Very well,' he said coldly, still suspicious.

'And talk to me.'

'What about?'

'Oh – atoms, if that's all you're really interested in. Or your grandmother. By the way, I take it that she is Mrs Belamie? Rather an odd way of spelling it.'

'Her husband, my grandfather, was French.'

'Oh, so this place, Weir House, is not an old family seat?'

'No. She bought it after he died.'

'And the pictures? How did she acquire those?'

'Most of them were his. He was a collector of fine arts and she carried on with his collection. The place is full of them. Quite useless, of course.'

'Except to turn into money for the atom bombs? Is that what you'd do with them if you acquired them?'

He gave her another of those suspicious glances, but her face was merely innocent and interested.

'Probably,' he said. 'All that money mouldering on the walls!'

The topic seemed unprofitable, so she tried something else.

'Tell me about the place, and the house. It must be big to have room on the walls for the pictures.'

He gave a deprecating shrug.

'Great barn of a place. A museum. A mausoleum. Can't think how she stands it, though she's usually in bed.'

'Then who'll be there besides us?'

'My brother and Miss Mellor, who went down yesterday. And the housekeeper and a sort of nurse-companion, and the servants.'

'Servants? Golly. I didn't know anybody in England had servants nowadays, except people like the Queen. I don't suppose she has to sweep the stairs at Buckingham Palace, do you?' with an irreverent little giggle.

'My grandmother pays them ridiculous wages, of course, or they'd never stay. The place is so isolated. There's not even a proper road to it without going miles round.'

'I wonder she can get servants to stay even by paying them, as you say, ridiculous wages.'

'Most of them are either elderly, or married couples.'

'How odd! With families?'

'There are some children about, but they have their own quarters and people to look after them and teach them as it's too far for them to go to school, the younger ones anyway. They're not allowed about the house, of course.'

'She must be quite a character, your grandmother. Fancy working all that out! It's really a sort of village, isn't it? Do they like it?'

'I suppose so, or they wouldn't stay. They all hope to get a bit of her money too.'

'Poor old thing, with them all waiting for her to die. Hasn't she any friends? Doesn't anybody go to see her, or to stay there?'

'Only my brother and I, and we only go when we're sent for.

We are expected to go at a moment's notice and also to leave in the same way. Sometimes we don't even see her.'

Eve digested this information and tried to picture what the place must be like, and the old autocrat who ruled from her bed by the sole power of her money. It seemed that no one loved her, not even her servants and certainly not this grandson.

He had picked up one of his newspapers again, and she set his arm free but continued to study him. His pale thin face, his eyes behind thick-lensed glasses and his narrow, apparently sexless lips showed no interest in her, a fact which piqued her even though theirs was no more than a purely business contract. She had dressed 'to do him proud' in a honey-coloured suit of summer tweed worn with a blouse of a paler shade, and though she often went without a hat, she had put one on for the occasion, a perky little affair of brown straw which matched her accessories, but he had scarcely even looked at her! It was a new experience for Eve Brayle and the little devil of mischief in her was determined to make him pay for it. With his magnificent ring on her fingers, he could hardly continue to ignore her before other people!

'Is it really worth it?' she asked suddenly.

He came back from his dull scientific journal with a start.

'Is what worth it?'

'This funny business of an engagement.'

His eyes bulged a little.

'You're surely not going to back out of it now? We're nearly there.'

'We needn't be actually engaged. I could be just a girl friend.'

'The whole idea is to be engaged. Nothing less than that would satisfy my grandmother.'

'Suppose she insists on marriage?'

'Don't you realise she might die at any moment? There wouldn't be time,' he said, but she saw that she had planted a most uncomfortable thought in his mind – also in her own. She would certainly not go as far as that, even if he were prepared to do so.

He tried to return to his reading, but every now and then gave her a furtive glance which revealed his disquiet.

They left the train at Helston and he began to fuss, carrying her big case and his small one and ignoring the porter.

'A car. I'm being met by a car,' he told the man irritably. 'Has it come? The car from South Cawer?'

'I couldn't zay, zur,' said the porter in a surly tone and Lewis pushed his way out of the station and looked about him.

An enormous car stood outside, a vintage Daimler which had been kept in superb condition, a uniformed chauffeur standing beside it. He looked about the same age as the car and as well preserved.

'Is this it?' she asked.

He did not answer but stalked towards the car, the chauffeur hurrying to relieve him of the luggage and, after a somewhat surprised glance at Eve, to open the door for them and usher them into the vast interior of the car. The upholstery had a musty, unused smell though it was spotlessly clean, and she gave a little laugh as she settled herself into one capacious corner. Her feet did not touch the floor.

'Do you think they've taken out the body?' she asked whilst the chauffeur was strapping on the luggage at the back of the car. It could easily have been accommodated inside.

'The body?'

'Well, it is rather like a hearse, isn't it? Though I've never been inside a hearse yet!'

'It's like everything else of hers, ancient and enormous. It's absurd to have a thing like this.'

'It's fun. I feel like Queen Victoria,' but his face did not change its expression of disgust as they started off on the final stage of their journey, which he had told her was ten miles.

She was fascinated as the car took them smoothly along the narrow, winding roads and soon they were within sight of the sea, at which she exclaimed with rapture.

'Oh, Lewis, it's lovely! So wild and lonely!'

'Yes, it's lonely all right, *and* wild. Nobody in their right senses would choose a place like this to live in when they could live anywhere else,' he said sourly.

'You wouldn't?'

'Not unless I had to. We've even got to take the cliff road and walk the rest of the way. The other's too narrow for this car. She might just as well have sent the staff car,' he grumbled and, sure enough, a mile or two farther on the car stopped and the chauffeur came to open the door for them.

'This is as far as we can go now, sir,' he said. 'I'll send the luggage up. Will you walk up, sir, you and madam?'

'What's the alternative?' asked Eve, hopping gaily out of the car. 'I don't know your name?' with an enquiring smile at the man.

'Hodd, madam. I expect you would prefer to walk up to the house?'

She looked past him at two small, sturdy donkeys waiting in the charge of a small boy and cried out in delight.

'Do you mean those? May I really ride one? What fun!' and she ran to where they stood and began fondling them, laughing.

'You surely don't mean to?' asked Lewis Belamie's shocked voice behind her.

'But of course! Isn't that what they're for, Hodd?'

'If you wish, madam,' he said, smiling involuntarily. 'I don't suppose Mr Lewis will want to ride, so the other one can take the luggage.'

'I shouldn't dream of it, of course,' said Lewis. 'You do what you like, but I prefer to walk.'

One of the donkeys was equipped with an old-fashioned side-saddle, but Eve ignored that, hitched up her narrow skirt to the edification of the grinning boy and sprang on the other one and sat astride it.

'Where do I go?' she asked.

'He knows the way, mum,' said the boy, and with a little urging the donkey started up the rough path, picking its sure way amongst the stones, whilst Lewis followed in his London-built shoes to their detriment.

She looked over her shoulder at him.

'Don't worry, *darling*,' she said saucily. 'I've been over the Pyrenees on one of these! See you at the top.'

She reined in the sure-footed little beast at the top of the path and waited for Lewis, feasting her eyes on the scene in front of her.

Smooth lawns of velvety turf spread from the top of the steep cliff to a grey old pile, hoary with age and, she felt, with history. No particular period could claim it, for evidently additions of all sorts, some of them incongruous, had been made to the original structure, so that it spread wide arms at either side, a flagged terrace with a wide balcony over it indicating what had been the actual house at one time. This part had deep, mullioned windows set into the walls, whereas some of the additions had almost modern windows and even here and there a French door. It was a curious, ugly conglomeration of buildings which bore no sign of being a human habitation except for the two gardeners working on the flower beds, which were ablaze with glory. Only afterwards did she discover at what enormous labour and cost these were encouraged and maintained right on the edge of that wild Cornish coast.

'It's – fascinating,' she said, when at last Lewis, panting and disgruntled, joined her. 'Ugly, but – fascinating. Perhaps because it's so ugly? There's no rhyme or reason in it. It's just as if people have come along and stuck a bit on just for fun.'

'You'd better get off that thing,' he said sourly. 'You can't ride up to the house on it.'

'Why not? There's nobody about.'

'That's what you think! For goodness sake, get off it.'

She laughed and slid to the ground and left the donkey contentedly grazing and went across the lawn with him, watched with interest by the gardeners.

As if they had touched a spring by setting foot on the first of the steps that led to the terrace, huge double doors opened to reveal an ancient manservant in the same green livery as the chauffeur's.

'This can't be real?' whispered Eve. 'We must be in a book.'

'It's real all right,' snarled Lewis, who had evidently not got over her donkey ride yet.

She slid a hand into his and smiled up at him.

'Mind your manners, darling,' she told him mockingly. 'You're bringing your future bride to the ancestral home, remember,' and when they reached the grey old retainer, she smiled into his impassive face.

Lewis took no notice of the old man but stalked across the wide hall and opened a door into what Eve supposed was the family sitting-room. By contrast with the out-of-doors, which was still illumined by a sun reluctant to leave a country on which it seldom shone so brightly and for so long, inside the room it was dark and gloomy. The deep-set mullioned windows were long and narrow and the walls, hung all round with enormous, heavy pictures (some of the Old Masters, thought Eve with a little shiver) seemed to absorb what light there was without giving any back. From the seat which ran along the row of windows two people rose, a man and a woman. Evidently Lewis had been right when he inferred that her undignified approach on the donkey had been observed!

No brothers could have been more different in appearance, except that they wore similar thick-lensed glasses which hid their eyes. Victor, the elder brother, was short and rotund and wore a bristling little moustache on his upper lip. If he were stretched lengthways, he could have come within at least an inch or two of the top of his companion's head, but as it was she towered above him, too thin and angular for grace. She might have come out of one of the high-fashion magazines, thought Eve, where the women seemed to have no possible accommodation for their food.

When Victor switched on a standard lamp, Myrtle Mellor moved into its light and the two girls regarded each other, Eve with her usual would-be friendliness, the other with unveiled hostility in every thin feature, especially in her eyes of pale, lustreless grey. Her dark hair was immaculately dressed, she wore a fashionably pale make-up with long, dangling ear-rings which seemed to accentuate the thinness of the bare shoulders rising from her elaborate evening gown of the wrong shade of blue. A paler shade might have softened the angular outlines, but this was an electric blue, well cut and obviously expensive but doing nothing for her.

31

She looked disparagingly at Eve's wind-blown halo of curls and honey-brown suit; she had taken off her hat and forgotten to put it on again, and such make-up as she had started with had disappeared during her hilarious ride up the cliff on the donkey.

Her hand met the other's limp clasp, which was no more than a touch, as Lewis murmured introductions.

'Miss Mellor – my brother – and this is, er, Miss Evelyn Brayle.'

As she greeted them, Victor showing rather more enthusiasm in his surprise than his fiancée, Eve ran her mind over the sort of clothes she had brought with her and those she had left behind. A telegram in the morning to Marcia would bring her something more elaborate. It was evidently to be a more dressy affair than she had imagined!

'I expect you would like to go to your room at once after your long journey, Miss Brayle,' said Myrtle. 'Dinner is at eight, and we have cocktails in here at half past seven. I hope that gives you time to dress, though you are somewhat late. Mrs Hodd will show you the way. I have given you your usual room, Lewis.'

Eve had become aware of someone entering the room behind them and turned to see a small, elderly woman, white-haired, fresh-faced, clad in black, who gave her a curious, not unfriendly half-smile.

'This way, Miss Brayle,' she said and turned to lead the way.

'You're the chauffeur's wife?' asked Eve in friendly fashion as they went across the hall and up a wide, carpeted stair-case darkened by more of the dull 'Old Masters'.

'Yes, the housekeeper, madam.'

'Have you been here a long time?'

'Most of us have.'

'Don't you find it rather lonely?'

'It's our home and Madame is very good to us. We shall find it difficult to settle down anywhere else when – when the time comes.'

They were the first kind words she had heard about old Mrs Belamie. Evidently the housekeeper, at least, was not looking forward to her death as Lewis, and probably Victor, were.

'Shall I see her at dinner?'

'Oh no, madam. She seldom leaves her room now, but I daresay she will want to see you afterwards.'

Perhaps that accounted for Myrtle's elaborate *toilette*, thought Eve, and wondered whether she had anything with her to match it. Lewis had given her no idea of the style in which they lived and she had packed only simple clothes.

Up they went, past the first floor with its many closed doors and on to the second floor, where Mrs Hodd showed her into a room which was large and gloomy with huge mahogany furniture and high windows which looked over the back and had no view of the sea.

'I hope you will be comfortable here, Miss Brayle,' said the housekeeper with a note of doubt in her voice now that she had seen Eve and approved of her. 'Miss Mellor told me which room you were to have.'

'I shall be quite all right,' said Eve cheerfully, though there was nothing about the room to make her feel cheerful.

'I'm afraid there isn't a private bathroom, but no one else will be using the one at the other end of the passage. There are no other guests.'

'That's all right, Mrs Hodd. Just show me where it is, will you? I think I've got time for a quick bath, haven't I? I feel messy after a day in the train.'

Mrs Hodd looked doubtful.

'Well, perhaps if you're very quick, but Madame likes meals to be served punctually.'

'Even though she's not there? I'll be very quick. I shan't be late. Oh, there's my case,' as another elderly manservant appeared with it.

Servants! The place was swarming with them!

The bathroom was small and inconvenient but at least there was plenty of hot water, and after a quick bath, she put on the only dress she had brought which might bear comparison with Myrtle's and which she had not imagined wearing at all in this remote place, having put it in for emergency only. It was of apricot and amber printed silk, short and sleeveless and as simple as were all her clothes but wearing the undoubted stamp of a famous house for those who had eyes to see. She wondered if Myrtle in her showy blue gown would have those eyes? Still, it was the best she had and she twisted her very good pearls round her throat, directed a little chuckle at Lewis's diamond ring and found her way to the sitting-room (which she found later was known as the Gainsborough Room) on the stroke of half past seven.

The brothers, Lewis in his ill-fitting dress clothes and Victor better upholstered in his, rose as she came into the room. At least Victor had better manners, and Lewis followed his lead. Myrtle sat before a low table on which was an array of decanters, bottles and fine glassware. She was evidently the hostess and meant Eve to know it, though it would have been more usual for the men to pour the drinks.

'What will you have, Miss Brayle?' she asked in her cold voice. 'Sherry?'

Eve hated sherry and was not going to be pushed off with it even if it were a ladylike drink.

'Something a bit more lively, I think,' she said briskly. 'May I have gin and mixed? Thank you, Lewis darling,' as he produced his cigarette case for her. 'Have you remembered to bring my special brand?'

'Er – I'm afraid not. Will these do?'

'Quite well,' she said. 'I ought to have reminded you. He is so forgetful,' turning with a smile to Victor. 'Still, I shall train him in time.'

Victor produced his own case.

'Perhaps you would prefer these, Evelyn?' coming to the other side of her. 'We can't call you Miss Brayle, you know!'

'I'm usually called Eve, and please don't call me Miss Brayle. After all, I'm going to be one of the family, aren't I, darling,' with a loving smile at Lewis. 'Yes, I'd like these better, though as Lewis has already discovered, I can smoke anything! Thank you,' as they both flicked on their lighters for her.

Myrtle's thin fingers amongst the bottles seemed to express her disapproval of the choice of gin and Eve wished rather

34

maliciously that she had asked for neat whisky or a 'Bloody Mary', though she doubted whether vodka appeared amongst the bottles, and anyway she hated it. Still, it would have been fun to watch Myrtle's reactions. Watching those fingers, she caught sight of a half-hoop of diamonds which in no way compared with her own magnificent 'engagement' ring. She still could not imagine why Lewis should have bought it for her temporary use, though it could have been to impress Victor and arouse Myrtle's jealousy. She decided that she did not like any of them. There was an under-current of bad feeling amongst them, though what else could one expect in the circumstances, with so much to be angled for?

Uncomfortably at the back of her mind she wondered whether old Mrs Belamie would be content to see her grandsons engaged, or if she would not require them to consolidate their unions by actual marriage. She was certainly not going to marry Lewis Belamie!

At dinner, in another vast, gloomy room, Myrtle sat at one end of the table and Victor at the other, leaving the sides to the younger brother and Eve, and it was Myrtle who gave quite unnecessary instructions to the well-trained servants, the old butler who had opened the door to the new arrivals and an almost equally elderly parlour-maid. Eve could scarcely restrain her amusement at being so assiduously waited on by the almost unheard-of luxury of servants and she longed to be able to give a description of the meal to Marcia. The appointments of the table were perfect, snowy embroidered linen, polished silver, gleaming crystal glass, whilst the dinner itself left nothing to be desired.

Myrtle gave Victor a disapproving look as he helped himself to more of a rich, thick sauce.

'I don't wonder you put on weight, Victor. If I ate the things you do, I should soon lose my figure.'

'Wouldn't do you any harm to put on a few pounds, my dear,' he said. 'I see that you're enjoying it, Eve. Take the sauce to Miss Brayle, Hibbert.'

'I'm afraid I love my food, and this is wonderful,' said Eve gaily, helping herself from the silver sauce boat.

'I should have thought you would be afraid of putting on weight,' commented Myrtle sourly.

'Aren't I lucky? I eat like a horse and never put on an ounce. It must be dreadful to have to count the calories all the time you're eating.'

'Food is not a particular pre-occupation of mine,' said Myrtle with curling lip. 'A little Melba toast, Hibbert, please. No, no potato thank you. Not for me, Corke, thank you,' as the butler was about to pour wine into her glass.

'A little water, madam?'

'Thank you, no. I never drink with my meals. You shouldn't either, Victor. It is definitely fattening.'

Having defied her over the sauce, Victor reluctantly refused the wine. Poor old Victor, thought Eve. She's got him under her thumb and if she has her way, he'll look half-starved, as she does!

Whilst coffee was being served, a message was brought to the effect that 'Madame' wished to see Miss Brayle and Mr Lewis.

Eve's eyes widened whilst Lewis went red and then pale.

He pushed back his chair and rose precipitately.

'Can't we finish our coffee first?' she asked.

'No, we'd better go now,' he said and made for the door.

On the way up the stairs, she asked him if he were afraid of his grandmother.

'Of course not,' he said irritably. 'It's only that when she sends for you, she expects you to go. She's a very old lady.'

'It's a good job she didn't send for us in the middle of dinner. I suppose she would have expected us to miss that as well as the coffee? It was a good dinner, wasn't it?'

'Yes.'

He evidently was in no mood for light conversation, his mind too much taken up with the impression his 'fiancée' would make on Mrs Belamie.

Meantime Victor and Myrtle, with the servants out of the room, discussed her.

'You could have knocked me down with a feather when old Lewis produced her,' said Victor. 'Who'd have imagined him getting hold of anyone like that? A damn' pretty girl.'

'I imagine he told her that he's coming into all this money,' said Myrtle acidly. 'You may think her pretty, but I'm afraid she's not my style, nor do I think she will be Mrs Belamie's. She strikes me as being flighty, and really that dress is much too short. It actually shows her knees when she sits down, and it's much too gaudy a colour, especially with that particular shade of hair – though that probably is not its natural colour.'

Victor gave a snigger.

'I wouldn't know about the colour of her hair and so on, but if she shows her legs, she's got something to show! Pass me the sugar, please.'

Myrtle moved it further from him.

'You've had enough,' she snapped and he shrugged and let it pass.

'Wonder just what Lewis did say to her about the money?' he said. 'After all, it's as likely to be mine as his.'

'Much more likely, I should say. Mrs Belamie has only got to look at her to see that she is most unsuited to being the mistress of a house of this size.'

He nodded.

'Yes. Probably. What I don't think she realises is that if he got his hands on it, Lewis would almost certainly sell it and the pictures for his infernal science and it would all go up in smoke, or come down in radio-activity or whatever it is. Wonder if I could give her a hint?'

'A bit difficult unless she broaches the subject. You know how touchy she is about it. Almost the only thing she's said about it is that she wants to see you both engaged to suitable girls, not even married to them – so far, at least.'

'Do you think we ought to spring it on Lewis and get married?'

'When you proposed it the last time we were down here, she told us to wait, said she intended to be at the wedding and didn't feel fit enough just then, though if you ask me, she's still as strong as a horse in spite of her age.'

'H'm. Yes. Perhaps we'd better not suggest it again just yet. Wish I knew what was going on upstairs and what she thinks of Eve.'

Up on the first floor, Lewis had opened a baize door which

led into an inner passage and another door at which he tapped nervously.

It was opened by a big, muscular woman with grey hair, who wore a nurse's uniform without the cap.

'Oh, it's you,' she said, looking past him to take a critical glance at Eve. 'You'd better come in,' and she opened the door wider to admit them.

Eve gasped at the proportions of the room. It seemed to stretch endlessly into the shadows and the lofty ceiling was dim in spite of the blaze of lights from a central chandelier. More enormous paintings covered what she could see of the walls, and here and there groups of statuary gleamed whitely. It was more like a museum or art gallery than a bedroom, and even the massive pieces of furniture were dwarfed by the size of the room.

Its focal point was a huge bed, a great gilded affair raised from the floor by a low platform, a canopy of thick silk brocade caught above it by fat, gilt cherubs. It was a monstrous bed, a fantastic, absurd bed. Surely no human could sleep in it, and yet, in the centre of the high, lace-edged pillows was a tiny face, made tinier by their great mound and the vast sea of brocaded satin covers.

The face was delicately painted and powdered and the hair that framed it was bright golden massed into little curls. Fragile, blue-veined hands with pink-painted nails lay on the satin coverlet, restless, eager little hands that seemed still to be seeking something fresh to grasp and to hold. On the wrinkled fingers a mass of gems sparkled with every movement.

An old, old woman, bedizened, painted, grotesque, pathetic, but there was one ageless, timeless feature about her, the brilliant eyes whose piercing blueness seemed to bore through Eve even at that distance.

One restless claw of a hand was lifted to beckon her closer and the girl found herself automatically obeying the imperative gesture.

'Come here, girl. Come closer so that I can have a good look at you. Not you, Lewis. I've already seen more than enough of you.'

The voice was thin and high-pitched but amazingly strong, every syllable clear.

Eve moved close to the bed, mounted the shallow step and stood gazing with fascinated eyes at the little creature with her painted mask of a face and her impossibly golden hair which might have been a wig.

'H'm. H'm,' commented the old woman, letting her eyes travel over the girl from head to foot until Eve felt she knew even what she had got on underneath. 'So you've come. What's your name?'

'Eve Brayle.'

'And you've got yourself engaged to my grandson Lewis? I wonder what for?'

For the first time Eve realised the cheapness of what she had done, a thing which in the presence of this old woman seemed no longer a prank but a paltry trick. She stood silently condemning herself, submitting to the ruthless scrutiny of the ageless eyes, eyes of a deep, vivid blue, bluer than her own which were more grey than blue.

'Well, there's no accounting for tastes, though I wonder what you see in him? My money-bags, perhaps? Did he tell you that if you married him, I might leave him a fortune, eh? Eh?'

For once in her life completely nonplussed, Eve could find nothing to say but simply stood there in the relentless gaze of those eyes which she felt could pierce her to the soul and find out everything that was hidden in it.

'Well,' said Mrs Belamie at last, 'perhaps I won't ask you.' (Having done so already!) 'But why should I mind? Money is power, power, and I love to feel its power. D'you know that? I like to make people rush to obey me, people I don't like. I enjoy making them *squirm*,' and the thin old voice took on a tone of worminess, burrowing and twisting in the earth, and chuckled as she spoke the word.

Eve, the tension suddenly snapping, laughed. She was no longer afraid of the old woman. In that revealing instant she had entered her mind and could chuckle at what she saw.

'It's fun to you, isn't it? You really enjoy it,' and she heard Lewis give a gasp just behind her.

Mrs Belamie nodded and laughed gleefully. The laughter was in her eyes as well.

'We're going to be good friends. You understand me. What did you say your name was?'

'Eve.'

'Ah yes. Eve. The name of the first of our sex. Let's hope you haven't wasted your apple!' and she laughed again.

The nurse came to the other side of the bed.

'You've talked enough for one day. You'll be able to see Miss Brayle again in the morning, you know,' she said authoritatively.

'Oh go away, Ford. I'm enjoying myself and who knows if I shall have any tomorrow. She'll go when I send her away and not before. Tell me, child. Have they given you a good room? Made you comfortable? Can you see the sea as you lie in bed? That's the one thing that never changes, you know, never grows old. Will you be able to see it as soon as it's morning?'

'I can't exactly see it from my bedroom, but—'

She was interrupted fiercely.

'Where have they put her?' she demanded of Lewis. 'That Myrtle, I suppose? I want her. Send her to me. No, not you, Lewis. You go, Ford. Tell her to come.'

The woman tut-tutted but went.

'Where have they put her?' she demanded again of her grandson.

'I – I don't quite know, *grand-mère*,' he stammered.

'Then you ought to have found out, seen she has a suitable room, one of the best. The Queen's Room. Yes, she shall have that.'

Victor and Myrtle could not have been far away. They were, in fact, standing just the other side of the baize door, apprehensive of what might have been going on in the bedroom, and the nurse returned with them at once.

'I don't want you, Victor. It's Myrtle I want. What room have you given her, eh? Eh?' aiming the last syllables like poisoned darts at the hapless Myrtle.

'A very nice large room on the second floor—'

'The second floor?' screamed the old woman in rage. 'The

second floor? That's for servants or guests of no importance. How dare you put the girl who's going to marry my grandson on the second floor? She's to have the Queen's Room.'

Myrtle stared and gulped.

'The – the Queen's Room?' she echoed.

'Of course. Is it ready? If not, it had better be made ready and she will stay here with me until it is. You go and see to it yourself. You like to give the orders. Well, now's your chance. Tonight, mind. Move all her things into it and come and tell me when it's ready. You two boys can go too. You stay with me, Eve. The second floor indeed!'

The room cleared as if by magic, leaving only the nurse and Eve with Mrs Belamie, who composed herself again though she still muttered 'The second floor! A servant's room.'

The nurse brought her something in a tumbler.

'You'd better drink this if you want to get through the night,' she said.

'Well, I do, so I may as well have it. What is it? Something nasty, I suppose?'

'It's a sedative, and you need it after letting yourself get all worked up like that.'

'Who's worked up? I enjoyed it,' she declared with a chuckle, but she took the tumbler and drank its contents. 'Ugh! Give me one of my peppermint creams. Have one, Eve,' offering her the box.

'I don't like peppermint,' said Eve calmly.

The nurse tut-tutted again, evidently expecting her to take one and eat it, but Mrs Belamie put the box back on the table beside her.

'Don't make that noise at her. Why should she eat it if she doesn't like them? She's got the courage to say so, and why not? The rest of you would eat them if you knew they were rat poison! I'll try that sometime,' with a diabolical little chuckle.

'You won't have the chance,' said Emma Ford grimly. 'I wouldn't trust you within a mile of it.'

'Afraid I might take it myself and end my miseries? Don't worry. I'm not finished yet. Too much to do. Go and draw the curtain back, Eve, the one opposite my bed. Now look out and tell me what you see.'

The girl did as she was told and stood there enchanted. Beyond the wide lawn, grey in the moonlight with the black shadows of the trees crossing it, the sea curled and foamed, never quite calm on that wild coast, and across it stretched to its far edge on the horizon the broad pathway of the moon, whilst far above it the stars were clear and bright. No sound broke the stillness but the lashing of the waves against the rocks, the sibilant whisper of the trees and the hooting of an owl and no sounds from the house disturbed the peace of the great room behind her. She might be alone in the world, in a solitude that yet brought no sense of loneliness with it.

The voice of the old woman broke the silence at last.

'Well? Like it?' she asked. 'Tell me what you see.'

'How can I? Such quietness and peace. As if nothing could ever change it. Perhaps eternity is like that?'

'Yes. Draw the curtains again. I wanted you to see it. I get out of bed and look at it myself sometimes. Yes, I do, Ford, and you know I do. However, I'm not getting out tonight. I've had enough excitement for today. I'm only going to stay awake until that Myrtle comes back to tell me the Queen's Room is ready, and then I'll let myself go to sleep. Do you know how old I am, Eve?'

'Lewis told me you are over ninety,' said Eve, coming back to stand by the bed.

'Nearly ninety-five. A good age, they tell me, and between ourselves, I'm going to make my century though they don't believe it. They'd like me to die tomorrow if they weren't so worried about who's going to get my money. Every time she comes down here Myrtle brings a black dress just in case. She'll look like a starved crow in it. Wish I could be here to see! Have you brought a black dress with you?'

'Well, I have, but I wear a lot of black. It suits me.'

'Promise me you won't wear it for me. Wear something like the thing you've got on tonight. That'd set them all by the ears!' with another fiendish chuckle. 'Come closer, child. I like that dress. Let me feel the material. H'm. Real silk, none of that artificial stuff. I thought so. And your pearls? Are they real too?'

Eve bent down so that the little claw-like hands could touch them.

'Yes, they're real,' she said.

'Bet my grandson didn't give them to you!'

'No, my father did.'

'Is he still alive?'

'No. I haven't any parents, scarcely any relations.'

'Well, I don't know that you're any the worse off for that. I've never had much pleasure or benefit out of mine. How old are you?'

'Twenty-two.'

'H'm. I can't remember ever being twenty-two, but I suppose I was once. You'll help me to remember. Lewis give you that?' taking her hand and looking at her ring, the only one she wore.

'Yes. Isn't it beautiful?' but she drew her hand back with that same feeling of shame that she should be deceiving an old woman who was being kind to her, but how could she tell her now? She would have to go through with it.

'Not bad,' agreed Mrs Belamie. 'Glad he had enough sense to give you something decent. Here, take this,' and she pulled one of the rings off her fingers. It slipped off so easily now. It was set with emeralds and small diamonds, old-fashioned but beautiful and undoubtedly valuable.

Eve drew back, her face flushing.

'Oh, I couldn't!' she said. 'You mustn't give it to me, really you mustn't.'

'Rubbish. I don't give much away, do I, Ford? Take it, girl, and mind you let Myrtle see it! Not that she's likely to miss it! Give me your hand. There, it fits quite nicely. I forget who gave it to me. I've had it so many years, but it's too big for me now. They all slip off now, even my wedding ring,' looking down at the thin, worn circlet of gold almost hidden under the load of gems.

Eve looked up beseechingly at the nurse, who merely nodded her head.

'She won't miss it,' she said.

Mrs Belamie, lost in who knew what dreams of the far-away past, did not even hear her and Eve, acutely uncomfortable, left the ring on her hand, where it seemed to burn her with its green fire.

Myrtle came back into the room, two spots of angry colour still in her cheeks.

'The room is ready, Mrs Belamie,' she said.

'The Queen's Room?'

'Yes.'

'Good. You may go now, both of you. I shall want to see you again in the morning, Eve, but not too early. Go out and enjoy yourself. I expect you swim, don't you? I'll send for you when I want you, but it won't be before twelve o'clock. Good night, Myrtle. Good night, Eve, my dear,' and she lay back on the pillows and closed her eyes, already half-asleep, whilst the two girls tiptoed out of the room.

3

Eve woke with a confused idea that she had fallen asleep in some museum or Buckingham Palace, where certainly she had never been.

Then she remembered and sat up and looked about her and laughed softly.

She was in a room as big, or almost as big, as Mrs Belamie's, and in a vast bed with four massive posts with curtains draped between them and forming a ceiling above her head. She had not been able quite to draw the curtains back the night before, but between them she got various glimpses of the room, the huge pieces of mahogany furniture that matched the bed, but thank heaven no 'Old Masters' on the walls. These were covered with an old-fashioned paper of trellis work and roses, and the pictures were water-colours in narrow gilt frames. The hangings of the bed were of gold brocade, and the same material hung from ceiling to floor at the many windows.

She threw back the bed-clothes and let her feet slide to the floor and they were almost lost in the thick pile of the white, rose-patterned carpet.

She chuckled again softly, wishing that Marcia were here to share in the fun. She wondered what queen had slept here to give the room its name. Elizabeth the First? She seemed seldom to have slept in her own bed, by all accounts, but though Weir House was so grand inside, it could scarcely compete with the Stately Homes at half-a-crown a peep.

She pulled back one of the heavy curtains, a job needing considerable strength, and saw that the windows opened on the wide balcony over the terrace.

It was very early, not quite six, and there was no one about and she went to the edge of the balcony, wearing only her pyjamas, and leaned her arms on the stone rail and thought about all the happenings of the evening before. In broad daylight, away from the macabre fascination of that vast room and the little old woman who dominated it, she could almost discount her part in the shabby trick being played on her. What was it to do with her, after all, how old Mrs Belamie left her money or by what means she was being coerced into leaving it to any particular person? She could not take it with her, and the people who had the best right to it were the grandsons whom she had brought up in the expectation of receiving it. It did not matter in the least to her, Eve, what use they made of it, though she would almost prefer the unpleasant Myrtle to queen it here to its being sold and turned into an hotel, which she felt was the only use to which it could be put. Without the almost frightening wealth stored up in the old pictures, the place made modern by 'improvements' and the old donkey track up the cliff turned into a proper approach for visitors' cars, it would be no more than a rather ugly house on the edge of the sea.

Still, if it became Victor's in the end, Myrtle would probably make the same 'improvements', so what did it matter? The simplest and the fairest thing would be to leave it between the two grandsons, of course, and let them sort it out for themselves, but she had gathered that it would be left to one and one only, and presumably to the one who could produce the more 'suitable' wife!

She chuckled to herself and went inside, for though the air was like wine, it was chilled champagne rather than, say, a Beaune. No one in their right senses could think her a more suitable person than Myrtle to be mistress of this place.

But was old Mrs Belamie quite in her right senses?

Oh well, she was here for a week, and London was sweltering in a heat wave, and she had no job and would have to continue the lugubrious search for one as soon as she got back, so why not enjoy this to the full whilst she had it?

She went through her bedroom into the adjoining bathroom,

of which she had not taken much notice the night before, being too much occupied with thoughts of the happenings of the day. Now she had time to look round her and laughed softly at what she saw.

A certain amount of modern plumbing had been put in. There was a fitted basin with taps instead of probably the jug-and-basin arrangement of the original, but nothing else had been altered in the room which, split into sections, could have accommodated a whole family according to modern standards of living in small boxes. In the middle of the floor was an enormous bath with a wide mahogany surround and brass taps representing lions' heads out of whose mouths the water gushed when she tentatively turned them on. Both mahogany and brass were brightly polished, and were probably kept so, for there would not have been time for such attentions in the half-hour it had taken on the night before to make it ready for her occupation. There was carpet on the floor. Modern or usual for a 'queen' of other days? At one side was a toilet necessity, mahogany-encased like the bath and, like it, having an ornate pattern of blue flowers on the pan. To use it, one had to mount a step which could have served no other purpose than to give a feeling of being enthroned to add dignity to an otherwise undignified procedure. A handle, also blue-flowered, was sunk in the surround to provide the necessary water and the lid which covered the whole thing might have served as a dining-table to seat at least six people!

Still, there was a plentiful supply of hot water and she climbed over the mahogany sill and could have drowned in the huge bath, which would have held four comfortably and still left space in the middle. How Marcia would have enjoyed this! Eve made a mental note of everything so that she could describe it when she got back.

It was not much later than half past six when, bare-legged and wearing little more than a yellow linen frock, her hair still damp from her bath and merely brushed into a careless, curly mop, she made her way cautiously down the wide, shallow steps of the staircase which had led to the first floor (the second flight had been narrower and steeper). A surprised maid, a young one at last, was on her hands and knees polishing the floor when she reached the hall.

Eve smiled at her in her friendly fashion.

'Isn't it a lovely morning? Is it all right if I take a look outside?'

'Oh yes, Miss. That be quite all right,' said the girl in a strong Cornish accent, and she got up to open the front door, though the top bolts proved too high for either of them to reach.

The maid began to drag a heavy chair forward, but Eve stopped her.

'I'll lift you up,' she said. 'Much easier than carting that chair about,' and in a moment she had lifted her up in her strong young arms and she had shot the bolts back, though protesting and giggling and casting a glance over her shoulder as if to make sure no one in authority saw them.

'Easy, wasn't it?' laughed Eve, setting her on her feet.

'I don't know how it would have been if Mr Corke had seen, Miss,' said the girl, 'but he baynt about this early.'

'Nobody seems to be but you and me. Tell me what your name is?'

'Sarah, Miss,' said the girl, shy again.

Eve nodded.

'You know who I am, I expect?'

'Yes, Miss. You be Mr Lewis's young lady. I don't expect he will be up yet. They mostly have breakfast in their rooms, but I could get you some.'

'Will you, Sarah? Presently? How shall I find you when I come back? I must just have a look outside first.'

'If you go into the dining-room and ring, Miss, it'll be me as'll answer it.'

'Thank you so much. I'll ring if I can find the dining-room again!' said Eve gaily and set off across the terrace.

The air was fresh and cold, for the sun had not yet warmed this part of the coast, and she lifted her face to breathe it in as she went across the lawn. London, which never got aired, would still smell of petrol and people!

She came upon the gardeners at work, and they stared at her and then, at her smile, gave her friendly grins.

'Isn't it a gorgeous morning?' she called to them, glad to share it with someone.

'Ah, it be that, Miss,' they agreed and went on with their work, and Eve, having reached the end of the lawn, turned along a small path which she thought might lead her to some means of getting down to the sea.

She found, instead, that it led further inland to where, behind the shielding belt of trees, there were fields, well-kept as was everything else apparently at Weir House, with a herd of cows grazing there.

She got over a style gingerly, for though she had encountered all sorts of animals in her travels with her father, she had never got over her nervousness of the placid English cow.

Crossing a corner of the field, her eyes warily on the grazing herd, she came to a gate, climbed it and sat on the top, spell-bound. Now she could see the sea stretching endlessly away, smooth except for the white horses some distance out but still far below her, empty but for two or three brown-stained fishing boats coming slowly into the little harbour below. There were cottages grouped around the harbour, small patches of pink and blue like the houses of toyland from where she sat. Small figures move about, people and dogs like toys again, and little wisps of smoke went up into the thin air from the chimneys but no sound came to her. She might be alone on top of the world.

And then, by some sixth sense, she knew she was not alone.

Slowly, as if impelled by some force outside herself, she turned her head and saw, seated negligently astride a hump of rock in the field behind her, a man who was observing her with a curiosity not unmixed with a sort of arrogant insolence. He wore a shabby, weather-stained coat over his open-necked shirt of washed-out blue, breeches and leggings, and an ancient deer-stalker cap was pushed back on a crop of dark, unruly hair.

His eyes were piercingly blue against the dark tan of his skin, and a sprig of yellow gorse was caught between brilliantly white teeth, giving him an odd, bizarre appearance from which the bold, faintly derisive smile did not detract.

She felt herself flush, and then, as he said nothing but

49

continued to regard her with that bold look, her eyes blazed and her little chin went up. She made a movement to get down from the gate, missed her footing, and to her outraged discomfort, felt herself caught in his arms and deposited on the ground on her feet.

'Thank you, but you need not have troubled,' she said icily. 'I was quite capable of getting down by myself.'

His amused eyes left her face to travel to a large patch of cow-dung in which she would inevitably have landed but for his timely rescue.

She followed the direction of his eyes with heightened colour, but nothing would have induced her to smile.

She felt impelled to meet his eyes again, however, and was aware now of a little sense of shock. Where had she seen, and recently, those same eyes of dark, brilliant blue? Or was it only his deep tan that made them seem so blue?

But when he spoke to her, she forgot his blue eyes in a surge of anger.

'So you are the new runner in the Matrimonial Stakes for the golden cup?' he asked, his tone matching that derisive smile.

He did not speak like a Cornishman, nor even like a countryman, though there was a slight touch of the Cornish in his accent, rather as if he had spent many years there than been born and bred to it, an educated voice but not, according to her standards, a cultured one.

She received only a vague impression of his voice, however; what he said made her too angry.

'How dare you speak to me like that! Who are you?'

He took off his disreputable deer-stalker and swept her a low bow, straightening himself again to his full height. He towered above her small person, big-framed, broad-shouldered, without an ounce of superfluous flesh on his muscular body.

'Who am I? A mere employee, lady. A creature who ekes out a precarious existence by the charity of others. "The rich man in his castle, The poor man at his gate." The rich man happens to be a woman, but the rest is me.'

His tone and that persistent smile mocked at her. She could not get under his guard. Except for Myrtle, he was the first unfriendly person she had found at Weir House and it was so unreasonable and uncalled-for that she felt helpless.

'Please let me pass,' she said with an attempt at haughtiness.

He had not replaced his cap, but he made her another bow.

'Lady, I would not impede your royal progress to the rich woman's castle for all the gold of Midas.'

She stood for a moment hesitantly.

'Who are you?' she asked again, though what could it possibly matter to her who this shabby man with the brilliant blue eyes and the derisive voice might be?

'I've told you. The beggar at the gate. Alms, lady. Alms, for the love of Allah, alms!' in the whine of the professional beggar.

Suddenly, terrified of she knew not what, though it was certainly not of this man who had in no way threatened her, she turned and ran.

His mocking laughter followed her.

She ran all the way to the house, though she knew he was not following her.

Corke, the solemn old butler, opened the door for her.

'I am sorry, madam. I did not know you were out,' he said. 'May I get you some breakfast?'

'Thank you, Corke,' she said breathlessly.

He would probably know who the strange man was, but she could not very well ask him.

'Perhaps you would like it on the terrace, madam? It is quite sheltered.

'Yes. Yes, please, and – I'm hungry, Corke,' suddenly discovering the fact.

His face relaxed into a momentary smile.

'Bacon and eggs, madam, and toast? Or would you prefer something else?'

'That'll be lovely,' she said, and sat down with a little bump in the chair he set for her.

Now she could think calmly and collectedly about that man.

He was certainly not the beggar he had declared himself to be, no idler or waster, so who and what was he? He seemed to know all about the happenings at Weir House and her position there as Lewis Belamie's fiancée. He had not even glanced at her hand to see the ring on her finger. In fact, he had not looked at anything but straight into her eyes, nor had she done anything but return that brilliant, mocking glance, yet she knew exactly what he looked like.

When Corke brought her breakfast, on a table with folding legs, she cast the strange man from her thoughts and attacked the food with the healthy appetite of the young and happily slim. Like the appointments of the dinner-table last night, those of the breakfast table were perfect, tea and coffee in silver pots, hot and cold milk, the covered dish of bacon and eggs on a hot-plate, a plentiful supply of toast, marmalade and honey, home-made yellow butter and a dish of thick, Cornish cream.

'Heavens, I really shall put on weight!' she thought, helping herself liberally. 'It's a good job it'll only be for a week!'

Presently Corke brought her the papers, which had come up by donkey, the boy riding one and the other loaded with a variety of goods. She commented on this to Corke, who seemed disposed to linger near her youth and brightness.

'Some of the things have to come up from the village, madam, but most of the food is supplied from the home farm. Would you be interested to see that?'

'A farm? Belonging to the house? Yes, I think I would. Perhaps I can get Mr Lewis to take me there.'

'I don't think either of the young gentlemen really care for the farm, but no doubt Mr Lewis would be pleased to take you there later on. Have you finished, madam?'

'I've eaten enormously,' she laughed.

'It's the air, madam, and Cook will be pleased that you've eaten a good breakfast. Young people ought to eat well.'

'Not when we're supposed to be skinny! I ought to starve for the rest of the day, but I don't suppose I shall. Good job I shan't be here long!'

'It's a pity, if I may say so, madam. Miss Ford says you quite cheered Madame up last night, and that she had a very good night.'

Eve had already learnt that Mrs Belamie was referred to by her staff as 'Madame' and she remembered that there had been a French husband, which probably accounted for it. It suited the old autocrat.

The two men came down when they discovered that Eve was already up and about.

'Good morning, Eve. I hope you slept well?' said Lewis formally.

She got up from her chair and, to his intense embarrassment, put an arm about his neck and kissed him.

'Wonderfully, darling, thank you,' she said gaily. 'The queen certainly had a comfortable bed! But, oh Lewis, have you seen her bathroom? You could hold a reception in it whilst you bathed!'

'I am afraid I've not seen the Queen's Room,' he replied stiffly. 'I have never known it in use before.'

'Aren't I honoured then? Is the whole house kept in such spotless order? There wasn't time to do any spring-cleaning before I was enthroned in it – and enthroned is certainly the word!' chuckling at the memory of the Queen's Bathroom, which she thought of with initial capitals.

'Would you like to go for a swim this morning, Eve?' asked Victor.

'Love to. How do we get down to the beach?'

'There's a path and steps, rather an effort, I'm afraid. I don't suppose Myrtle will want to come, but I'll ask her. Can you be ready in half an hour or so?'

'I'm ready now,' said Eve, oblivious of the fact that she had only just finished a large breakfast.

'We need not go just yet, but as I understand that my grandmother would like you to visit her again, it would be as well to be back in good time.'

'Not before twelve, she said.'

'She sometimes changes her mind so it is better to be prepared. She isn't used to being kept waiting,' said Lewis, casting a nasty little smile at his brother.

It was evidently a matter for congratulation that Eve had been asked so soon to pay the old lady a second visit.

Half an hour later they were on their way to the beach Myrtle had elected not to go with them, and Eve had changed into an enchanting little suit specially made for the purpose and consisting of a little circular skirt and a jacket of brightly patterned drip-dry cotton worn over a brief swim-suit of elasticised satin to tone with it.

When they showed her the little path which she had over-looked earlier, she ran ahead, leaping down the steep steps cut in the rock, and was already in the water when they arrived more slowly and carefully at the bottom, peeled off their very correct flannels and college blazers behind a rock discreetly and waded gingerly into the water.

Eve could not repress a grin at sight of them, Lewis long and skinny and Victor like a little barrel in his bathing trunks which must be kept up by suction, for he had no definite waist and hips on which to moor them.

They were reasonably good swimmers, however, though they warned her not to go out too far because of the under-current, which she had already felt tugging at her legs as she swam.

When they came out, the two men went behind the rocks at once to dress, but Eve lay stretched out on a flat rock in the sun and closed her eyes in dreamy contentment.

She might not have been so contented had she known that the man she had met earlier that morning had paused at the top and was looking down at her. Her skin was beginning to turn golden already, for she never had to endure the pink and red stages of sunburn, used as she had been all her life to tropical suns. He saw the graceful abandon of the outstretched limbs against the grey rocks, her face turned to the sunshine, her pale silvery gold hair seeming a part of the sun itself, and with a small grimace, he turned away.

It was none of his business, of course, but why on earth should a girl like that think it worth while to sell herself to a drip like Lewis Belamie for the old girl's money? For of course that was all it was, and she had not even the certainty that Lewis would get it! It could just as well be the abominable Myrtle, but you could never tell with the old girl. Anyway, onlookers usually had most of the fun.

Exactly at noon, the summons came to all of them to attend, and they went in procession up the stairs, Eve in her yellow linen again, Myrtle wearing a cotton dress, white patterned with red which did not suit her any better than the evening frock of electric blue, the two men immaculate now in white flannels and their blazers.

Eve gave a little squeak of laughter outside the baize door.

'It's like having an audience with the queen,' she said.

'Ssh!' warned the others as the nurse opened the door and ushered them into the inner hall.

'How is she this morning?' whispered Victor.

'A bit uppish. Better mind your p's and q's,' replied the nurse in the same tone and opened the door into the bedroom.

They advanced to the bed, Myrtle leading but Eve hanging back a little behind the two men.

The room was darker than it had been by artificial light, for the curtains were drawn against the sunlight which was not kind to wrinkles and the freshly painted cheeks. The corners of the room lay in shadows, but a small, electric light under a pink shade threw its rosy glow over the central figure in the bed.

'Good morning, *grand-mère*,' said Victor. 'I'm glad to hear that you slept well.'

'Don't crowd me, don't crowd me!' snapped the old lady. 'I want to breathe whilst I can. As to sleeping well, you'd have been glad, all three of you, if I'd slept well enough not to wake again.'

'We don't want you to die, *grand-mère*,' put in Lewis feebly.

'You're a liar,' said Mrs Belamie, and Eve could have sworn that she heard the echo of 'that man's' laugh from a corner of the room, but how could she have done? Apart from Mrs Belamie and the nurse, there were only the four of them in the room.

The old lady was peering with her bright eyes amongst the little group by the bed, and suddenly Eve thought of those same eyes of intense blue which she had already seen once that morning – in the face of that man!

Good heavens, she was haunted by that maddening memory! A lot of people had blue eyes.

'Where's that girl? What's her name? Eve. Where is she?' asked Mrs Belamie querulously.

Eve stepped forward reluctantly and the others made way for her. She laid her hand gently on the wrinkled fingers.

'I'm here, Mrs Belamie,' she said.

The hand closed tightly round hers with a surprisingly strong grip.

'H'm,' she said. 'H'm. Nice. I like that yellow dress. Why don't you wear something simple like that, Myrtle, instead of looking like a pillar box daubed with white paint? Not yellow, though. Wouldn't suit you with your sallow skin. You'd look more like a decayed cabbage stalk, worse than a pillar box.'

Eve felt a wave of sympathetic resentment. The old lady said the most outrageous things and evidently did not mind how much she hurt people. Myrtle, whose face had gone brick-red, fortunately did not attempt to reply and Mrs Belamie looked down at the hand she still held.

'Where's your ring?' she demanded. 'The one I gave you last night?'

'I – it's a bit loose. I was afraid I might lose it,' said Eve haltingly.

As a matter of fact, she had managed to conceal it from Myrtle last night, and had purposely not put it on this morning for fear of giving offence.

'Rubbish. What would it matter if you did? I've got plenty more and you might as well have them as anybody else,' with a baleful glance at Myrtle, who was still flushed. 'Go and get it. Put it on. Wear it,' and Eve scuttled out of the room, pausing when she was outside at the realisation that she, as well as everyone else, rushed to obey.

For a moment she was tempted to go back without the ring, defying the old autocrat. Then she decided that she might as well do as she was told. It might make it easier for the others, since Mrs Belamie was certainly not in a good mood.

She went back wearing the ring and Mrs Belamie took her hand again to make sure. She caught a nasty look from Myrtle but she could not have prevented the gift of the ring, and anyway she would leave it behind when she left.

'It's not loose,' declared Mrs Belamie, examining it. 'It fits you much better than it did me. It's the only emerald thing

I've ever had. I've never liked them. Can't remember who gave it to me.'

'I can,' said an unexpected voice from the other side of the room – the voice of 'that man'! 'It was that Italian count, or so you told me once.'

Mrs Belamie threw a glance in the direction of the voice.

'You still here, Felix? What for?' she asked testily.

He came lounging out from the shadowed corner. Except that he wore no hat and had thrown aside his jacket, he was dressed just as he had been that morning, even to the boots and leggings. Even in this big room he looked huge, dwarfing the other two men.

'You wanted to talk to me about those new heifers, remember?' he said, coming to stand near the bed.

'H'm. Yes. All right. You can go, the rest of you. Not you, Eve. I like to have you near me. You don't fidget about or say idiotic things to me,' which was hardly fair as none of them had said anything for a long time. 'Well? What are you waiting for? I told you to go, didn't I? Do you want my stick about your backs?'

The three of them turned and hurried out of the room, and the man Mrs Belamie had called 'Felix' laughed.

'Good for you, old lady,' he said. 'Three blind mice, see how they run!'

'Yes, and I would cut off their tails with a carving knife if they didn't.'

'Mine too?' he asked and took a seat on the side of the bed, to Eve's astonishment.

'You? You haven't got a tail. At least, I never see it wag.'

'Perhaps I'm a bob-tailed sheep-dog? Or a guinea pig?' he said, and she gave a dry cackle of laughter. She did not seem in the least to resent his taking a seat on her bed, though Eve guessed that none of the three who had just left the room would have dared to do so.

'You can go as well, Ford,' said Mrs. Belamie. 'Miss Brayle will stay with me till you bring me my luncheon. What am I having?'

'Sweetbreads done in milk and a pear condé,' said the nurse.

'Pah! Invalid stuff! Why can't I have a steak, or some fried fish and chipped potatoes, and fried onions with the steak?'

'You couldn't chew the steak if I gave it to you, and you can't digest onions and the doctor says you're not to have fried fish, that's why.'

'Doctors! What do I want with doctors? He only comes so that he can send me in a bill.'

'Well, do as you like. I'll give you fried fish tomorrow *and* chips, but don't blame me if you die of it,' said the nurse equably.

'Well, perhaps you're right. I don't want to die yet and I'm not going to. Too many things to see to. I'll have the sweetbreads and the other mess, but not pears. Can't stand them. I'll have raspberries.'

'The seeds get under your plate.'

'Well, whose plate is it, yours or mine?'

'Yours, but I have to get them out.'

'That's what you're paid for, isn't it?'

'Amongst a few other things, I suppose. O.K. raspberries,' and with a final settling of the pillows, she marched out of the room.

'I can't think why she stands you,' said the man, Felix.

'Same reason as everybody else. For what I pay her.'

'Include me out!' he said with a grin.

'Oh – you! Dunno why you stay.'

'Could be because you'd never get anybody else to do what I do?'

'Huh!' she grunted non-committally. 'What do you think of this child?' turning again to Eve, who had remained standing by the bed.

He rose to his feet and came round to where she stood and looked her up and down with that same derisive grin of the early morning, and her face flushed hotly.

'Not bad,' he said. 'Not bad at all. Pretty. Nice shape. Good legs. I like her hair, too. Same colour as yours, but a bit lighter.'

Mrs Belamie cackled delightedly and Eve would have left the room in high dudgeon but was held firmly by the hand.

'She's not one of your prize heifers, you know! What about those heifers? Are they any good? Worth keeping for milk?'

'We've got all the milk we can do with, but we can sell more cream if we breed 'em now. Or butter. Always a call for that and the pigs'll be needing the skim soon.'

'Will they take Phoebus or is he getting a bit rough?'

'We can use A.I.'

She cackled again.

'Not much fun for the cows, though they won't know it, poor things. All right. Do what you like about them. Going to stay for lunch?'

'And play gooseberry to two pairs of turtle doves? Not much,' he said. 'I'll be getting along now. I'll call in for a bite in the kitchen on the way out. So long, old dear,' and he smiled at the old lady, gave Eve a contemptuous nod and strolled out.

Mrs Belamie chuckled.

'Surprised, eh?'

'A bit. Who is he?' asked Eve, trying to smooth down her ruffled feathers.

'Felix Welby? My other grandson.'

This time Eve really was surprised.

'I didn't know you had three,' she said.

'Born the wrong side of the blanket. You might as well know about it. The rest of 'em do. My daughter's child. Name's Belamie, I suppose, if it's anything, but I've never let him use it. I made Welby up. Never knew the father's name. She was dead when I got there.'

'And you brought him up?'

'More or less. Not like the others, my son's boys, of course, but I had him fed and educated and in due course found him a job.'

'Here?'

'Yes. He owed me service for all the years I'd kept him.'

'But he is your own grandson!'

'Yes, but he cost my daughter her honour and her life.'

Mrs Belamie's mouth grew thin and hard, and her chin jutted out in defiance of the girl's thoughts.

Yes, Felix Welby was like her, far more like her than were either of the other two, and not only in the eyes but also in mouth and chin. His could, she felt, be just as hard. They were birds of a feather, neither prepared to yield an inch. Unaccountably, she shivered.

'That wasn't his fault,' she said.

'He was the living result of her folly. My daughter was a lovely girl. I was married when I was barely twenty and I had to wait a long time for her, twelve years. Two years later my son Louis was born, but I always loved Helen best. After my husband died, she stayed with me, went to a day school here in England. All the men were after her. She was so beautiful. But somehow she didn't want to marry. We were so happy together, such friends. Then when we were on holiday in France, I came home because my son's wife had nearly died losing her first child. Helen wanted to stay on in France. She was nearly thirty-two and it didn't seem to matter so I – left her there. I never saw her alive again. She simply disappeared. I didn't know where she had gone nor who she had gone with, but I had one letter from her saying that she was all right, very happy but living with a married man as his wife. She did not tell me his name, did not tell me where to find her. It nearly broke my heart. Then I had a telegram from her to ask me to come to her, to a place near Rouen, but she died before I got there. The child lived. The doctor's wife was looking after it. There was no one else, no man, and the name the doctor knew her by was Belamie. She had left a note for me. I could scarcely read it. It was all smudged with her tears. She asked me to call the baby Felix. Felix for happiness, though I felt she had had little of it. I brought the child home and put it with foster-parents. I could not bear even to look at it for some years. Then, when he was about sixteen the foster mother died and her husband did not want the boy so I brought him here. He was big enough and strong enough to work on the farm but he's never lived in the house. I found an old woman to look after him in a cottage on the estate but when my son died and I took over the care of Victor and Lewis, I told them the truth about Felix. I thought they had a right to know, but

there's never been friendship between them, nor have I ever
thought of Felix as my grandson. Thirty-two years ago my
lovely Helen died. Thirty-two years of bitter sorrow and futile
regret. I'd have forgiven her everything if she had trusted me,
but she didn't. And all I've got left of her is Felix. I've never
loved or wanted him, but – well – we are friends now, I suppose. He works well for me. I pay him but he knows he's not
going to get anything out of me, except perhaps the cottage he
lives in. He's the only one who's not waiting for me to die
because he knows he'll lose his job.'

The thin voice had been growing weaker. Now she was
almost exhausted and lay back against the pillows, grey-faced
under the rouge.

'I ought not to have let you talk so long,' said Eve
anxiously.

The blue eyes opened again.

'I'm all right. I've liked telling you. Perhaps you'd better
send Ford in. She won't be far away.'

Eve hurried to the door. The nurse stood in the inner hall,
waiting like a faithful dog.

'She wants you to go to her. I'm afraid I've let her talk too
much.'

'Once she starts, nothing can stop her. Don't worry. It won't
have hurt her. I've put her lunch back a bit. Telling you about
Felix Welby, has she?'

'You know about him?'

'I've been with her more than twenty years, my dear. I know
everything about her, and about him. Don't you worry now.
she won't die till she wants to, and that's not yet. Go down to
your lunch, and I wouldn't say anything about Felix to the
others. Just as well if they think you don't know,' and with a
reassuring little pat, she went into the bedroom and left Eve
to go downstairs.

She did not see Mrs Belamie again that day, nor did she ask
Lewis to take her to the farm. She did not want to see Felix
Welby again, though she told herself it was because now that
she knew who he was, she might feel embarrassed.

But the next day, after lunch, she decided to go to the baize door and knock on the wooden frame of the door to ask the nurse how Mrs Belamie was.

Before she could knock, the door opened and the nurse came out with Felix. Her impulse was to turn and run, but she would not give him that satisfaction, so, ignoring him, she spoke to the nurse instead.

'Oh, Miss Ford, I came to ask you how Mrs Belamie is,' she said.

Felix interrupted.

'Now isn't that nice? Such a well-behaved guest, isn't she, Emma?'

Emma Ford turned a half-laughing, half-angry face to him.

'It's very nice of Miss Brayle to come,' she said.

'But of course she'd come! She's going to marry one of the young hopefuls, you know. There's only one woman I'd ever marry, and that's you, Emma darling,' and he seized her buxom form in his arms and planted a smacking kiss on her cheek.

Eve turned to go without the information she had come for, and she heard a laugh, a smart slap and the swing of the baize door as it closed behind the nurse.

The next moment Felix had caught up with Eve and barred the way. She had intended to escape to her room, but he was too quick for her.

'My women always treat me rough,' he said. 'I hope you don't behave in the same way towards your intended? By the way, I congratulate you on your approach to our Gorgon. I don't mean yesterday. I mean the night you came. I was outside and I saw you at her window, drawing the curtain aside. She must have asked you to do so and to admire the view. You did extremely well, that look of rapture on your face, the half-drawn gasp of enchantment which I could only imagine. It was a pity that most of it had to be wasted on me because of course with your back to her, the old lady could not see the act, but your performance was really superb. I've got to hand it to you. Tell me, though, as a matter of interest and to assist me in my study of feminine psychology, was it all done impromptu or had you rehearsed it in front of the mirror?'

She had listened in helpless anger to the tirade, but she could not escape. He had her in a corner of the passage, his hands stretched out on the angle of the banister.

'Why do you talk to me like this? How – how dare you?' she almost spat at him.

He laughed lazily. There was no possibility of help coming. Myrtle had gone to lie down, she had refused an invitation to go into the village in the small staff car which the two men had borrowed, and at this hour of the day, the servants were having their dinner.

'Dare? Do you use the word "dare" to me, you small thing?' he asked and before she guessed his intention or could frustrate it, he had swung her up in his arms and set her on the broad ledge of the banister, where she sat with her legs dangling, with a sheer drop of some twenty feet down to the hall below.

'Don't struggle,' he warned her, holding her there firmly. 'I'd hate to see you spread all over the floor down there. Whilst you rely on me, you'll be perfectly safe.'

'Let me get down at once,' cried Eve, but softly in case her voice could penetrate the baize door.

'What are you going to do? Scream for help? Have one of the servants come up and rescue you from the bold, bad man?'

She sat perfectly still and rigid. The last thing she wanted was for one of the servants to witness her predicament, neither did she intend to struggle against the strong, brown hands that held her. The earthy, masculine smell of him was in her nostrils, a smell of the open-air and the sea, of farm animals and good tobacco and tweed. She wondered if she would ever get rid of the memory of it.

'It's no good your either fighting me or standing on your dignity with me,' he went on in his slow, lazy voice. 'You'll have to accept me as a permanent source of annoyance, at least whilst the old lady's alive. They all do, even the divine Myrtle and the fish-faced Belamie *frères*, or I ought to say Myrtle and *one* fish-faced Belamie. I'd almost forgotten you are going to marry the other – always supposing you play your cards well enough to secure the golden prize for him! I shouldn't actually marry him, if I were you, until you've made

63

quite sure about that. Without the money, Lewis is no catch for a girl like you. You could do much better and you're young enough to be able to wait a year or two. Still, if you play your cards right, I don't mind betting that she'll have her lawyers in the place in a day or two and everything fixed up.'

'How – how perfectly *beastly* you are,' said Eve in a voice whose fury had to be concentrated into a small compass.

It was infuriating and humiliating to be at his mercy like this.

He laughed softly.

'You know, you're extremely attractive when you're angry, Eve,' he said, 'though actually Emma Ford's more my style. More substantial, for one thing.'

'Let me get down,' she said fiercely, 'and if I never see you again, it'll be too soon.'

'Now isn't that just too bad? Because you will be seeing me again. I'm dining here tonight, for one thing. I do sometimes, you know. The dog that licks up the crumbs from the rich woman's table is sometimes permitted to sit in a chair. I'm always underfoot. Also you won't be able to keep up the business with the old lady without me. She'll expect me to show you round the estate, and visit the farm. Scratch the pigs' backs, you know, and be bright about cows. I know you'd rather go hand in hand with dear Lewis, with the chance of sly kisses behind the hay-rick and a bit of a cuddle in the byre, but he doesn't know a thing about the place and would hate to get his shoes dirty. Also – he'd lose you amongst the stalls and pig-styes whereas I'd never lose you, Eve, never!'

His voice had changed, perhaps unconsciously, had become softer, had lost its derisive note and its scorn and she caught a glint of something that was not mockery in his blue eyes.

'Let me get down,' she said with as much dignity as she still possessed.

'Please,' he said.

She swallowed and then repeated the word meekly.

'Please.'

'Please, Felix.'

'Please, Felix,' she said in a small voice.

64

He tightened his hands about her waist and swung her lightly down, but he still held her there, his big hands almost spanning her waist. Holding her, he marched her down the corridor and stood her in front of a long mirror set in the wall panelling.

'Look at yourself, Eve Brayle, you little scrap of nothing in your white dress – lovely, entrancing little Eve. What the hell do you mean by saying you're going to marry Lewis Belamie, that yard of flat pump-water? You aren't in love with him. You couldn't be.'

It took a desperate effort for her to look away from the blue eyes reflected in the mirror. They were so like old Mrs Belamie's, but with youth in them, real youth not the desperate clinging to life of the old. They were so much alike, those two, ruthless, autocratic, wringing every last drop out of life as she felt he could do in equal measure if he cared to.

She gave an involuntary shiver and forced her eyes from his.

'What is it to you? I can marry anyone I like.'

'Or just one you love? That isn't Lewis. What is it to me? Nothing really, except that I don't like to see people make a mess of their lives and speculate afterwards as to where they went wrong.'

'Why should you assume that I am going to make a mess of my life?'

'My dear girl, look at Lewis. Just think of him since happily he is not with us at the moment. Could life with him be anything but a mess? He's got his head in the clouds but his feet are not on the solid earth. And how much do you think you're going to get out of the old lady's estate for yourself even if he does get it? I'm all for getting money, if you like it and can get it honestly, but what would you do with it? A flat in town all chromium and square furniture with a cocktail bar? If that's what you want, I really do sympathise with you for having to take Lewis on as a necessary preliminary!'

'I suppose you imagine I should be better off with you?'

Now why on earth had she said that? The words had just popped out in her anger. He had certainly not given her any reason for saying them. She felt like some small insect trying to sting a bar of iron for all the effect it had on him, for he threw back his head and laughed.

'Good Lord, no! I'm no woman's man nor ever shall be. I adore your sex as a whole, but to have one woman clinging to me for life – no! One woman to order all my comings and goings? One woman walking down the aisle with me dressed like a Christmas cake and with that "Gottim!" expression on her face? Never, my dear, never! Also I've got no claim to the old lady's estate, so you couldn't get it through me, if I were willing. Far better pin your hopes on Lewis.'

'You're quite the most conceited, insufferable creature I've ever met or am likely to meet,' she cried, beside herself with fury. 'Please take your hands off me!'

He laughed again and let her go and she ran into her bedroom and slammed the door. The sound of his laughter echoed in her mind when the thick door had shut it from her ears, mocking, derisive, contemptuous. She was angry with herself and with him, perhaps the more with herself because she was humiliated by disgust of what she was doing. Whilst none of them had been real people, not even Lewis as a person whom she knew, it had been no more than a silly prank to get away from London and the search for a job because of the nostalgic longing for the sort of life she had always lived, easy, comfortable, moving on somewhere else when conditions were boring or unpleasant, finding the hot sunshine or the cold of snow and ice, always adventure and excitement shared with her beloved father, the only real companion she had ever needed.

Just a prank when Lewis had suggested it – but now it was no longer that because the people had become real, old Mrs Belamie with the money her wrinkled, bejewelled hands would cling to until they relaxed in death, the two brothers whose only thought was how to get their hands on it, the hard-eyed, tight-lipped Myrtle whom she could not conceive of having any softness and love for Victor – and Felix Welby, who taunted and despised her, Eve, as being one of them.

The awful, paralysing thought was that she minded his opinion of her! In the middle of their bitter words to each other, his eyes had softened and he had called her 'lovely, entrancing little Eve', and her heart had turned to water and she had no longer wanted him to release her, but the next moment he was full of scorn for her again, lashing her into impotent fury.

Why should she mind what he thought of her? What was he to her?

The bitter thing was that she did mind.

When she heard the men talking as they crossed the lawn, she went downstairs.

'Lewis, I want to speak to you,' she said, and Victor went into the house and left them together.

'What's the matter?' he asked uneasily.

'I can't go through with it. I want to go back. I'm not staying.'

He caught hold of her arm and walked her a little farther from the house, his eyes following Victor and seeing Myrtle on the terrace.

'Why? What's the idea?'

'I'm in a hateful position. I've had enough of it. It's beastly.'

'It's no different from what it was when you said you'd come.'

'I hadn't met people then. Now I have – Mrs Belamie – and—'

'And Felix Welby?' he asked furiously.

'Yes, but he doesn't count. It's Mrs Belamie. She's been good to me. I think she likes me, and I feel cheap in trying to deceive her and playing a trick on her. I want to go, tonight if possible.'

'You can't. There's no train,' he said weakly.

'Then first thing in the morning. I'm not staying. You can tell them anything you like. Say I've broken off the engagement. Anything you like,' and she wrenched off the ring and tried to give it back to him but he would not take it.

And just at that moment, Emma Ford came running out of the house towards them.

'She wants you, Miss Brayle. You'd better be quick. She's raising the roof,' and she caught the girl's hand and hurried her away, Eve with the ring still clutched in her hand. 'I

67

couldn't find you till I saw you out here. Thank heaven I did! They're all running about like rabbits for you.'

There was nothing for it but to put the ring back on her finger. She had no pocket in her dress.

'Must I really go to her?' she asked as they ran.

'Good heavens, yes! You're all expected to be at her beck and call at a moment's notice.'

The nurse was breathless by the time she had fairly pushed Eve into the room where Mrs Belamie was sitting upright in bed, her eyes blazing, her face red, her voice shrill as one of the maids, hastily summoned, was trying to reassure her.

As soon as she saw Eve, there was a complete metamorphosis. She lay back against her pillows, her eyes ceased to flash fire and her hands to beat the bed-clothes and she smiled triumphantly.

'Oh, there you are, Eve. You can go now, both of you. No, I don't want that,' thrusting aside the bottle of tablets which the nurse had hurriedly picked up from the table and scattering the contents all over the floor. 'You can go, do you hear? You can pick them up afterwards.'

When they had gone hastily from the room, the nurse giving one meaning look at Eve as she went, Mrs Belamie laughed delightedly.

'Where were you?' she asked.

'In the garden – with Lewis.'

'Well, you've got plenty of time for love-making, if that oaf knows how to do it. Shouldn't think he does, does he? Well, you needn't tell me. You must see something in him that I don't see – unless it's my money you're after. Is it?' fixing the girl with her eyes.

'No!'

Mrs Belamie patted her hand.

'Do you know, I believe you. That Myrtle, well of course she is after it. She fancies herself as mistress here. Putting you on the second floor, indeed! Do you like the Queen's Room?'

'It's palatial,' said Eve.

'Comfortable?'

'Yes. Very.'

68

'Now tell me what you've been doing today. You haven't been to see me all day.'

'I thought you'd send for me when you wanted me.'

'You don't have to wait for that. I want to see you every day, every day, mind. Not the others. Just you. Did you swim this morning?'

'Yes, it was lovely.'

'I used to swim when we first came here, but that was many years ago. I don't think I could manage it now, though I'd like to set them all by the ears by threatening to!' with a shrill, elfish laugh. 'They want to be sure I've altered my Will first. Now tomorrow I want you to go over the estate and to see the farm. You haven't seen it yet?'

'No.'

'Felix had better show it to you. He knows all about it. I'll tell him,' and she rang the hand-bell on the table.

The nurse, who had been standing outside, came instantly.

'Tell Felix Welby I want him.'

'Now? He's coming to dinner tonight,' she said.

'All right. That'll do, but I want to see him as soon as he comes. Tell Corke. That's all. You can go again now. No, not you, Eve. Stay and talk to me. Tell me about yourself. What do you do in London? Got any money?'

Eve managed to summon a little laugh.

'Not much,' she said. 'I – I work. At least, I try to. Actually I'm out of a job at the moment. I shall have to look for another when I go back, but the trouble is that I'm not much good at anything.'

She realised at once that she had made a mistake, for the old lady was quick to seize the advantage.

'Then you need not go back just yet,' she said with satisfaction. 'The rest of them can go back when they like, but you can stay. It's nice to have someone pretty to look at for a change. I think one of these days I'll get up and you shall take me for a drive. I can, you know. One of the servants can wheel me in my chair along the top road so that I can get into the car. Yes, I shall like that. Not tomorrow because you're going to the farm, but the next day perhaps. I'll tell Ford. And she needn't think she's coming with me because you and I are going alone and I'm going to buy you something pretty. Now tell me. Have you got a pretty dress? Something really pretty – you know, fluffy and frilly?'

Eve remembered, with something of a shock, that only that morning she had telephoned to Marcia to send her some more clothes, and Marcia had said that she would go to the flat during her lunch hour and dispatch a case to her. It would be on its way already, and if she carried out her intention of leaving in the morning, it would come after she had left and someone would have the trouble of sending it back. She had not told Marcia what to send, only that she wanted some 'grander' things than what she had brought with her, the silly idea in her mind at the time being that she would out-shine Myrtle in her harsh blue!

Perhaps she had better wait until the following day, after all. But how was she now to explain to Mrs Belamie why she wanted to go? The old lady's voice was still rippling on, making more plans. Eve caught words here and there and gradually found her attention riveted on what she was saying.

'Yes, that will be a good idea. You'll like that, my dear, and it's a long time since we had any festivity here. I shall stay very quietly all day so as to be equal to it. We'll postpone the drive till another day. Get a pencil and paper. There's one in the desk over there. We must make sure not to forget anybody. People will come from quite a distance, you know, perhaps even from London. We must put them up in the house, of course. Mrs Hodd will see to that. Then there is the orchestra. Band, I suppose you call it. We used to have one from Truro but that was a long time ago. Ask Corke if he remembers who they were. Dear me, I suppose half the people who used to come are dead now, but they will have children, grandchildren probably. Have you found the paper and pencil? I'd better ask Ford who's still alive,' and she rang the bell again with vigour. 'Oh Ford,' she said when the nurse appeared, 'I'm going to give a ball.'

Emma Ford stared at her.

'Have you gone crazy, or what?' she asked.

'Is it crazy to want to liven things up a bit? Now don't argue. I've made up my mind. Find my little red book and go through the names and you can telephone to find out who there is in the families to come. It's to be next Thursday. Tell Mrs Hodd and Corke I want them. And you'd better send for my grandsons and Miss Mellor. I'll tell them.'

'You're quite mad, of course,' said the nurse crossly, but she found the red book and gave it to her, exchanging a helpless look with Eve as she did so.

'Write these down, Eve,' and she began to read out a list of names, giving scandalous comments on each as she did so, and was only interrupted by the arrival of Felix Welby, to whom she told her scheme at once.

He chuckled.

'Good for you, old lady,' he said. 'Do you a power of good.'

Mrs Belamie flung a triumphant glance at the nurse, and at Eve, who had said nothing and was completely flabbergasted by the whole idea.

'There, you see? At least one of you has got a bit of sense. Why shouldn't I give a party?'

'No reason on earth if you want to,' said Felix, sitting on the end of the bed.

He had altered his appearance completely, and was wearing a dinner-jacket suit and white shirt, immaculate and perfectly fitting, his thick dark hair well brushed, his blue eyes twinkling as they met their counterpart in his grandmother's face.

'You're got up like a dog's dinner,' she said. 'Is that to impress Eve?'

His eyes flickered over the girl with an odd look in them which she could not interpret.

'I doubt if anything I said or did could impress Miss Brayle,' he said mockingly, and she felt her face flame.

How perfectly beastly he could be!

'I want her to see the farm tomorrow. Arrange a time with her and come and fetch her. Just Eve. I shall want the rest of them. They may as well make themselves useful and there will be plenty to do. You'd better go and get ready for dinner, Eve. Felix, you stay with me. And don't fuss so, Ford! Anybody would think I was dying, and I'm not, you know, not by a long chalk.'

Eve took her departure thankfully but as she made a rapid change of dress, she was realising that she could not go back tomorrow, as she had planned. Undoubtedly before the morning too many wheels would have been set in motion and she could not disrupt the machinery now.

4

OVER dinner that night, all the talk was of the proposed
ball.

Victor and Lewis and Myrtle thought the whole idea was
absurd and, since there had been no entertaining at Weir
House for many years, impossible to achieve. Felix, on the
other hand, was all in favour of it whilst Eve sat silent, saying
nothing.

'Of course, it won't come off,' said Victor. 'She may issue
invitations, probably to people who're dead, but who would
not come, and at a moment's notice like this?'

'Don't make any mistake,' said Felix. 'Plenty of people will.
They'll come if only out of curiosity, and at this very moment
Emma's got the job of ringing up hundreds of numbers to
find out whether people are still alive and the names of their
surviving families. They'll come all right,' and he chuckled
with glee.

'She's even talking of a special train from London.'

'And how are they going to get here when even the top road
won't take a car of any size?'

'She's going to have a fleet of small cars to transfer them to,'
said Felix.

'Suppose it's pouring with rain?'

'Believe me, they'll be prepared for that rather than miss
the show!'

'It's a ridiculous idea! She hasn't been out of bed for weeks,
and yet she proposes to dress and come down!'

'You bet she will, too! Even the thought of it has put new
life into her and she's going to have the regalia sent from the

73

bank for the occasion,' laughed Felix. 'I hope you girls have got your best bibs and tuckers. You, Myrtle?'

'I shall have to send to London for something,' said Myrtle angrily. 'I've nothing suitable. Perhaps if I telephoned Charisse in the morning, they might have something. They know my fitting. What about you, Eve?'

'My friend is sending me a few more of my clothes, and I shall have to make do with what she sends,' said Eve. 'I don't think I matter much.'

There was a gleam of satisfaction in Myrtle's eyes.

'Well, of course, people know me, even down here, and as I shall be regarded more or less as the hostess, I shall have to be suitably dressed,' she said.

'I thought it was the old lady's idea to be her own hostess,' put in Felix drily.

Even when they were all together, Eve noticed that he never referred to her as his grandmother, and seldom by name, though she knew that they were all aware of the relationship and acknowledged it to the extent of having him to dine with them though he was no more than the farm manager.

Myrtle's face coloured a little and she gave him a hostile glance. It was clear that there was no love lost between the two.

'I imagine she will only make a very brief appearance and then it will devolve on me as Victor's fiancée,' she said.

'Surely on both of you?'

Eve interposed quickly.

'I can assure you I shouldn't want to be in any such position,' she said, 'so you can count me out. I am only a sort of interloper.'

'Don't talk nonsense,' said Lewis irritably. 'You've just as much right here as Myrtle. You're engaged to me.'

He was looking at her appealingly, remembering that she had said she was giving up the pretence and returning to London, though from the discussion on clothes it seemed apparent that she was going to stay for the ball.

Eve shrugged her shoulders.

'It really doesn't concern me very much,' she said, and Felix changed the subject.

'I understand that you want to see the farm tomorrow, Miss Brayle.'

Miss Brayle, when he had called her 'lovely, entrancing little Eve'!

'It was Mrs Belamie's suggestion, Mr Welby,' meeting his eyes for the first time, two blue steel daggers in hers.

'Her suggestions are always law. What time shall I call for you?'

'Any time you like.'

'Say half past nine? I'll bring a horse for you. You do ride, I believe?' blandly.

She could not repress a little smile.

'A donkey, anyway.'

He must have heard of her arrival at Weir House.

'You wouldn't prefer that means of locomotion?'

'No. I can ride most things.'

'I hope you'll bring a quiet horse for Eve, Felix,' said Lewis pompously.

'I said I could ride most things, but thank you for your solicitude, *darling*,' she said sweetly.

'I can assure you that I'll take the greatest care of your beloved, Lewis. As much as if she were my own!'

It was really maddening the power he had to bring the angry colour to her cheeks!

'Shall we adjourn for coffee?' suggested Myrtle in her grand hostess manner. 'We'll have it on the terrace, Corke.'

The old butler pursed his lips but merely inclined his head and was quick to draw Eve's chair back for her as she rose.

'I won't stay for coffee,' said Felix. 'I've got a few things to see to. Half past nine, then, Miss Brayle?'

'I shall be ready,' said Eve frostily.

'I don't like Felix's manner,' said Myrtle when he had left them, strolling across the lawn and whistling to the dogs which were not permitted in the house. 'He is almost insulting, and seeing what his position is—'

She broke off as both the men glaced uneasily at Eve, but she made no comment.

'I mean that he is only the farm manager,' amended Myrtle lamely.

'He has been here a good many years and has got a bit above himself,' said Victor.

'We can change that when—'

Myrtle stopped, flushing, and busied herself with the coffee cups.

Presently Lewis asked Eve to stroll in the garden with him and she got up reluctantly, knowing what was coming.

'You didn't mean what you said this afternoon about going back, did you?' he asked when they were out of earshot of the others.

'I did at the time, but all this business of the ball has caught up on me and I can't very well. Mrs Belamie would be so – hurt by it. But it can't go on. I must tell her, or you must. Invent some excuse, a quarrel or something. Unfortunately I let out to her just now that I haven't a job to go back to, and she asked me to stay on after the rest of you have gone. I didn't know what to say or how to get out of it, but of course I can't. The sooner I can get away from here, the better.'

'She asked you to stay? I knew you'd made a good impression, but to ask you to stay!'

He was obviously pleased, even showing some excitement.

'I'm not going to, of course.'

'Eve, couldn't you – wouldn't you—'

'Definitely, no, Lewis. It's cheap and – absolutely immoral.'

'Eve – I know how it sounds – sudden and all that, but during this day or two here, I – I—'

She interrupted him with a little incredulous laugh.

'Lewis, if you have any thought of actually proposing to me, don't. You're not in love with me any more than I am with you, and at least we needn't pretend to each other.'

'I – I'm not sure that I'm not,' he stammered, red-faced.

She laughed again.

'Don't be silly. Of course you're not. How could you be?'

'You're – you're very pretty, Eve.'

'But not at all nice, or I shouldn't have agreed to this sort of thing just to get out of London in a heat wave,' and she turned to go back to the house, followed rather disconsolately by Lewis.

It had not occurred to Eve to bring riding clothes with her, so the next morning she appeared in grey slacks and yellow sweater just as Felix arrived on a powerful-looking grey leading a spirited chestnut.

Lewis was quick to object.

'You can't be going to put Eve up on that?'

'Why not? She says she can ride most things.'

'Isn't that the one that threw Hodges yesterday?'

'Only because he didn't know how to manage her.'

'How do you know Eve can?' demanded Lewis.

Eve herself interposed. The mare was curvetting about on the leading rein, showing her mettle, and though Felix had her well in hand, the girl suspected that he was allowing her to show off a bit.

'I can try,' she said coolly. 'Hold her for me, Mr Welby, will you?' and when he had dismounted from his own horse and controlled the mare sufficiently, she leaped into the saddle with the least possible help from him, though she gave a gulp and felt her heart miss a beat as the mare reared again and tried to unseat her.

'All right,' she said. 'Let her go,' and as he did so, they were off and away, the mare choosing the direction and Eve having to exert all her not inconsiderable powers of horsemanship to keep her seat.

Felix watched her for a moment and then laughed over his shoulder at Lewis and vaulted on to the grey and sped after her. He had seen in a flash that she knew what she was doing, but he did not forget that only the day before the mare had thrown the experienced stable lad.

He caught up with her but kept behind her whilst the mare, with flying hoofs, headed for the fields, took the stile at a bound and made for the open common. Eve kept her seat with grim determination, and after a time the mare, knowing the rider was master, settled down into a steady gallop.

Felix drew alongside and laughed.

'Good for you,' he said. 'That's one in the eye for dear Lewis. May I be permitted to congratulate you?'

She was breathless, flushed and laughing.

'I'd rather have died than let her unseat me!'

'Yes, I think you would. Going to let her have her head for a bit? She's been eating it off.'

'May I?' she asked and, not waiting for permission, gallopped off at a spanking pace, the grey keeping by her side, until the mare had had enough and was cantering quietly enough.

'I loved that. It's been a long time.'

'You've ridden a lot though?'

'Yes, ever since I was a child. I rode with – with my father,' her face changing as it always did when she spoke of him.

'He died?'

The question was asked gently, and she nodded, looking straight ahead of her as the horses cantered along together peaceably.

'Six months ago.'

'And it made all the difference to you?'

'Yes. We – we always had a lot of money, or I thought we did, and I never had to think about it. Afterwards – well, there just wasn't any, and it left me not knowing quite what to do.'

He was silent. Perhaps that explained, and in a way excused, her engagement to Lewis Belamie, who, even without his grandmother's money, would never be a really poor man. Felix himself, though he had been brought up always to have enough, had never known what it was to have too much of anything but work, and he had accepted the need to work, would never have desired any other lot in life.

But what must it mean to a girl like Eve, always to have had too much and suddenly to have nothing?

'Well,' he said, 'how about turning back now? We're a long way from the farm.'

They rode back sedately, Nina, the mare, having shown what she could do and perhaps recognised a kindred spirit in the girl who rode her and reined in at the stable yard, which was orderly and very clean.

Hodges, the stable boy, came forward rather sheepishly to help Eve to dismount, but Felix was before him and, taken by surprise, she found herself sliding from the mare into his arms. He held her lightly, smiling with that faint shadow of mockery in his eyes again, and set her on the ground before turning to the boy.

'You see? Meek as a lamb, aren't you, my beauty?' he asked, fondling the soft nose and producing an apple from his pocket for her and another for his own horse, Tristram. 'Think you can manage her now Miss Brayle has shown you how to do it? This, Hodges, is Miss Brayle who is going to marry Mr Lewis,' managing to give the words that light twist of scorn which flicked her on the raw.

'Her won't do it again, zur,' said the boy, rubbing his seat ruefully.

'Well, you'd better see that she doesn't, or you'll be out on your ear as well as your seat,' said Felix good-humouredly. 'Look after both of them. We shall want them again when we're ready to go back. Coming, Miss Brayle?' to Eve, who was stroking the nose of another horse looking out over the door of a loose box.

'That's Bessie,' he said. 'She's in foal to Tristram. A winner, I hope.'

'Do you hunt them?'

'No. Hunting isn't much in my line. I don't like to see anything hounded to its death, but luckily there isn't much hunting round here. I prefer point to point.'

He opened the door of the box and ran his hand knowledgeably and affectionately over Bessie, produced another apple for her and went on the next box.

'Are they your own horses?' asked Eve.

'Yes, the only things in the world that belong to me,' he told her with a smile that was now frank and unmalicious. 'That's why I could put you on Nina without asking anybody's permission. I might give her to you as a wedding present. I shan't be able to keep her, anyway.'

'You mean you'll leave here when – when Mrs Belamie dies?' asked Eve, shocked into an indiscretion.

'Of course,' he said shortly. 'You don't imagine that either of my cousins will want me hanging about then, even if they

79

keep the place? You know about the relationship, I suppose?'

She flushed and looked away.

'Yes. Mrs Belamie told me. I – I'm sorry.'

His eyebrows went up.

'Are you? Why? You don't need to be. I've had much more out of life than people born with only one parent usually get. I've been fed, clothed and educated according to my station all my life. I'm even permitted to dine in the ancestral hall with my family, as you observed last night.'

He spoke in a light, bantering tone from which she could not divine his real feelings about his position. Did he really mind?

They left the stables and came out into a yard, again spotlessly clean, where there was a range of byres in which the cows were being milked. He caught the look of apprehension in her eyes and laughed.

'Afraid of them?' he asked teasingly.

'I don't mind when they're tied up, but they always look so fierce when they're loose in a field.'

'You wouldn't make a good farmer's wife then, would you? Good thing you're going to marry a harmless atom bomb instead of a fierce cow.'

She flung up her head and met his eyes.

'Why do you keep harping on that?'

'Do I? Well, I won't any more. Let's leave these wild beasts and go into the other sheds. This is where the milk is cooled as soon as it leaves the cow,' showing her the rivers of milk cascading down the shining metal slats to be piped into the huge churns.

'What do you do with all that milk?' asked Eve, fascinated.

'We use a lot of it up at the house, and for cream and butter and cheese. The farm workers have all they want, too, and any we have left over is sold in the village. Haven't you met any of the children yet?'

'What children?'

'The ones up at the house. Most of the servants are married, and the younger ones have children who live in the houses and

80

additions at the back. It's all quite feudal, you know, with the old lady as the overlord. There's even a school, though some of them go into the village every day. You must ask Lewis to show it all to you. Oh, I forgot I wasn't going to mention him again!'

This time his smile was friendly and held no mockery and, in spite of herself, she found herself returning it.

'She's quite a character, isn't she?' she said.

'I'll say she is! She intends to come to that ball, you know. She'll be dressed up to the nines and ablaze with the full regalia. I hope you'll have something to wear that will stand up to comparison with Myrtle in all her glory?'

She laughed.

'It depends what my friend sends me. I asked her to send a few more clothes. I didn't know you dressed for dinner here.'

'Oh, we live in great style! The old lady's idea, of course. She lives up to the standards of her own childhood.'

'What will happen to the servants when – when someone else takes over?'

He gave a shrug.

'They'll have to go, I suppose, though it will mean losing their homes. Nobody else would keep up this style, nor probably be able to,' and he broke off a bit of cheese from the great lumps ready to go into the press and commented on it to the buxom woman who was superintending the making of it and walked out of the big dairy.

At the entrance of a low building, he paused and handed her a stick.

'What's this for? Am I going to need protection against something?'

'It's to scratch the pigs' backs with. They like that little friendly attention,' and he took her into a concreted passage, as spotless and perfectly kept as the rest, where on either side were pens and small sheds in which were pigs of all sizes, many of them with the rosettes which showed a winner.

She wrinkled her nose.

'We haven't had time to give them their usual bath in

lavender water,' he said gravely, and she laughed, and gingerly scratched the back of a huge sow, which wriggled and grunted with pleasure.

'Aren't her babies sweet?' she asked. 'What do you do with them all?'

'I'm afraid one of them is destined to be your dinner tonight.'

Her face changed and she gave a little shiver.

'Ugh, I don't like the idea of that. I shan't have pig.'

'Must happen, of course, but I can't say I like the idea much. In fact, that's one of the things I don't like about farming. What I'd really like to have been is one of the game wardens in the big national reserves in South Africa where the idea is to preserve rather than to kill.'

'Have you ever been in one?'

'No, I've never been out of England though I was born in France. Have you been in one?'

She nodded and described it to him and he listened with deep interest as they left the piggery and went slowly back, passing two great bulls in their strong enclosures whose furry heads he stopped to stroke, and across the field where hens, segregated to their colour and breed, clucked and scratched.

'But you're obviously happy here, aren't you?' she asked at last.

'Happy? Yes, quite,' he said shortly and she wondered whether, after all, he felt the difference between his position and that of the Belamie men. After all, he was just as much the old lady's grandson.

'I suppose you wash these as well as the pigs and cows?' she asked mischievously, pausing by a flock of pure white Leghorns, and catching at a chance to change the subject.

He grinned.

'Oh yes, certainly. We have a hairdresser who comes to shampoo them and dress their feathers every Saturday night,' and she laughed with him.

They came to the farm cottages, neat and well-kept, each with its own patch of garden. One, small and thatched, stood a little apart from the others and he indicated it with a nod.

'That's where I live,' he said. 'May I give you a cup of coffee before we go back?'

She glanced at it with interest.

'Thank you. I'd like that,' she said, and he went with her to it and opened the door which led directly into a comfortable living-room, a man's room, with deep leather chairs and well-stocked book shelves, its two small windows curtained in brown velvet.

She exclaimed with pleasure.

'This is very nice. Who looks after it?'

'I do. I used to have an old woman who came in every day to "do" for me, but when she got past it, I managed for myself. Sit down, won't you? I'll put the coffee on.'

'Can't I do it?'

'Thanks, I can manage quite well,' he said and went into the adjoining kitchen.

How odd that she should be here in his home with him, and on friendly terms, after the episode of the day before! She had felt a wild, unreasoning hatred of him only a few hours ago; now she felt – what?

Whatever it was, she crushed it down and refused to think about it and whilst he came in and out with cups and a box of biscuits, she wandered about the room, noting in particular two pieces of framed needlework, flower pieces exquisitely worked and carefully hung to catch the light.

'These are lovely,' she said.

'Yes. My mother did them. I've got a lot of her work. I'll show you some more if you're interested. After she died, the old lady packed away everything she had done, everything that could have reminded her of her, photographs, everything, and after I had come here to live, she sent them to me without a word. She has never referred to them, never spoken to me about her. She might never have existed.'

'Yet she has not forgotten. She told me about her. She said she was her favourite child,' said Eve thoughtfully.

'She never forgave her over me.'

'Yet she provided for you.'

'She considered that her duty, and once I was old enough, I

was given a job here so that I could repay her. Oh, I'm not complaining. For one thing I like farming, and for another I'm glad of the opportunity of getting out of her debt. She pays me a wage, you know. About the same amount as the head cowman gets,' with a smile which held no rancour.

'You're just as much her grandson as Victor and Lewis are,' said Eve with slight indignation.

'No, not just as much. I didn't have a father. I'm not a Belamie and I certainly couldn't inherit. I expect the water's boiling. I'll go and make the coffee,' and he left her again.

Eve pursed her lips as she wondered about old Mrs Belamie and what she really felt for this man, who was not only the son of her favourite child but who was surely the grandson of whom she could have been fonder than she ever could be of either of the others? And Felix himself? He was a man in every sense of the word, hard-working, self-reliant, self-educated except for the minimum provided by the State, whilst Victor and Lewis had had the advantages of a public school and university and had professions. Felix did not even own the land he farmed, and was paid only the same wages as a head cowman.

Eve felt that, in Mrs Belamie's position, she would have been more proud of this unacknowledged grandson than of either of the others, but Felix showed no resentment and no jealousy; in fact, though he treated the old lady with far less outward show of respect, she felt that he cared for her a great deal more than the two whose only interest in her was how much they were going to get from her when she died.

His dogs, a labrador and a dalmatian, discovering that he was at home, came bounding to him, and with them a fat tabby cat with a family of nondescript kittens. She jumped on his knee when he sat down and from that place of safety surveyed imperturbably the mingling of dogs and kittens, whilst his big hand stroked and fondled her.

The thatched cottage, small though it was, gave Eve a feeling of home, the home she had never really known in her wanderings. Here was peace and comfort and friendliness which she was strangely loth to leave for the grandeur of 'the big house' but presently she rose reluctantly, dislodging from her lap two of the kittens which had scrambled on to it.

'I shall have to go back,' she said, and did not know she had said it with a sigh. 'There's probably all hell let loose at the house and a hundred things to do. May I – may I come another time to see the things you were going to show me; your mother's things?'

He, too, had risen from his chair, setting Mrs Miggs, the cat, gently down. In the little room he seemed bigger than ever, towering above her.

'Yes, if you really want to,' he said, and the spell which had held her was broken, for he spoke again in that tone of half-amused contempt. 'You must get Lewis to bring you some day,' and she knew that he had introduced purposely the name of her 'fiancé'.

She did not reply but went out into the sunshine with a feeling of anti-climax which he had deliberately produced.

'Will you mind if I send Hodges with you to bring the horses back?' he asked. 'I'm rather busy.'

'I'm sorry to have taken up so much of your time,' she said shortly.

'It's all in the day's work since Madame decreed it,' he said and called to a man working near to go to the stables and warn Hodges to saddle Nina and another horse.

'Not Tristram,' he added. 'He'd better ride Bruce.'

By the time they reached the stables, the two horses stood saddled, and he put his hand ready for her foot but she ignored it and swung herself up without his help.

'Thank you for showing me the farm, Mr Welby,' she said frostily, not looking at him.

'It was a pleasure, Miss Brayle,' he replied in the tone she hated, and she set Nina off at a good pace, leaving Hodges to follow her.

How hateful he could be – and yet – how kind and friendly! Would she ever really know him?

She was absorbed immediately in the arrangements for the fantastically conceived affair which, since the idea emanated from the old lady, everyone called a 'ball'. The whole place

85

seemed to have gone mad with the hurrying and scurrying, orders and counter-orders, Mrs Belamie sitting up in her bed and organising everything from there like a spider for whom others weaved the web. Her energy and will-power were amazing. She knew everything that had to be done, had everything in her grasp, had servants always at hand running in and out of the room which many of them had never seen before but who now knew it only too well.

Emma Ford was chiefly concerned with looking after her, giving her various 'pieces of her mind' in her downright fashion, insisting on periods of rest when everyone else was excluded from the room, but the old lady, waging constant war against her for her insistence, seemed to have taken on a new lease of life and to be growing actually younger in all the turmoil.

'Let me alone, Ford. I'm all right. A bit of excitement is what I need after being shut up here all this time. Any more of your nonsense and I'll get out of bed and go downstairs myself and put a stick about the backs of those lazy sluts,' but at least she did not do that, though Eve, dashing about and running up and down stairs, felt she would not be at all surprised to see her down there.

She caught occasional glimpses of Felix, calm and amused in the midst of all the turmoil, but he did not speak to her, busy with his own multitudinous orders. Myrtle was in a hectic state, trying all the time to appear the king-pin, the pseudo-hostess who was actually in charge though the old lady treated her as being of no more importance than anyone else.

Eve had to vacate the Queen's Room to make accommodation for some of the London visitors and found herself pushed into a tiny, remote room but felt it to be of no consequence. In any case, she was so tired when she finally got to bed that she slept just as well on the hard little iron bed as in the Queen's luxurious four-poster. Phalanxes of men arrived to polish to a glass-like finish the floor of the long gallery where the main dancing was to take place and which had been long unused, stacks of food and drink arrived hourly and white-capped cooks took over the kitchens, enough flowers and plants to fill a market arrived on the morning of the 'ball' and florists transformed the whole place with them. An orchestra appeared and added to the noise and confusion by the practising which Eve felt was entirely unnecessary.

By the afternoon people from a distance began to arrive, and though Eve herself had sent out many of the invitations, she was amazed at the number who came in the special train and were conveyed to the house by the stream of hired cars small enough to negotiate the narrow 'top road'.

At last, with all the house guests accommodated, some of the sitting-rooms turned into bedrooms with the hired beds which had been brought in, Eve retired thankfully to her cubby hole to dress. Emma Ford had mounted guard outside the baize door and would allow nobody in, sitting there, a solid, substantial figure, all the afternoon and evening.

'Will she really come down tonight,' asked Eve, pausing on her way towards the back staircase.

'If she doesn't collapse and die first,' said the nurse grimly.

'She won't, will she?' asked the girl anxiously.

'Not she! If she were dead, her ghost would walk, but heaven help us all tomorrow. Can't you get half an hour's rest, Eve? You look ready to drop. You haven't stopped running for a couple of days.'

'I'll be all right. I wouldn't miss it for the world, after all this!'

'Have you got something pretty to wear? Myrtle will be dressed up to the nines. She went hours ago to start getting ready.'

'What's she wearing, do you know?'

Emma's round face creased into wrinkles of laughter.

'One of the maids saw it spread out on the bed. A sort of snake-skin, green and all over sequins, oh very grand, very grand!'

'Golly! They'll certainly notice her,' giggled Eve. 'Well, nobody will bother about me and that suits me fine,' and as the bell rang imperiously from the bedroom, she scurried away.

When she was dressed, she surveyed herself in sections in the small mirror which was all she had. Amongst the things Marcia had sent her had been a white dress which she had never had occasion to wear since her father's death. It was very simple, with the simplicity which only the famous *couturier* could have achieved though it took a discerning eye to appreciate the fact. The filmy chiffon lay in close folds over the small breasts defining them cunningly, and below the tight little waist the material billowed to her feet, floating out as she moved in a soft cloud of chiffon. She had no jewels except her pearls and the two rings gleaming on her fingers, Lewis's and Mrs Belamie's emerald.

She was filled with the excitement of youth and danced a few steps in the tiny space available, her feet twinkling in their silver slippers. Outside the cars came and went in a continuous stream, those small hired cars into which all the guests were being crushed, probably furious at being transferred to them but having no option. Fortunately it was a fine night!

At last she went down to mingle inconspicuously with the crowd, and Lewis, who had been waiting for her, greeted her querulously.

'I wondered where on earth you were. You ought to have been here to receive people instead of leaving it all to Myrtle.'

'She's quite capable of receiving them alone and will have loved it,' she said.

'You're just as important as she is,' he said angrily, and she looked at him and laughed.

'Oh, Lewis!'

'Well, you are.'

'Don't glower at me now I have come or people will think we've had a row. Oh!' as she suddenly caught sight of Myrtle queening it amongst the still arriving guests.

Myrtle certainly glittered and gleamed in her gown of emerald-green satin embroidered in a lavish pattern of green and gold sequins, fitting her tall, thin form tightly save where it swirled about her gold-sandalled feet. It really was like a snake-skin, she thought with a giggle, and to add to the illusion she wore a flexible gold bracelet set with emeralds high up on one thin arm and a load of diamonds on her fingers.

Really diamonds? wondered Eve as, brought by Lewis to stand beside Myrtle, she caught the other's disparaging and triumphant look at her white gown and her pearls; not that Myrtle believed for a moment that they were real, of course. She soon saw, to her chagrin however, that the younger girl was attracting more attention than she was in spite of the glittering new gown, and when all the guests had arrived and she was free to dance, she expressed her disapproval acidly to Victor.

'That girl, dressed up like a bride,' she said. 'I wonder that Lewis likes her behaving like that, dancing with all the men. *I* prefer to dance with you, Victor.'

'Thank you, dear,' he replied meekly, reluctantly abandoning his intention of trying to get a dance with Eve who was passing from one man's arms to another's in gay succession. It was a long time since she had enjoyed herself so much and she turned her mind resolutely away from the thought that in a few days at most this would be over and she would be back on the unskilled labour market.

During one dance, a clumsy partner stepped on the hem of her dress and tore it, and though she laughed the incident away, she was obliged to run up to the bedroom being used as a cloak-room and ask the maid in charge of it to do a quick repair.

'Just cobble it together, Lucy,' she said.

'Oh, Miss Eve, your lovely dress! What a shame,' said the girl.

'It doesn't matter. I don't suppose I shall wear it again,' she said, caught back for the moment into the days when she could afford to throw her things carelessly aside, but going back down the stairs again, she remembered rather grimly that that might be true for quite a different reason, unless she decided in the end to marry Phillip.

She paused at the foot of the stairs to look into the long gallery, whose double doors had been thrown open for the occasion when a well-remembered voice sent her spinning round to face Felix Welby, the last person she would have expected to find there at that moment. He was faultlessly dressed in white tie and tails and was obviously a guest.

'May I have the honour?' he asked, his voice and eyes mocking her and before she could refuse, she felt his arm come about her and sweep her away through the doorway amongst the dancers.

She was angry but helpless, remembering the terms on which they had parted, he coolly sending her back to the house with a groom after those moments when she seemed to have come almost near him, and the antagonism which he could so easily and maddeningly arouse, returned. He looked at her frosty eyes and tight lips and laughed and held her closer.

'It's no good, you know,' he said softly.

'I don't know what you mean.'

'No good putting on airs with me and trying to go all dignified. I can see what you're thinking, that I'm a cad, a bounder, that I'm stepping out of place to presume to hold you in my arms seeing who and what I am, and you my cousin's fiancée and an aspirant for the Belamie stakes, but you can't escape at the moment, can you? So why not relax and just dance with me?'

What could she say or do? It was not only her helplessness that kept her silent. She knew that she was experiencing a new sensation and, though she wanted to fight against it, she felt herself relax as they danced. He was the perfect partner, moving effortlessly to the rhythm of the music so that instinctively her steps followed his without any conscious thought.

Then he paused. The long gallery was at the back of the house, but double doors leading to a small drawing-room had been opened and the room cleared to give the dancers more space, making the room L-shaped, and either by accident or design he had drawn her into this part which had a french window opening on the terrace.

Her breath came quickly. She did not want to go out there with him, but had no power to resist him, still held by the enchantment of the dance.

'Afraid?' he asked her mockingly.

'Of course not,' she said, her head high, and she stepped over the low sill and went with him.

The night engulfed them with its moonlit magic and she

gave a little shiver and almost turned back. There was a look of startled appeal in the eyes that caught his for a moment though she did not realise it. His arm still held her.

'You need not be afraid,' he said, and now his voice had lost that note of mockery. 'You're quite safe with me. I wouldn't let anything happen to you. I haven't brought you out here to make love to you. I just want you to see something for the first time by moonlight. Not frightened any more, are you? Or cold?'

'N-no,' she quavered, feeling his arm tighten about her as they walked to the end of the terrace and down the three steps into the garden.

'Where are we going?' she asked in a whisper.

'Not far, but I don't think you will have seen it yet. Few people think of coming here. It hasn't the same magic in the daytime.'

His arm still warmly about her, he led her through a path where she had not been before, a dark path between high masses of rhododendrons and instinctively she pressed more closely to him.

'I don't think I like it,' she said with a little shudder.

'You will in a minute,' he promised her and at that moment they came to the end of the rhododendrons and she stopped with caught breath.

They stood at the entrance to a pathway between two rows of trees which, arching overhead, led to the very edge of the cliff where the moonlight lay in silver across a smooth sea stretching out to the horizon, unearthly in its majesty and ageless magic.

'Oh!' she breathed softly and he let his hand slip from her so that she stood alone, enchanted, moving a few steps from him without even being aware that he had set her free.

He stood watching her, a strange look in his eyes. The moonlight filtering through the arch of the trees made her look unreal, a part of itself in her white dress, with her hair of silver-gold and her face, pale in the moon's beams and only the line of her lovely mouth giving her the beauty of a living, breathing woman rather than the white statue she might almost have been. His hands clenched against the desire to touch her, to hold her and his lips quivered at the sight of her warm mouth and the thought of mad kisses there in the moonlit darkness which might bring her wholly to life.

As if she sensed his thoughts, she turned towards him, reluctantly at first and against her will, her lips parted a little and the quick breath coming from them. Then she moved, her hands going out to him, and the next moment she was in his arms, her eyes closing as his mouth, hard and firm, met her own.

'Eve – my small darling – my beautiful,' he whispered against her lips.

For a long moment she stood there, past, present and future forgotten, nothing remembered or felt but that close hold and the pressure of his mouth to which her whole body surrendered in a delirium of happiness such as she had never known before. Mind and body were in a tumult which were aware of neither time nor space.

Then she tore herself from him as memory flooded back, a kind of horror in the eyes that stared, wide open now, into his and her hands went to her lips as if to hide them.

'Oh,' she breathed. 'Oh – Felix!'

He would have caught her in his arms again, but she backed away from him and he interpreted after his own fashion that look of horror in her eyes. His lips tightened and there was mockery in his own again.

'What are you remembering?' he asked harshly. 'Lewis?'

'Yes.'

The word was a mere breath of sound.

'I suppose I might have remembered him too, but I didn't. All I could think of was you and how lovely you are. I should have remembered, of course, that you belong to him – or rather to what he might be going to get out of the old lady,' and he gave a short, mirthless laugh.

'You don't understand,' she said and wondered wildly if she should tell him the truth. Yet how could she, when he was facing her with that look of smiling contempt, when she felt herself to be so cheap, so unworthy? If he had shown the smallest sign of tenderness, she might have told him, but she could not.

She turned from him with a strangled sob and ran back through the dark path to the house, the path no more dark and gloomy than her thoughts.

5

As she reached the house, she saw Lewis's thin, angular figure on the terrace and he came towards her angrily.

'Where on earth have you been?' he asked.

She was breathless from running and from the emotion which had stirred her and she stopped, putting out a hand to catch the stone balustrade at the foot of the steps.

'I've been looking for you everywhere. *Grand-mère* has just sent word that she is coming down. What on earth have you been doing?'

'It was so hot in there. I went to have a look at the sea,' she managed to say, not daring to turn her head to make sure that Felix had not followed her.

He seized her by the arm and hurried her up the steps and along the terrace.

'And you had to choose that time! You might have known she was coming down and of course you must be there. For goodness sake, come along,' and he almost pulled her into the room where the guests had evidently had word that the old lady was arriving, for though the orchestra was still playing, most of the dancers had stopped dancing and were standing in small groups expectantly.

They made way smilingly for Lewis and his 'fiancée' whom they naturally thought had been together outside, and Eve drew a breath of relief. For the time being, anyway, she must keep up the pretence, and she was aided to it by the sight of Myrtle in her glittering green gown standing well to the fore with Victor and beginning to move towards the main door of the room.

She went forward, propelled by Lewis, thinking with a gulp of relief what a blessing it was that Myrtle had not seen her go out with Felix.

And then, enthroned in state in a wheeled chair, Corke pushing it and Emma Ford walking beside it, came the little old lady.

She wore black velvet, and diamonds sparkled at every conceivable point, a tiara of them set in her impossibly golden hair, diamonds round her thin old neck and throat, diamonds on her stick-like arms and her hands like claws, even diamonds winking on the high-heeled black velvet slippers on her tiny, useless feet, the trailing velvet of her gown having been carefully arranged so that they could be seen.

A gasp of sheer amazement and admiration went up from the assembled guests, for in spite of the golden hair and painted face which in themselves were ludicrous, she was a magnificent sight to which they paid the homage of that gasp.

Corke, who had had his orders, wheeled the chair slowly down the length of the room and from it Mrs Belamie inclined her head in a regal gesture to left and right, smiling her acknowledgement of her guests' greetings, delighted with the impression her appearance was making.

Early in the procession, Myrtle and Victor had pressed forward to be at her side but Eve was thankful that Lewis had not succeeded in forcing her to take up a position on the other side when the old lady, with an imperious gesture, signed to them to keep back.

'Don't crowd about me, you two,' she said. 'I've come to greet my guests and I see quite enough of you. You look ridiculous in that hideous gown, Myrtle. What is it supposed to be? Are you in fancy dress as a snake or something?' and at the intentionally cruel rebuff, poor Myrtle drew as inconspicuously as she could into the background.

Mrs Belamie's eyes, brightly malicious after the encounter, alighted on Eve who, feeling desperately sorry for Myrtle (who wouldn't be?) had drawn back behind Lewis.

'Who's that you're hiding, Lewis? Eve? Come here, my dear, and let me see you. Now that's how I like to see a young girl looking. That's a very pretty dress, and you can walk beside me. No, not you, Lewis. Just Eve. You're blushing child. That's a thing I like to see as well. Come along. Put your hand on the arm of my chair to steady it. Corke's such an old fool that he might tip me out, mightn't you, Corke, eh? Eh?' craning her scraggy neck to look round at him maliciously.

'No, Madame,' said the old butler imperturbably.

So, to her great embarrassment, Eve found herself walking in state in the procession, the cynosure of all eyes when they had satisfied themselves by staring frankly at the old lady and her jewels.

When she had toured the room, the chair was placed in a small enclosure which had been roped off for the purpose.

'I'll send for you when I want you, Corke, and I don't want you either, Ford, fluttering about like a sick hen. My guests will look after me. Oh, there's Felix. Come and sit beside me, Felix, and tell me all the scandals you know about everyone. You go and dance with Lewis, my pretty, but come back to me again,' dismissing Eve with a nod as Felix lounged up to the old lady and drew a chair up beside her.

Eve felt her face flame but she did not look at him, glad for once to be under the protection of Lewis.

'You did splendidly,' he said as they moved off together. 'Myrtle's nose was properly out of joint.'

'Poor Myrtle. Mrs Belamie was most unkind to her,' said Eve, with genuine feeling.

'Well, look what a sight she's made of herself! And she's no beauty at the best of times. Can't imagine what Victor sees in her.'

'What you see in me?' asked Eve tartly. 'No, that's not quite fair. I think he's genuinely fond of Myrtle.'

Lewis, who danced so loosely that it was almost impossible to follow his steps, made a sudden grab and drew her nearer.

'So am I of you,' he muttered. 'You knock 'em all into a cocked hat in that dress.'

She gave a dreary little laugh.

'You don't have to pay me compliments, you know, and for

goodness sake keep your feet off it. It's already been torn once,' and they finished the dance in silence.

She wished he had not returned her to the enclosure which held the wheeled chair, for Felix was still there and whatever he had just said had delighted the old lady, who was cackling with eldritch laughter.

He got up to offer Eve the seat of honour, but the old lady gave him a little push.

'Go on, Felix. Dance with Eve. Hope you'll make a better job of it than Lewis did. You can stay and talk to me, Lewis, if you like and don't stand there looking like a wet week because Felix has taken your girl. I wouldn't blame him if he did more than dance with her, either!' with another malicious little cackle as the two moved off together.

'Do you mind so much?' he asked her, as he put his arm about her and drew her close. 'I couldn't very well help it, could It?'

'Did you want to "help" it?' she asked in a low voice.

'No. Above all things I wanted you in my arms again. Have you forgiven me?'

'For the unforgiveable things you said?'

'Those, too. But for kissing you?'

His cheek lay against hers, his whisper close to her ear, her soft hair brushing his face. He felt her quiver and tightened his arm about her.

She could not speak. How could she possibly forgive the things he had said? And yet she was remembering, more than those, that moment when he had kissed her and she had come very close to heaven.

'Eve – Eve darling – can't we be friends?'

'How can we be when you think such beastly things about me?'

'I don't really think them.'

'Then why do you say them?' she asked, and for a moment tilted her head back so that she could look at him, hurt bewilderment in her eyes.

He put his cheek against hers again. He could not look into those eyes and remain sane, he felt.

'A form of self-defence. You're going to marry another man and even if you weren't, I shouldn't be in the running. I haven't even got a name,' with the first touch of bitterness she had heard from him on his own account.

How could she tell him that that did not matter, that if he loved her, nothing else in the world would matter?

The next moment his mood had changed.

'Let's do some fancy business. Wonder if the band can play a cha-cha? Can you do it?' and when she nodded and laughed, wondering where on earth he had learned even its name, he spoke to the band leader who obligingly changed the rhythm from the rather sedate measures they had thought would be more acceptable up to now.

Many of the older couples sat down, including Victor and Myrtle, but the younger people stayed on the floor and turned the dance into a gay frolic. When it ended, Felix took Eve back to Mrs Belamie, who had thoroughly enjoyed it, clapping her hands and tapping with her little high-heeled slippers.

'Bravo! Bravo!' she cried. 'How I'd have enjoyed dancing like that a few years ago! Where did you learn that, Felix, you rascal?'

'That's a bit of my murky past,' he told her, laughing. 'One of the things I get up to when I take a day or two off in the big, bad city, but I've never danced it with anyone like Eve. You ought to teach Lewis the Latin-American rhythms!' but this time, though he deliberately introduced Lewis's name, there was none of the former malice in it, only a faint sound of regret.

'I don't think he'd be particularly good at it,' she said and laughed.

'Well, children,' said Mrs Belamie, 'I think I've had enough. The only place for the very old and the very young at this time of night is bed,' and though she looked strained and tired, she was regretful. 'Find Corke for me, Felix, will you?'

'I'll be your chauffeur myself, old lady,' he said.

'All right. Say goodnight to all my guests and thank them for the pleasure they've given an old woman. I don't feel equal to doing it myself. Come with me, Eve, my dear. No, not any of the rest of you. I'm too tired to be bothered with any-body else.'

They stood up respectfully whilst she made her royal pro-gress down the room, but there were no smiles and waves now, just a very old lady going thankfully to bed and when they reached the hall, the double doors were closed behind them and the music had started again.

'Get one of the young manservants to carry me up,' quavered Mrs Belamie.

'I can do that,' said Felix, and he lifted her gently and tenderly in his arms, a feather weight to his strength, whilst Eve following with her wrap.

Emma Ford was waiting anxiously at the top of the stairs and he carried the old lady into her bedroom and deposited her gently in a chair. For once she made no protest at being treated as an invalid for she was clearly very tired.

'You can leave me now, both of you,' she said. 'Ford will look after me. I've had a wonderful time, and don't send for that old fool of a doctor tomorrow. You may kiss me, Eve, my child.'

Eve bent and kissed the cheek that seemed as thin and dry as tissue paper, sweetly perfumed and powdered.

'Good-night, dear Mrs Belamie,' she said with a little catch in her voice and a lump in her throat and turned swiftly to go. How could she ever tell her the mean trick she was playing on her? Yet how could she go on with it? The next day, come what may, she would insist on returning to town. Lewis must sort it out after she had gone.

As she turned to leave her, Felix deposited a smacking kiss on the withered old cheek and was rewarded with a cackle and a smart slap from the jewelled fingers.

'Get along with you,' she said, 'and you needn't think there's anything coming to you,' but the laugh ended in a sigh as if she regretted something beyond her powers to remedy.

'Do you think I don't know that?' Felix said with a grin, and he followed Eve and caught her up in the little hall be-tween the two doors. Instinctively she paused and gave him a troubled look which he could not begin to understand and once again she might have confessed to him her duplicity but she found in the eyes that met her own that look of mocking contempt. Would she never know where she was with this strange man?

'You see how wise you are in sticking to Lewis!' he said. 'If you go on playing your cards like this, the game is definitely yours. That kiss was a master-piece. I congratulate you.'

She clenched her hands.

'You're hateful,' she said.

'Much better, and safer, to feel like that about me.'

'Oh – I hate you,' she said and opened the baize door and fled from him.

Lewis was waiting for her at the bottom of the stairs, looking supremely satisfied with himself and her.

He put his arm through hers and pressed it.

'Thank you, Eve. You've been wonderful,' he said, and because Felix was close behind her, she turned and lifted her face to his.

'Kiss me, darling,' she said, and though she was aware that he was staggered by the suggestion, his lips came swiftly to hers, dry, thin lips which gave her no pleasure.

'Now take me to supper. I'm starving,' she said gaily and kept her arm in his as they made their way to the room where an elaborate buffet supper had been prepared.

He disengaged his arm and looked anxiously at the crowd about the tables.

'I'll see what I can get,' he said in a worried tone. 'Will you wait here?'

She nodded and he began in his nervous fashion to edge between the people.

'Excellent. Full marks for a most impressive display. I hope you won't starve to death whilst dear Lewis finds something for you,' said a mocking voice in a whisper at her elbow, and the colour flamed in her face but she did not turn her head. A moment afterwards, she saw his tall figure making its way out of the house. He had not stayed for supper or the rest of the dance and she knew a moment's sick longing to follow him to the peace and quiet of his little house. What was the matter with her, to have any such desire to follow and be alone with such a hateful man who had plainly no need of her?

That night, though she had every reason for being able to sleep, she slept fitfully and was awake early and glad to get up, though the rest of the house, except for the servants, was wrapped in slumber. Putting on a white swim-suit and a short wrap of towelling, she slipped out of the house to which order was being restored and down to the little cove and, throwing the wrap aside, waded gratefully into the water. It was ice-cold and made her gasp for the first few moments but by the time she had reached the rocks that jutted out a little distance from the shore, she was glowing with warmth.

She climbed up and sat gazing out to sea, her hands nursing her knees.

She was going to miss this badly when she had put it all behind her. She had no illusions about herself. She did not want to be a working girl, accepting cheerfully and without complaint the conditions on which so many thousands of girls, girls like Marcia, lived. Yet the only alternative was a wealthy marriage, presumably to Phillip Shawn, and her mind veered away from that with a feeling of revulsion such as she had never felt before. Though she had said repeatedly to Marcia, lightly and gaily, that she could never marry Phillip, she knew now that that had been at the back of her mind all the time as her only possible escape.

Why was she so sure now that she could never marry him?

The answer came to her with appalling clarity as she sat there, alone and facing life as she had never let herself face it before. It lay with the one man who had ever been able to rouse her to an answering thrill.

Felix Welby.

It was no use telling herself that she hated him because he had shown her that he despised her. Whatever else had happened between them, whatever else he may have said, she would always remember the moment when she had been in his arms, her whole body and mind in tune with his, and his voice when he had called her his 'small darling', his 'beautiful'. Remembering that voice and his lips, she dropped her head on her knees in mingled loathing and delight. It was so easy at this moment to forget that he could be utterly beastly as well!

She raised her head with a start at the sound of his voice close to her. She had believed herself to be alone.

'Felix!'

The love that had been in her thoughts still trembled in her voice.

'May I come in?' he said, and she moved to make room for him beside her but could not command her voice to speak more than that startled name.

'I didn't expect to find company when I came out here,' he said. 'Oughtn't you to have slept late? Or couldn't you sleep?'

'Not – very well,' she managed to say.

'Friends at the moment or enemies?'

He was pleading with her and, weak as ever where he was concerned, she responded to the appeal with a fugitive little smile.

'Friends,' she said in a low voice.

'Then look at me as you say so,' but she shook her head and he laughed.

'Cigarette?' he asked and this time she did look at him.

'Out here?'

He took from a small pocket in his swimming trunks a packet wrapped in a waterproof covering and offered them to her. Without thinking, she took two and put them between her lips and when he offered her a light from the same waterproof covering, she lit them both and absent-mindedly put one of them into his mouth.

'Now who taught you to do that, I wonder?' he asked, amused, and she coloured. 'Some other man?'

'My father,' she said shortly, and the smile died from his face.

'Tell me about him, Eve.'

She hesitated and then began to speak of that beloved being as she had never yet been able to do even to Marcia, told him something of their life together and the perfect comradeship that had exited between them, neither of them needing other friends or companions though they had made a host of acquaintances all over the world.

'People don't understand and blame him for leaving me high dry, but he didn't expect to die so early and leave me, and he had made and lost other fortunes but had always been able to make more. It was just one of those things. I don't blame him. I couldn't. Wherever he is, and I feel he must be somewhere, he won't know any happiness because he left me like this. I wish I could reach him somewhere and let him know that I shall be all right, that I shall win through somehow.'

She realised that she had given him a fresh opportunity to gibe at her for getting engaged to a man who had at least expectations of a considerable share in a large fortune, but he did not take the opportunity.

'I think you will,' was all he said. 'You've got courage. You're not the sort to go under.'

'You don't really know anything about me,' she said in a low voice and once again was tempted to tell him of how she had got mixed up in the life of Lewis Belamie, but she did not tell him, and when he spoke again, it was of other things, of the farm and his life on it, a life which evidently filled his thoughts, occupying his whole mind.

She was emboldened to ask him a question when he paused.

'If you love the place and your life here so much, Felix, why doesn't Mrs Belamie give you some security? She must know what it means to you.'

She had spoken thoughtfully and with only his well-being in her mind, but she saw at once that she had said the wrong thing. His face and voice changed instantly.

'If you are thinking that I'm the better horse to put your money on, you'd better think again, little lady. Stick to Lewis. I'm not in the running. I was scratched before the start.'

She sprang to her feet.

'You're hateful. How can we possibly be friends when you think and talk like that?' and in her fury she missed her footing on the slippery rock and fell headlong into the sea.

He sat watching her imperturbably for a moment and then realised that she was in difficulties. Her face appeared above the surface of the water, a look of agonised dismay upon it, and then was completely submerged. In an instant he was beside her and had caught her and upheld her in his strong grasp.

'All right. I've got you. Don't struggle or you'll drown us both,' and he caught her under her arms and, swimming on his back, brought her quickly and easily into the shallows and carried her, in spite of her protesting struggle, to the firm, dry sand and set her free.

'If you can't swim well enough, you shouldn't have gone out so far,' he told her shortly.

'I can swim,' she said indignantly. 'I got cramp,' rubbing her legs.

'Through falling off the rock in a temper. You can't take liberties with a Cornish sea. Here, better let me do that. You're only stroking them,' and pushing her hands aside, he massaged her limbs firmly until the muscles were free again.

'Thank you,' she said meekly but still with that undercurrent of anger, humiliated that he had had to come to her rescue, and he grinned.

'Put on your shoes and then I'm going to walk you up and down before you climb back.'

'I shall be quite all right,' she said haughtily, but when she had put on her shoes, he took her arm firmly in his and made her walk up and down the little cove briskly.

He did not speak to her until they had returned to the rock on which she had thrown her wrap, but when she had put it on, she hesitated. She did not want to leave him like this; she did not want to leave him at all. She was torn between hate and something perilously like love, though she knew that what she thought of as 'love' was no more than his appeal to her senses. It was dangerous to stay, yet it tempted her. No man had ever made her feel like this, afraid to go, afraid to stay.

He saw her hesitation and smiled.

'Have breakfast with me,' he suggested.

'Here?'

'I've brought mine with me. That's one of the benefits of not having any woman to fuss round me. There's plenty for two, if you can manage hard-boiled eggs and coffee,' and he picked up a little case and unloaded it. 'Three eggs, that's one and a half each, a stack of rather thick bread and butter, and a flask of coffee with only one cup, I'm afraid. That do? I take it you came out without breakfast?'

'Yes. Everybody else seemed to be staying in bed.'

He poured some coffee for her in the top of the flask.

'You have first drink,' he said. 'We can't be anything but friends when we're sharing the same cup.'

Her hand shook as she took it.

'How can we be friends when – when you're so beastly to me, Felix?'

'I'm not really. It's only that I have to keep reminding myself that you're not for me and never can be. Let's leave it at that, shall we? And I won't be what you call beastly to you any more.'

She sat on the rock and shared his breakfast, wondering whether they could ever be friends with both hatred and love between them, but if this was an hiatus between the two, she was prepared to enjoy it whilst it lasted.

'The rollers are coming in,' he said. 'Can you surf-ride?'

'I've never tried.'

'All right. Finish up and I'll teach you. There are some surf boards tucked away in one of these little caves,' and he left her whilst he looked for them and brought back two.

She was quick to master the art and after a few duckings, could ride the long rollers almost as well as he.

'It's the most glorious sensation in the world,' she cried when she had managed to bring the board right in, and stay on it. 'It's almost like ski-ing!'

'Let's rest a minute and have a cigarette. You're a very apt pupil but don't overdo it.'

He produced his packet again but this time she took only one and lay back on the flat, sun-warmed rock, her eyes closed, a little smile on her lips.

He lay and looked at her, her face sun-brown and sea-wet, the drops clinging to her lashes and to the lips at which he dared not look too long. Without make-up, they were as red and alluring as they had been in all her war-paint. To him, as a man of the open-air with little use for the ballroom, they were infinitely more alluring just as she herself was supremely attractive in her white suit, her limbs carelessly free.

He dragged his eyes away from her.

'You've done some ski-ing then, I take it. Where?'

'Oh, lots of places – Grindelwald, Wengen, St Moritz, and in Norway and Sweden. Have you?

He laughed.

'No, I stay here. I'm not one of the fortunate, or perhaps unfortunate, rich. There isn't any ski-ing in Cornwall.'

'Don't you ever go away?' she asked curiously. 'Are you always here?'

He nodded, pulling bits of seaweed from the rock. She watched with a queer fascination his strong, ruthless fingers.

'I like it. Besides, it's my job.'

'But no one has to work all the time. Don't you ever have a holiday?'

'I could have one, I suppose, but the old lady would be so astounded if I did. By feeding, clothing and educating me up to the point when I was able to begin to repay her, she considers that I owe her a debt until I have cleared it. Quid pro quo.'

She glanced at him. Neither face nor voice expressed any bitterness. He was merely stating a fact which seemed reasonable, but she flared up in his defence.

'That's utterly unfair!' she said hotly. 'You're her own grandson. What else could she have done but look after you?'

He smiled.

'Several things. For instance, she need not even have brought me back to England. She could have cast me adrift on French charity. As it was, she gave me a name and arranged for me to be looked after, and not in a charitable institution either. I was comfortable and well cared for.'

'To get the quid pro quo out of you!'

This time the smile became an amused chuckle.

'Thank you for getting so het up on my behalf, but there's no need. I'd much rather pay my debt.'

'And when she dies? Will you consider it paid in full?'

'Oh, definitely. I shall be free then to start a life of my own.'

'With no capital and no job?'

'I can always get a job. No man in this country need be out of work. I'm thirty-two and fit and strong and I have no wife or dependants. Your sympathy does you credit, but I assure you it's misplaced. Let's forget it, shall we? Do you feel all right now? No after-effects of having come near to drowning?'

'No, but – suppose you hadn't been there?'

'I don't imagine it would have happened if I hadn't been there. I made you mad, didn't I?'

'Yes.'

'What if I hadn't brought you back but had just gone on swimming with you – swimming—'

'We'd have drowned eventually, I suppose.

'Or found some world of our own? Some undiscovered island, a kingdom with a king and queen and no subjects—'

She wrenched her eyes from the deep blue of his in which there was mockery, mischief, absurd fantasy – but something else as well. She could not trust her voice to speak. Her heart was beating unevenly.

'How if we had found that island, Eve? Do you know what I would have done with you?'

She shook her head but she knew.

'I'd have loved you, my sweet. And you'll never know love now, since you're going to marry dear Lewis! What a waste!'

If he had not turned so suddenly to derision, she would have been in his arms, blurting out the truth of that engagement, throwing herself on his mercy, claiming the love he had seemed to offer for one magic moment and had then snatched away.

Angry and hot-faced, she sprang to her feet.

'Oh, I shall never understand you!' she cried.

'Nor I you, my sweet,' he said lightly. 'Since you can't pretend that you're in love with him, not to me anyway—'

She cut him short. Her hands were clenched at her sides. She wanted to hit him, to wipe that smile from his face, but that was not her way. And what difference would it have made, pitting her puny strength against his? That was her trouble. She felt so utterly helpless against him.

'Why shouldn't I love Lewis? Because he's different from you, gentler, a man with brains and not just a – a—'

'A great hulking brute who can only work with his hands?' he suggested, supplying her with words when she paused, that maddening smile still on his face.

'In your insufferable conceit, you see your own type as the only one women can admire,' she said furiously.

'Not at all. I don't expect or want to be admired. So we leave it at that, do we? That you're in love with dear Lewis?'

'Yes,' she said, and turned and left him, running up the cliff path and never pausing until she had reached the top and was out of his sight.

When the bend in the path had hidden her, Felix Welby sat looking at the empty sea, his hands clasped between his knees and no smile now on his face.

For the first time in his life, a woman had come to invade it and that woman was going to marry his cousin, going to marry him for the sake of their grandmother's money, he was quite convinced, and for no other reason. He ought to despise her as he pretended to her that he did; but he could not. The truth had been made plain to him in that moment when he had seen her frightened face just before it disappeared under the water and he had gone in after her. He would have done the same had she been any woman, any man, but in that instant he had known that, beyond all reason and common sense, he loved her.

His life had been singularly devoid of love. No mother had ever loved him, no father ever been concerned for his welfare. His foster parents had been kind but not affectionate and when he had discovered, as he did at an early age, the relationship of his grandmother, there was nothing to love in that distant and austere being, only the need to be grateful to her. At school, he had kept himself apart from the others, knowing that he had no real home or background or parents and resenting any suggestion of pity, fiercely proud and independent. He could have had many friends, for he did well at school and in the playing fields, but he spurned all offers of friendship out of school hours and all the time he did not spend with his books was spent in willing work on the farm.

The animals were his friends and on them he lavished the

love of a heart which he had never thought of as being lonely. He could do anything with animals, especially the sick ones that need special care and he would have liked to become a veterinary surgeon, but never expressed the wish to anyone, perhaps because he knew it would be useless to do so. It would have meant years of study, of being kept by Mrs Belamie, whereas from the moment he left school, she and his foster parents had made it clear he must begin to recompense her for the amount of money she had spent on him.

He was far ahead of his years when she brought him to Weir House as an assistant to the then overseer of the farm, and was still not twenty when she dismissed the overseer and put the whole responsibility on his young shoulders.

It had been an even lonelier life than with his foster-parents, but it had not troubled him. He had made the acquaintance of his cousins but had not particularly cared for either of them. He supposed that the household at the big house, and the villagers in South Cawer knew who he was though no reference was ever made to it in his hearing. He had the entrée to Weir House since it was often necessary for him to go there to discuss affairs with Mrs Belamie and he made free with it and with Victor and Lewis without creating any feeling of embarrassment. His attitude to his grandmother had grown with the years into the casual friendliness in which no trust was displayed on either side, and she had always made it clear to him that he could expect nothing from her when she died. He was perfectly content that it should be so, asking no more from her than the ability to repay his indebtedness to her. Since they understood each other completely, a queer feeling of friendship had grown up between them. He was the one person amongst all the horde of relations, friends and servants surrounding her who had nothing to gain from her death and nothing to hope for.

He could easily have married. Many of the village girls had their eye on him and would have been pleased and flattered by his attentions, but he was friendly with all but desired none.

Once Mrs Belamie had spoken to him about it.

'I wonder you don't find yourself a wife, Felix. I know I don't pay you much, but if you found a suitable girl, I'd pay you a bit more and she'd help you with the farm, making the butter and so on, a strong, willing girl.'

He had smiled his lazy smile.

'Pay for her keep, you mean? Quite apart from the fact that I don't fancy any of the girls I've met, not as a life partner, anyway, I've an idea that I'd like to keep my wife as more or less an ornament.'

The old woman gave him a wry smile.

'Think yourself too good for the village girls, I suppose?'

'Not at all. Many of them are too good for me. After all, I can't even offer them a name of my own, can I?'

'Do you mind that? Would you feel better if you were called Belamie?'

'Certainly not. I'd inevitably be associated with what you've got to leave then. No, I'm quite content to be Felix Welby for the rest of my life, but I'm not going to make myself answerable to any woman for either my name or lack of one.'

She gave him a keen, appraising look and nodded her head with a faint sigh.

'Yes. You're proud. As proud as I am, as proud as Lucifer. If I'd known how it would all turn out – well, I didn't know, did I? And now if I gave you my name, you'd refuse it, I suppose.'

'You never spoke a truer word, old lady. You've ordered my life so far, and I've jigged about on the strings you've pulled, but don't try to find the one that says I'm to marry, and whom I'm to marry because you won't find it,' and he had laughed and gone away.

But what would the old autocrat say if she knew that the only girl he would dream of marrying, always supposing that she would have him, was the affianced wife of one of her respectable, legitimate grandsons? After her money too?

'You're a fool, Felix Whatever-your-name is,' he apostrophised himself with a bitter little laugh. 'You'd better stop your dreaming and get back to where you belong, to the muck-heap!'

6

WHEN Eve returned to the house, she found the two brothers and Myrtle gathered on the terrace, obviously in deep discussion, and Lewis turned to her in evident relief. For once he did not ask her where she had been, because it was self-evident.

'Oh, there you are, Eve! I want to talk to you whilst you're having your breakfast. You could have had it sent up, you know.'

'I don't want breakfast. At least – I've had some. I – I took something down to the beach. What do you want to talk about?' suspiciously.

He took her arm in an ostentatious manner and walked her into the house to be out of earshot.

'It's *grand-mère*,' he said in a hurried whisper. 'Anybody might have thought she'd sleep late this morning, but she didn't. She's sent for Pawnsford, her solicitor, you know. You can guess what that means.'

There was excitement in his usually colourless voice and a gleam of satisfaction in his eyes behind their thick glasses.

'Lewis, I meant what I said. I want to go back to London. Now.'

'You can't, Eve. Do be sensible.'

'I am being sensible for the first time since I agreed to such a hare-brained scheme as yours. Goodness knows why I did agree. I must have been raving mad. Anyway, I'm going back – now, today. I'm just going up to dress and pack and if you won't arrange a car for me, I'll walk.'

'To Helston? It's ten miles. Don't be childish,' he said

irritably, and then changed his tone to one of pleading. 'It's not for much longer. Only perhaps for today. Don't spoil everything now. You know what a good impression you've made on *grand-mère*—'

'That's just it. I didn't know she would be like this. You didn't tell me. I had quite a different idea of her. Now I know her, and I can't be a party to deceiving her. I want to go—'

But at that moment Emma Ford came in, looking for her, relieved to see her.

'Oh, there you are, Miss Brayle! She wants you, and you're not even dressed! You'd better hurry. She's like a cat amongst the pigeons. Nobody knows which of us she's going to pounce on and claw to bits. You're the only one who seems able to keep her quiet.'

Eve gave Lewis a helpless, frustrated look but he pushed her towards the door.

'Of course you must go to her,' he said. 'For heaven's sake don't keep her waiting.'

Frowning, she went with the nurse up the stairs but had only reached the baize door when they heard the sound of Mrs Belamie's little brass bell which could sound like a gong when the old hands clanged it vigorously.

The two outside the door exchanged looks.

'She sounds furious. Better go in as you are,' said the nurse and gave her an unceremonious little push through both door-ways and into the bedroom where Mrs Belamie sat up in bed clanging the bell in a fury.

'Oh,' she said at sight of Eve. 'So they've found you at last. Go away, Ford. You're no more use than a sick headache.'

'And when you get your sick headache, you'll be shouting for me,' said the nurse imperturbably. 'I wonder you haven't got one now, with all the fuss you've been making. All right. I'm going. You needn't shout any more for Miss Brayle. She's here and I'll leave you with her,' which she did promptly.

Mrs Belamie gave her thin little cackle of laughter and laid down the bell.

'Come here where I can see you,' she said. 'H'm. Been swimming, have you? Take off that coat thing so that I can see you,' and when Eve had rather shyly obeyed and come forward in her trim white wool suit, the old lady nodded approval.

'Very nice. Covered yourself decently. Don't wear those indecent things they call bikinis, do you?'

'I do sometimes, but this is more comfortable for a real swim.'

'Who've you been with?'

Eve was tempted to lie but somehow she could not do so.

'I went by myself, but – afterwards Felix Welby came. We've been surf-riding. At least, he was teaching me.'

'H'm. How d'you get on with him? Like him?'

Eve had not wanted to be asked that question, to be obliged to answer it, but with the old lady's bright, intelligent eyes piercing her, she could not avoid it.

'No,' she said explosively, after a revealing pause. 'I – I dislike him intensely.'

Mrs Belamie chuckled and patted the hand she had been holding.

'Ha! No need to be so violent about it,' she said. 'I usually feel that way myself about him. A rude young man. No proper respect. Now, what I want you for is to make sure that you are going to stay with me for a few days. I don't want the others. they can all go back – and they will, once I have seen Pawnsford. They know I have sent for him?'

'Y-yes,' admitted Eve reluctantly.

The old lady chuckled again.

'I meant 'em to know so that they could all go back. But not you, my dear. You haven't any job to go back to so there's no reason why you shouldn't stay to cheer an old woman up. I like to have you about. You're very pretty, though what you can see in my grandson Lewis is more than I can imagine. Now that old fool Pawnsford will be here any minute. He may be here already, but it won't hurt him to cool his heels. He'll charge me for it anyway. You go and get dressed and tell the others that I say they can go as soon as they like, but that you are staying,' and she seized the little bell and rang it imperiously, giving the girl a little push.

This was the third time she had been pushed around this morning, Eve thought, first by Lewis, then by the nurse and now by Mrs Belamie herself. Who were they to push her around like this, as if she had no will of her own?

She opened her mouth to protest but Emma Ford came sailing in like a busy, well-manned barge and practially shoo-ed her out of the room. She found herself outside the firmly shut door before she could say a word.

And now what? Of course she didn't want to stay. Of course she must go with Lewis and the others. Of course she must end for good and all this fantastic situation – and yet there had been an odd appeal, a sudden softening, in the voice that had begged rather than commanded though the words had been as autocratic as ever.

Perhaps she had better stay behind when the others went, just for a day or two. She would have an opportunity to put things right, to confess the trick to which she had been a willing party, after which Mrs Belamie would not be able to get rid of her fast enough.

What she refused to let herself think was 'Perhaps I shall see *him* again – not that I want to. Of course I don't.'

She dressed slowly, hoping that by the time she went down, the rest of the over-night visitors would have left. Her little room was at the back and she could hear the sounds of their departure in the fleet of small cars which would convey them to Helston or to the points at which they could transfer themselves to their own cars. Luggage was being carried out and good-byes said, Myrtle on hand to receive as proxy for Mrs Belamie their thanks and congratulations on a successful party. Myrtle would be enjoying that!

She went to the window and peeped out. Yes, there was Myrtle, dressed in that particular shade of dull brown which became her so ill, though she was unaware of it. She had no sense of dress at all, thought Eve. Poor Myrtle! Well, after to-day, with both grandsons suitably 'engaged', she would probably be secure as far as the old lady's money was concerned, and once she, Eve, had left Weir House, even if she had not brought herself to confess the truth, Lewis could do what he liked about his 'fiancée'. It would not matter any longer to her and she would certainly never come here again!

When the last car-load had left, she went downstairs. Myrtle threw her a glance of veiled triumph.

'I should have thought you would at least be down to say good-bye to the guests, Eve,' she said.

'I'm sure my presence would not have been missed with you there to do the honours. Oh, coffee! Good. It's just what I could do with,' said Eve, settling herself in a chair as a maid brought in the silver tray and set it on a small table near Myrtle.

The three of them were clearly on edge, glancing now and then towards the open door through which they hoped the solicitor might materialise.

'I suppose there's no need to wait for Mr Pawnsford to join us?' said Victor.

'I can always ask for some fresh coffee to be brought.'

'He'll probably need something stronger than coffee after he's finished the session with her. I'll have mine white, Myrtle.'

'You'll have it black, and without sugar. You've put on weight disgracefully since we've been here,' retorted Myrtle, passing a cup to him which he took with an expression of disgust, but took just the same.

'What shall we do this afternoon?' asked Lewis. 'If we can get the staff car, I thought we might take a run to the Lizard. It's really too ridiculous of her not to have had the road widened or even to keep a small car of her own.'

'I've been thinking over the possibility of making a road up to the front where the donkey path is. It would mean taking a bit from the lawn but it would zigzag to avoid too steep a gradient,' said Victor thoughtfully, taking from his pocket a piece of paper on which he had evidently been taking notes and measurements.

'Always assuming, of course, that you are left the house,' put in Lewis coldly. 'As far as I am concerned, there is no need to discuss roads. I should sell the place. Who'd want to live here, anyway?'

'I would, for one,' put in Myrtle, 'and I agree with Victor about the need for proper roads. Apart from our own car, visitors would be able to come right up to the door without this absurd business of having to change into hired cars.'

Eve had sat in silence, listening to their heartless discussion on what they were going to do when their grandmother died, and Lewis seemed suddenly to have become aware of her silence.

'I don't think Eve would want to live here, would you – darling?' bringing out the endearment awkwardly, as he always did.

'Don't any of you think of Mrs Belamie herself? Or care for anything but what she may leave you?' she asked with curling lip. 'I want her to go on living. Why shouldn't she? She enjoys her life. Look how she was last night. I think it's perfectly beastly of you to be apportioning her goods between you whilst she's still alive.'

'Good for you!' said a quiet, amused voice behind her and they all turned, startled and a little uncomfortable, to see Felix there. 'How is the old lady after last night's jollification? Not in the state you'd all like her to be, I take it – all, that is, with the exception of Eve.'

'We haven't seen her this morning,' said Myrtle acidly.

'Eve has, haven't you, darling?' asked Lewis proudly.

'She is quite well,' said Eve, colouring and refusing to meet Felix's eyes after that first glance.

'Splendid,' he said with a bland smile. 'Is there anyone with her now, do you think, or can I go up?'

'Pawnsford is here,' snapped Victor and Felix laughed.

'I'm sure that makes you all happy – or worried?'

Before anyone could think of a reply, a maid came into the room with a note for Victor, which he slit open hurriedly and then sat staring at it until the maid had gone.

'It's from her,' he said. 'Written by Ford, of course. She says we're to leave today but that Eve is staying on!'

'What on earth for?' asked Myrtle indignantly. 'Of course, you and Lewis will be wanting to get back to your offices, but if Eve is to stay, then of course I shall stay too. Someone must be here to attend to things with a *visitor* in the house,' giving Eve a baleful glance.

'She says that the three of us are to go,' said Victor uncomfortably.

'It's preposterous, practically turning us out, me included. I shall speak to Ford about it, and to Mrs Hodd.'

'I shouldn't, if I were you,' said Lewis. 'Certainly Eve must stay.'

There was triumph in his smile.

'I'd rather go with you,' put in Eve quickly.

'You can't do that. Of course you must stay.'

'Why not let her go, if she wants to?' suggested Felix in his lazy voice as he lounged against the window-frame and lit a cigarette.

Immediately Eve decided to stay, if only because he wanted her to go!

'There's no immediate need for me to go,' she said. 'I can stay for a day or two,' and now she flung him a defiant glance which he received with a tantalising smile.

It might have been just what he wanted and had calculated on that particular reaction! She could not change her mind again, but she was determined that she would not stay more than the requisite few days and would be careful to avoid him.

Myrtle left the room in high dudgeon, but returned discomfited a few minutes later.

'Mr Pawnsford is still with her, but I saw Ford and she is most insistent that Mrs Belamie means me to go and Eve to remain, and she says it is most unlikely that I shall be able to see her today. We are not even to say good-bye. I may say that I strongly object to Ford's attitude. Who is she to say we are not to be allowed to see Mrs Belamie even when Mr Pawnsford has gone?'

'She is the nurse, after all,' said Lewis complacently. 'I'm afraid there's nothing for it but to come along with us, Myrtle. Can we catch the 12.5 from Helston? There's a connection which will enable us to get lunch on the train. Will you order the staff car for us. I'd like a word with you, Eve,' taking her arm and leading her out to the terrace.

She forestalled what she knew he was going to say, disengaging her arm from his and facing him squarely.

'If you're going to ask me to use whatever influence I've got to get your grandmother to leave you the house, you may as well save your words, Lewis. I definitely refuse. It's probably too late, anyway, if it's her Will she is discussing with the solicitor.'

'It won't be too late. It will only be a draft that he'll take back to Helston with him to get it ready for her signature—'

'It's no good. I won't do anything, and if she drives me into a corner, I shall be quite frank about the situation and tell her the truth about you and me.'

'Eve, you wouldn't do that? Not when you've made such a good impression that she has asked you to stay?' he begged. 'It will only be for a day or two, I'm sure. She's never asked Myrtle to stay.'

'I'm not staying on your account, Lewis. I've hated deceiving her like this and I'm staying solely because she wants me to, me myself, and not as your fiancée. I – I've got very fond of her, and I don't in the least want her to die, as apparently you and Victor and Myrtle do.'

He had taken her arm and would not release it, holding on to it with a dogged persistence, and now walked her down the terrace steps and out into the garden.

'Eve, I – there's something I must say to you. It's about – money.'

'Oh, not still that!' she said angrily. 'That's all you think of, you and the others. For heaven's sake, give it a rest!'

'Not quite that. I mean – not just my grandmother's money. It's for you. If you're going to stay here, you'll need – let me—'

He was clearly so embarrassed that her anger vanished and she laughed.

'Lewis, you're surely not going to offer me more money?'

'I know you haven't got much and I couldn't – can't – I mean—' he floundered.

'Don't go on. I understand what you mean and I assure you I'm in no immediate need, and I've got my return ticket,' she said, still laughing though his suggestion annoyed her.

'You wouldn't take more money from me?'

'Of course I wouldn't. Don't be absurd.'

Lewis drew a deep breath. He was going off the diving board into the deep end, but he had made up his mind.

'Eve—'

There was still time to change his mind, but he was not going to change it. He was going to take the plunge.

She gave him a quizzical, encouraging smile, having no idea what was in his mind.

'Well?' she asked.

'Eve – you've been very decent about this – about the whole thing – and – I understand how you feel about not taking money from me when we're not even engaged. I'm not a marrying man. Girls have never meant anything to me but – if my grandmother leaves me Weir House, or anything substantial in her Will – I'll – I'll marry you, Eve.'

He had left the diving board, had taken the plunge. It was too late now to draw back and he waited for the icy waters to close over his head.

She stared at him in complete stupefaction and then, collapsing on a near-by seat, she went into paroxysms of laughter. That was the last thing he had expected!

'Oh Lewis – Lewis!' she gasped between the peals of laughter.

His face was scarlet with indignation and affront.

'I fail to see what amuses you. I make you a perfectly honourable proposal of marriage—'

She stopped laughing but was mopping her eyes, her face still twitching.

'Can't you see how funny you are? How really terribly funny it is for you to be proposing to me, and in such terms?' she asked quaveringly.

'I am sorry that you consider a proposal—' he began stiffly, but she cut him short.

'Lewis, really! You don't want to marry me any more than I want to marry you. I'm sorry I laughed, but even your proposal had reservations. You want Mrs Belamie's money in the bag first.'

'Without it, I should hardly be in a position to marry at all,' he said, still bitterly affronted but with the sneaking relief of knowing that he had somehow been saved, that he was still on dry land, still by some miracle safe.

She tucked away her handkerchief and rose and put a hand on his arm consolingly.

'Forget it,' she said. 'I suppose I ought to consider it an honour that you might be willing to go to such lengths to repay me, but there's no need for any such sacrifice. Believe me, when I can leave here, I shall very gladly put the whole stupid affair behind me and shall never, in any circumstances, want to see or hear of you again, any of you! Let's go back to the others, shall we?'

If Victor was sour towards her because she was to stay and they to go, Myrtle was positively vitriolic. She frankly accused Eve of manœuvring the invitation.

'Of course, my dear, you can't be expected to know Mrs Belamie as we do,' she said acidly, 'or you wouldn't feel so triumphant at having engineered this invitation to stay. She doesn't think any more of the people who play up to her, and actually she's laughing at you behind your back.'

'Oh well,' said Eve tranquilly, 'there isn't much she can find to laugh at at her age, and if I've done her a good turn by letting her laugh at me, I'm glad.'

'Very clever! I suppose you might as well make the most of your chance of staying on at Weir House.'

Felix, who had been a silent, interested spectator though he had been out of earshot whilst Eve and Lewis had had their conversation in the garden, spoke in the lazy drawl of amusement which characterised his detached observation of the four of them.

'Myrtle means that when she and Victor have come romping home in the Matrimonial Stakes, *you* won't be welcome here any more. You'd better be careful, Myrtle. Even if Eve has no legal right here as part owner, a lot of people like her and you may find you need some sort of added attraction to lure them here when Mrs Belamie is no longer knocking about as a side show.'

In spite of herself, Eve laughed. His position as a mere spectator of what he called the Matrimonial Stakes made him so secure that he could afford to be irreverent.

'I don't know that I'd be keen to be regarded as a side show,' she said. 'Don't worry, Myrtle. I assure you that I shan't expect to be invited to Weir House after this visit.'

Myrtle gave them a withering look and turned to go into the house.

'Come along, Victor,' she said sharply. 'I had better see about the packing since apparently we are being turned out,' and when Victor went obediently, Lewis followed them after a sheepish glance at Eve.

Felix set a chair for her and offered her a cigarette.

'Myrtle's green with jealousy,' he said with a satisfied smile.

'You really enjoy seeing them all at one another's throats, don't you?'

'I've got a ringside seat, but you're one of the contestants, remember. Pity you can't sit beside me and enjoy the spectacle. You wouldn't be so likely to get hurt in the brawl, either.'

'What makes you think I'm in the fight at all?'

'Dear Lewis's betrothed? You can't very well help it, can you?'

At the old mocking tone, which he seemed able to turn on and off at will, she flushed angrily and then with that essential sense of fairness which was typical of her, realised that this was how he must see her, for it must be obvious to him that she was not in the least in love with Lewis. If only she could tell him the truth! But what would he think of her, taking a hundred pounds for this masquerade? If only she could pay it back to Lewis and be free of it! Yet how could she? Where on earth was she to get a hundred pounds from? And if she made a clean breast of it to Felix, would she ever be able to make him understand why she had accepted it? Her reasons now seemed so inadequate, money owed to her dressmaker, money borrowed from Marcia, money for all sorts of odds and ends which she could quite well have gone without, taxis when she could have done what other working girls do and gone by bus, meals in expensive restaurants instead of the self-service tea shops, clothes when she fancied them and not sensible clothes because she needed them.

Looking back at the girl she had been, it was incredible that she had been that girl such a short time ago. Why had she changed so utterly and, she felt, irrevocably? She still wanted all the things she had wanted before, but not at the price she paid for them. Paid or received? The former, she felt, for it had cost her her own self-respect – and, scarcely acknowledged even by her secret self, that of Felix.

She knew that he was watching her, waiting for the anger he could so easily raise in her, but she did not reply or look at him. Had she looked, she would have seen something new in his expression, surprise, interest, speculation, for her mobile face with its sudden changes always intrigued him. He could not understand her nor her thoughts, and as she remained silent after his gibe, he spoke again.

'Has he been trying to rush you into marriage? He'd be a lot safer married to you rather than just engaged, you know.'

'Has it anything to do with you?' she asked in a chilling voice.

'To some extent I'm an interested party. You see, if Victor and Myrtle won the prize, they would live here as lord and lady of the manor, and they would be quite prepared to let me stay on under the same conditions as I now enjoy. If the prize goes to Lewis, he'd sell it – and even if he didn't, I wouldn't stay here.'

'Why not?' she asked unthinkingly, but regretted the question immediately.

'With you here?' came the swift question and for once she was thankful for the intrusion of Lewis who came towards them from the house, giving Felix a baleful glance.

'We shall have to go now if we are to catch the early train,' he said. 'Haven't you anything better to do than hang around, Felix?'

'Any amount of things, dear Cousin Lewis, but I felt it only courteous to be about to speed the parting guests,' said Felix with a grin.

'We're not your guests,' snapped Lewis and the other man, with a shrug and another tantalising smile, ambled away.

'I can take a hint,' he said over his shoulder as he went. 'No doubt you want to take a tender farewell of your fiancée in private. Be seeing you, Eve.'

When he had gone, Lewis spoke petulantly.

'I hope you won't be seeing too much of him when we've gone.'

'There won't be any occasion to,' said Eve serenely, and led the way into the house where Victor and Myrtle were waiting, their faces still hostile and aggrieved. Myrtle did not even take a formal farewell of Eve, but Victor kissed her, with some enjoyment she felt, and she submitted to a cold kiss from Lewis's thin, tight lips and pushed him away almost hysterically and went up the stairs, not even waiting to see them leave.

The maids were moving her belongings back into the Queen's Room which Mrs Belamie had said she was to have, and as she helped them, she was aware of a feeling of enormous relief in the absence of Lewis. She could still smile to herself at his proposal of marriage, but it had put the whole situation on a different and most undesirable basis. At least she need never see him again, though she was determined that somehow or other she would return that hated hundred pounds. Until she had done so, she would never feel her self-respect restored.

When she went down to luncheon, however, she found two places laid on a table on the terrace.

'Is Mr Pawnsford having it here?' she asked Corke.

'No, Miss Eve, he would not stay,' and at that moment Felix appeared, smiling at her with impudent good humour.

'I was sure you would not want to eat alone now that the others have gone,' he said, and held a chair for her whilst Corke disappeared into the house.

'Why should you assume that?' asked Eve tartly.

'I did not want to leave you to lonely reflection so soon after being deprived of the stimulating presence of your fiancé,' said Felix with his imperturbable grin to which, in spite of herself, she was finding it difficult not to respond. He was an impossible person. She could not think of a suitably crushing answer and his smile changed into a beguiling friendliness.

'Must we fight all the time, Eve? Couldn't we at least pretend to be friends?'

'If we must,' she said ungraciously, 'but you might have waited for an invitation.'

'I did, actually. My grandmother issued one, a royal command,' he said, and she coloured at the neat turning of the tables and as Corke came back at that moment, Felix took his seat opposite and began a desultory conversation about nothing at all.

Corke, like all the staff, was very partial to Mr Felix. Though they were aware of his equivocal position in the household, he never traded on his relationship to Mrs Belamie and was their stalwart defender when difficuties arose with the old autocrat and had got his way on many occasions when some injustice threatened.

He chatted entertainingly to his almost silent companion throughout the meal and against her will she found her ruffled feathers being smoothed down. He really was a most annoying person. How could one possibly remain seething with indignation when he completely ignored any cause for it?

At the end of the meal, he rose to take a look at the sky.

'Nice fresh breeze blowing from the right quarter. I think I'll go for a sail.'

'Haven't you any work to do?'

'It's my half day. I take that when I can, which isn't every week. Ever done any sailing? Like to come?'

She hated the knowledge that she would like it beyond all things.

'Mrs Belamie may want me,' she said lamely.

'We can send and ask her.'

'I couldn't do that!'

He came to the table and stood looking down at her.

'Not afraid of her, are you? It's the one thing she can't stand, and the chief reason why she dislikes her grandsons, her legitimate ones that is. She does, you know. I'm not in the least afraid of her, and you need not be.'

She waited for the gibe about her position here to follow, but for once it did not.

'No, I don't think I'm afraid of her,' she said thoughtfully.

'She's never given me any reason to be, but – I'm her guest, after all. I can't just go haring off without a word.'

He found an old envelope in his pocket, scribbled a few words on it and gave it to Corke, who was serving the coffee.

'Send this up to Miss Ford, will you? And tell whoever takes it to wait for an answer,' and to Eve, 'Shall I pour out? Black or white?'

'Black, please. What did you say in your note?'

'Told her that if the old lady doesn't want you, you're going sailing with me. Know anything about sailing, by the way?'

'A bit. My – my father was very keen on it.'

He had noticed the slight hesitation when she spoke of her father and knew that the wound of his loss was taking a long time to heal. He spoke of it gently.

'You still miss him badly, don't you? You can't live with the dead, you know. You must let life close over it, though there will always be a gap.'

She nodded and tears threatened her eyes, as much at the gentle kindness of his tone as for that unremitting sense of loss.

'We were very close. I don't think I realised how close until I didn't have him any more. I know I've got to get over it, and of course I shall in time, but when I do things for the first time without him – sailing, for instance – the memory is very poignant. I've felt that a lot since I came here. It's the sort of life we used to live, rather grand and spacious and – dignified,' looking at him with a smile whose bravery he felt. 'I suppose that's really what tempted me to come, but – I ought not to have come. I don't belong to these things or to the sort of life any more. I've become a working girl, or that's what I ought to have become, though so far I have not had much success!' with a laugh at the memory of her various short adventures into the working world.

Again she had unconsciously given him an opportunity for one of the old gibes, but again he did not take it. He was re-assessing his opinion of her and trying to make sense of her engagement to Lewis Belamie. Was there not something to be said on her side, after all? A girl brought up to all the luxuries of life, suddenly bereft of them and left high and dry to fend for herself?

But, in heaven's name, why Lewis Belamie? Had he told her fantastic tales of his expectations and his position?

He was still pondering this when a maid brought a verbal message in reply to his note.

'Miss Ford says that Madame is resting and does not want to be disturbed, but that if she wakes, Miss Ford will tell her where Miss Brayle has gone.'

'So that's all right,' said Felix. 'Want to change or anything?'

'Yes. I think I'll put on slacks and a sweater. Will you wait or shall I be able to find you?'

'I'll wait. I came in my ramshackle old car that will almost climb the cliff in spite of its age. Will you mind?'

'Not a bit!'

She ran off, feeling suddenly gay and light-hearted, and the mood stayed with her during the rest of the afternoon. Workmanlike in grey slacks and a scarlet sweater, she revealed to him more than the 'bit' of knowledge to which she had admitted. She was an expert 'crew', knowing in an instant what was required for her and he soon found that he could take risks which gave them an added thrill in the stiff breeze which would soon have overset a less experienced pair.

'Oh, I love it!' she cried when they both hurled themselves to the side to counteract the swing of the sails as the little yacht heeled over in the wind.

'And I love you,' he thought, looking at her lithe figure, her eager, laughing face covered with salt spray and the short, blown curls of spun, silvery gold, but she was completely oblivious of him as anything other than the perfect companion for the gay adventure.

When they had had enough, they drew in closer to the shore which was sheltered by the cliffs, hauled in the sails and drifted, his hand lightly on the tiller.

'Where did you learn so much about sailing?' he asked her.

'In many places. Chiefly Bermuda.'

'Where the Bermudan rig came from?'

126

'Yes. That was a battle! I went overboard a good many times before I learned to stay in the boat, but with sharks about I soon learned!'

'Just the two of you handling those huge sheets?'

She nodded, her smile reminiscent, and now that she was getting over the first difficulty in speaking of her father, words poured from her as she described their life together, the places where they had made temporary homes, the interesting and amusing and not always by any means high-born or rich people they had met. She made Richard Brayle a vivid personality to Felix, colouring him with her love and admiration. To the man who had always been lonely, without any background of family life, this father-and-daughter relationship seemed a perfect thing, and he realised more and more the shock to her whole life when in an instant all that was snatched away from her, leaving her bereft not only of that beloved companion but also of money.

He could even, partially at any rate, understood how she had become engaged to Lewis Belamie. He was certainly not the father-figure, but he would appear solid and substantial, a man devoted to his life-work, not making any demands on her or causing any emotional upset for which so shortly after the death of her father she would be unwilling and unprepared.

But what did she think about Lewis now? She was coming back to life. That was clear. Would she not ask more, much more, than he would ever be able to supply?

The sunshine had gone and he realised it suddenly and looked up at the sky apprehensively. There was more than the threat of rain, for already a few spots had fallen.

'We'd better scurry back,' he said. 'Not much wind now, but there should be enough to take us home before there's a real downpour,' and in an instant she had scrambled to her feet to help him adjust the sails to catch what breeze there was.

When they reached the mooring buoy a short distance from the shore and had reefed the sails neatly, they had to scramble over a few boats and wade through the shallow water. He offered to carry her, but she refused the indignity laughingly, rolled her slacks above her knees and dropped over the side and they waded companionably to dry land and to his car.

'Friends?' he asked, and she nodded without looking at him and ran across the grass and into the house, and after a moment's hesitation, he followed her.

Instinctively she waited for him on the terrace. Neither of them wanted the day to end, poised on the dangerous brink between enmity and more than friendship.

'You'd better get out of your damp clothes,' he said. 'How about – later on? Will you invite me to dinner?'

She wanted to refuse, not because she did not want his company but because, whilst he was in this mood, she wanted it too much. She must be mad to let this happen to her, yet she nodded again.

'If you like,' she said and ran into the house and left him.

When she had bathed and changed into one of her simple cotton frocks, white with a scarlet belt, it was not yet time for dinner and she went to the baize door, pushed it open hesitantly and found Emma Ford in the little passage, seated as usual in the comfortable chair she kept there. They exchanged the smiles of good friends.

'Do you think I could go in for a little while?' whispered Eve.

'Yes, I expect she'd like you to. She turned me out, but I never mind that, bless her,' and she opened the door into Mrs Belamie's bedroom and put her head round it.

'Here's Miss Brayle,' she said. 'Like to see her?'

'Of course I should,' said the old woman querulously. 'I get enough of my own company and you haven't been near me for hours. I might be dead for all you know.

'Nonsense. I've been with you ever since Mr Pawnsford left, and you turned me out only quarter of an hour ago,' said Emma robustly. 'Anyway, whilst Miss Brayle's here I'll go and get a breath of air and I hope you'll be in a better temper when I come back. I wonder why I put up with you.'

'You'll stay with me until I die because of what you hope to get out of me, like everybody else,' grumbled the old lady, but Emma laughed and opened the door more widely to admit Eve and closed it behind her.

Mrs Belamie chuckled. They were old enemies and the best of friends, as the girl knew.

'Thank goodness she's gone and I've got someone young and pretty about me again. Pull up a chair where I can see you and tell me what you've been doing all day.'

'Felix came to lunch and this afternoon we've been sailing. Did Miss Ford tell you?'

'She said something about it. Enjoy it?'

'Yes, I loved it. It started to rain, though, so we had to scurry back.'

'H'm. Ha. Like him?' It was the second time she had asked that question.

The blue eyes searched her face with a certain malice in it.

'I don't know,' said Eve frankly. 'Sometimes I hate him, but we had fun this afternoon. He has a bitter tongue, though, when he likes.'

'I expect you think I'm not fair to him, don't you?'

'It isn't my business how you treat him, is it?'

'No, but you've probably got your own opinion. Felix and I understand each other. He knows he's got no claim on me and no expectations and that what he does here is only payment for what I've done for him. I need not have done anything, you know.'

'He's your grandson, after all,' ventured Eve.

'He's my daughter's shame,' snarled Mrs Belamie.

'That's not his fault. He couldn't help how he was born.'

'The sins of the father's, and the mother's. Anyway, I did what I considered my duty to him.'

'Don't you ever think it might be galling to him to know that? And it seems he has amply repaid you in the way he keeps the farm.'

She wondered at the urge she felt to defend Felix, and the old woman chuckled nastily.

'He doesn't need you to speak for him, and I don't know why you should. It's none of your business. What's it to you? It's Lewis you're going to marry, though I don't know how you can be such a fool, a girl like you. For the money you think he's going to get, I suppose? And this house?'

Eve rose precipitately, her face pale with anger.

'Perhaps I'd better go,' she said, but the old woman caught at her arm.

'No. Sit down. Sit down, girl. I'm just a disagreeable old woman. I suppose Lewis has got his points so we won't discuss that any further. You won't leave me, Eve? You'll stop a few days? I – I'm a lonely old woman, too. Probably my own fault but – you won't let me scare you away?'

Eve felt a pang of pity. To be old and unloved and to know that they all wanted her to die and leave them her money!

She covered the thin old hand with her own warm young fingers.

'No,' she said, 'I'll stay if you want me to, but you mustn't say things like that to me again. It – it isn't true, you know. I don't think about your money and I don't want any of it. I'm fond of you. You know that, don't you?'

The aged face softened and there was a film of actual tears over the piercing blue eyes.

'Yes, I do, my dear, though heaven knows why you should be. We won't talk any more about Lewis or Felix. Talk to me about yourself. Tell me some more about your father. He was a scoundrel, of course, to leave you without any money, leave you to earn your living or to make a good marriage, but you loved him, didn't you?'

'More than anyone in the world,' said Eve shakily, and she sat down again and they talked of the places they had been to, some of them known to Mrs Belamie in her youth, though unbelievably changed now, some quite new to her.

When Emma Ford came in with her dinner on a tray, they were absorbed and happy and Mrs Belamie dismissed the girl reluctantly.

'We'll talk some more tomorrow,' she said. 'You do me good, doesn't she, Ford?'

'You're certainly a bit more pleasant than you were,' said the woman with a grim smile behind which lurked the real affection she had for her cantankerous old employer. 'Eat your dinner now, and then I'll come and settle you down for the night. You've had a tiring day and ought to have rested after all that festivity last night.'

'Rest? What do I want with rest? I shall have quite enough of that when my time comes. What have I got?' lifting the covers to look at the clear soup and the beautifully prepared and served morsel of fish, each on its special hot-plate.

Eve smiled and bent to kiss the delicately perfumed cheek.

'Good night, dear Mrs Belamie,' she said.

'Good night, child,' replied the old woman absently, all her attention now occupied with the inspection of her meal, and Eve slipped away.

It was only after she had done so that she remembered that she ought to have mentioned that Felix was coming to dinner.

7

THE DAYS flowed peacefully and happily by. One week passed, and then two, and finally three, and apart from odd days of mist and rain, the summer weather held and Eve spent most of the time out of doors and most of it with Felix.

It was not that she neglected Mrs Belamie. She spent some time every day with her, reading to her from the newspapers and entering into lively discussions on the ways of modern life of which the old lady strongly disapproved, or from old-fashioned novels which Mrs Belamie declared beat the novels of today 'into a cocked hat'. But, with the sun pouring into the room, the old lady quickly grew tired, or said she did, and sent her young guest away to make the most of the weather.

'Go and swim, my dear, or get Felix to take you sailing. I've told him to look after you. You don't want to spend all your time with a sick old woman who's always grumbling. That's why I pay Ford more than she's worth. I don't know why I hang on to the unwanted remnants of my life – except to keep Victor and Lewis wondering how much they're going to get! You've not fixed a date for your wedding yet, have you?'

'No,' murmured Eve uncomfortably.

Mrs Belamie gave her wheezy chuckle.

'No need to hurry about that. Much better to wait till I'm out of the way, though if I were a young man and engaged to a girl like you, I wouldn't wait a day in case you slipped through my fingers. Get along with you now, and send Ford to me.'

Released from her willing attendance on the woman who was certainly old but not at all sick, Eve pushed out of her mind that unwelcome thought of Lewis, though it was entirely due to him that she was here. He wrote to her every few days, stiff formal letters dictated to his secretary and typed by her, urging her to stay as long as Mrs Belamie wanted her. Once he sent her a cheque, which she promptly returned with one of her equally formal letters, making no comment on his wish that she should remain at Weir House.

It was easy enough to forget him in between those letters, spending so much time with Felix who had ceased to gibe at her or to provoke a quarrel, so that her relations with him were friendly, if with a certain reserve of which both were conscious. Most mornings he joined her without previous arrangement for her early swim and came back to the house for breakfast with her and, again without arrangement, at some time later in the morning she walked over to the farm, making light of the distance now that he had shown her all the short cuts. He was making preparations for an early harvest, fearful of rain setting in at the normal, later time and, walking through the fields with him, she became knowledgeable about matters in which she had previously taken no interest, though often he had occasion to laugh at her naïve comments.

Until he could start the harvest in earnest, however, he seized several opportunities to go sailing with her, and when they returned from such carefree afternoons they were both aware of the increasing danger of their association, nor did he ever, by word or touch, seek to take advantages freely offered him by their growing intimacy. She stopped wearing her 'engagement' ring but though he noticed the fact, Lewis's name was now never mentioned between them. She began to long for him to speak of Lewis, even to jeer at her as he had done in the past, for if he did, she felt she might pluck up courage to confess the truth about it in spite of what his reactions might be, but he seemed quite content now with her friendship.

One wet evening towards the end of the third week since the others had gone, when she had not seen him all day, she was feeling listless and dispirited and tried to make herself believe it was only the change in the weather. She had dined alone after spending only a few minutes with Mrs Belamie, who had sent her away on the plea of feeling tired.

'Wouldn't you like me to sit with you whilst Miss Ford has her dinner? I won't even talk. You may be able to sleep,' she said, but Mrs Belamie shook her head wearily.

'No, my dear. You go and amuse yourself. I'd rather be alone, and Emma will soon be up again.'

It was very seldom she called her devoted nurse by her Christian name. When she did, they knew that she was not feeling in her usual good health and liked being cossetted.

Eve stood by the bed for a moment and then bent down to kiss her. The old hand went up to touch the girl's cheek in an unwonted caress.

'Thank you, my dear. You've been very kind to a grumpy old woman. I haven't forgotten you.'

Eve drew away in sharp distress.

'Please, Mrs Belamie. Please – no. I didn't stay with you for that.'

'I know you didn't. Bless the child, you've got tears in your eyes! What on earth for?'

'You're so kind – to let me stay in your lovely house – to be so good to me,' quavered Eve, dashing away the tears and smiling through them.

'Oh, get along with you. I wanted you to stay for my own sake. Don't you know yet that I never do a kindness, or anything I don't want to do? Run along now. I'll see you in the morning.'

Eve went down to her solitary dinner and afterwards wandered into the long, narrow room known as the Music Room because at one end of it there was a grand piano. She had heard it being tuned, but it was never used and she opened the keyboard and touched the notes softly, almost fearfully. She had not touched a piano since her father's death. For one thing there had been no opportunity, but if there had been she would not have taken it. She had no great talent, but she had been well taught. Richard Brayle had had the soul of a musician without any ability to express himself in music, and he had given his daughter the opportunity of such expression though aware that she had no real talent. She could never have become a concert pianist but, more to please him than from any great desire herself, she had learnt a certain mechanical precision and had a feeling for music which she was not able to develop or express. It had remained a pleasant accomplishment from which both drew some private satisfaction whilst recognising her limitations and they had spent many quiet hours of enjoyment of the old composers without catching their magic or being able to translate their souls into sound.

She had thought never to attempt to play again after his death and had felt no desire to do so, but tonight, lonely and filled with that strange depression and foreboding, she longed inexpressibly to be back in the past, to recapture some shadow and echo of the girl she had been even whilst she knew she would never be that girl again.

Finally she drew out the stool from under the piano and began to play tentatively, softly, with a melancholy which took her first into Brahms and then into the sad, slow cadences of certain movements of Beethoven's quieter sonatas which seemed filled with the passionate longings of the great man to hear with his physical ears what could be conceived only in his soul.

And suddenly the tragedy of the deaf man swept over her and her hands fell silent on the keys and she bent her head on the instrument and gave way to her own feeling of desolation and loss. What was left to her? Where was she going? Drifting, inadequate, with no goal and no desire, what would happen to her in the endless years ahead?

Her shoulders shook with great, silent sobs which did not bring the relief of tears – and suddenly she felt a hand touching her, gripping one shaking shoulder firmly, drawing her head until it rested against his body and she was held there in a strong, comforting clasp. The blessed comfort seeped into her mind so that she knew she was no longer alone, no longer so utterly desolate.

Then his voice spoke to her softly.

'It's all right. Don't try to talk. Cry if you want to. There's no one here but me, and I understand, my darling – my dearest.'

She knew that he did not understand. She did not understand herself. The whole thing was too complex, but at that moment he was an anchor, something she could cling to.

'Felix – forgive me – I'm not like this, really. It was just that – I was suddenly so lonely, afraid—'

'Of what? Of life in general? It gets us all at times. Life's all we have and we've got to get through it alone, make our own mistakes, bear the responsibility of them, choose our own path alone, always alone.'

'Felix – I don't want to be alone. I'm frightened—'

He bent and lifted her from the stool into his arms, so small, so fragile, so pathetic and helpless, and his lips came to hers, at first with the kiss of comfort to a frightened child, then at the contact with the kiss of a man and a woman, close, vibrant, and her lips parted to receive his.

Then suddenly they drew apart as the door was flung open and Emma Ford stood there, her face distraught, her eyes wild with distress.

'Eve – I heard you playing – Felix – Felix, she's gone! All in a moment like that—'

They ran to her, Felix the first to reach her as she stood grasping the side of the door to steady herself.

'*Grand-mère*?' he asked, though he had never referred to her like that before. 'She's – dead?'

Emma nodded, her eyes wide with anguish.

'Yes. I asked her if she was all right. I thought she was looking strange. Then she said, quite clearly and calmly, "No, I'm going to die" and just fell back on the pillows – dead.'

He took charge immediately.

'I'll come,' he said. 'Have you done anything yet? Sent for the doctor? Not that there is anything for him to do if she's really gone, but we must get him. Look after her, Eve. I'm going up. Perhaps you'll telephone to the doctor? His number is on the pad by the telephone in the hall. Then give Emma a brandy, a strong one, and have one yourself. I'll ring Corke as I go through. The other servants will have gone to bed. He'll know which of them to disturb,' and with a comforting touch on Emma's shoulder, he went past her and towards the stairs.

By morning, the whole large household knew that Mrs Belamie was dead and it was the measure of the iron grip in which, from her bed, she had held them that for the moment they felt lost and bewildered. For years they had anticipated it but had not actually visualised it and were stunned by it. Everything devolved on Felix, and on Emma Ford once the initial shock had passed.

He stayed in the house that night, insisting that as there was nothing she could do, Eve went to bed. They had returned to their former basis of friendship, their moment of passion and revelation as if it had never been, and when they met in the morning over a snatched breakfast which was served to them by an awed, wide-eyed maid, he was business-like and authoritative.

'Hadn't I better leave?' she asked. 'Nobody will want me here.'

'Please stay. I've notified Pawnsford but there is a lot to do, telegrams to be sent, arrangements to be made by telephone. This is a list of people to be informed by telegram, Victor and Lewis first, of course, then other relations. Will you see to it? Use the telephone in the hall. I'll use the one upstairs. And see that Emma has something to eat, will you? Poor old Corke is not capable just now. After you've sent the telegrams to relatives, come and find me, will you? There are the notices for the papers and so on, and then the immediate arrangements for the funeral, which will be a full-dress affair. Not cremation unfortunately, which is the only decent way of disposing of unwanted remains!' and for a moment his face twisted into one of the old grins. 'The dear old soul would not have wanted that, and would have wished to be accompanied on her last journey by all her relatives and associates in their decent suits of black. Have you got a decent suit of black, by the way?'

She nodded.

'Are you sure you will want me to be there, Felix?'

'But of course! As Lewis's betrothed and a possible beneficiary, you must certainly be at the gathering of the vultures,' the smile fading from his face and leaving it grim.

Eve, with nothing she could possibly say, left him.

The brothers, accompanied inevitably by Myrtle in deepest mourning, came down later in the day and Myrtle immediately took over, assuming the position of one of the chief mourners and setting the staff, who had never liked her, against her by her dictatorial ways.

'Of course, you must move out of the Queen's Room, Eve,' she said. 'It will be wanted for more important guests who will have to remain over night.'

'Nothing of the sort, Myrtle,' put in Lewis before Eve could reply. 'Eve is just as important as you are, as my future wife.'

'*I'm* not in a room like that,' snapped Myrtle.

'Oh, what does it matter?' asked Eve wearily. 'Of course I'll move into whatever room you like. I'll go and do it now,' but when she was taking her dresses out of the wardrobe and folding them for the packing which she would soon be doing, Lewis came into the room.

'Why should you be moved out of here, Eve?' he asked, his annoyance plain. 'I'm not going to let you be put on by Myrtle and relegated to the background.'

'Oh, Lewis, why keep on about it? I don't mind in the least where I sleep. It's only for a day or two anyway. After the funeral I shall go back to London and be finished with the whole business. You can't have any more use for me now so please go away and don't hinder me.'

'Why aren't you wearing my ring?'

She snatched it from a drawer and put it on.

'I've told you I'll keep up the fiction until I leave this house,' she said angrily. 'Then you can have it back, and I only wish I could cast off all the memories of the whole disgraceful episode as easily.

He still barred her way between wardrobe and bed.

'Eve – I asked you to marry me – and I meant it,' he stammered.

She gave a look of contempt.

'Oh, that! There was no need for you to have been so gallant, though I suppose I ought to appreciate it. Do you know anything about the Will?' she asked suspiciously, on a sudden, unpalatable thought. 'Has it made a condition that we are to be actually married? Because this is the end and my answer is definitely no.'

'I don't know anything about it and what the conditions are. I – I'm fond of you, Eve, and I should really like to marry you.'

She hesitated between laughter and anger, and the laughter won.

'Thank you for the compliment, Lewis, but the answer is still no.'

'Couldn't you care for me just a little?'

She became grave again after that little burst of laughter.

'I'm afraid when I marry, I should want a lot more than that on both sides. I shouldn't want just to be able to live with someone, but not to be able to live without him and you and I would never feel that. Please let it end here, Lewis. I'm desperately sorry and ashamed of having entered into this. That's all I can say about it.'

He still hung about as if wanting to say more, but at last he left her. He seemed to have accepted it, and she heaved a sigh of relief.

Dinner that evening was a solemn and uncomfortable meal, though Eve felt that the solemnity was only because in the room above them an old woman lay dead and not yet buried and the discomfort only from private speculation about what her death would mean to them. Felix was not present, and except for Corke and Emma Ford, whose eyes were still red with weeping, and herself, she felt that nobody was thinking of Mrs Belamie herself except with relief that at last her life was over.

'That gathering of the vultures,' Felix had called these, her closest relatives and all those who would be coming from far and near to see what pickings, if any, were for them.

Sick at the thought, and at the sight of Myrtle in funereal black and the black ties which Victor and Lewis had probably had in readiness for a long time (for no one had dressed for dinner that night), she slipped out of the house as soon as the meal was over and made her way to the top of the cliff, where trees and a jutting ledge of rock shielded her from view from the house.

But someone was there before her. She did not see him until she had rounded the corner of rock and she drew back with an involuntary 'oh' of surprise and dismay.

'No, don't go, Eve,' said Felix. 'If you came here to be alone, I'll go if you want me to.'

She hesitated and then took the few more steps to the ledge of rock from which he had risen.

'No,' she said. 'Only – I can't go on quarrelling with you. I came here for a bit of peace.'

'Agreed,' he said and sat beside her, and for a few minutes they were silent.

Then she said softly, 'I wonder where she is now? Is she anywhere at all? Is she young again by now, do you think?'

'She was never old. It was only her body that was worn out and tired. No one can be called old who loved life as she did – and she did, you know. She got a kick out of keeping us all at loggerheads with one another and especially at keeping *them* guessing,' with a gesture of his head towards the house. 'Yes, I think she's alive somewhere and will be taking a keen interest in all the proceedings. Well, we're going to do her proud, with all the trappings, purple velvet for the pall and so on. They think it's madness to spend so much money on it, but Pawnsford's with me in this. What do you think about it, Eve?'

'I think you're right. She loved to be treated like royalty, and as it's for the last time, why shouldn't she be? It's her own money that's being spent.'

'They don't think it is any longer,' he said grimly, and she fell silent again, gazing out over the sea, thinking of the dead woman who had loved her long life, no matter what sorrows it may have brought her and finding it impossible to believe that everything had ceased for her when the body no longer functioned.

'Felix,' she said suddenly, 'what do you really believe in? Anything?'

'I don't know. Not the orthodox things I was taught as a child, and that probably you were too, anyway. I'd like to, of course. In the so-called progress of the world, we've lost a lot of things that must have been a great help in the business of living, a firm belief in life after death, meeting and knowing one's friends again, being able at last to look at life from a distance and understanding the pattern. I've probably been through the lot and, as old Omar said "Came out at that same door wherein I went". The Church today has no answer to give though probably more people are thinking and wondering than ever before and reaching out, metaphorically as well as actually, towards the stars. All the churches have to offer is the symbol of a dying man on a cross, which frankly has always horrified me. As a child, I hated going to church and could not keep myself from renewing that agony of horror week after week until I was old enough to stay away. Surely it is the resurrection that is the important thing, not that hideous political execution which, after all, was meted out in those days to many others. I think I believe in the resurrection, not of the body of Christ though that mysteriously disappeared, but of the spirit which re-clothed itself in the form of the body for the purpose of recognition. That I believe in – or I think I do. I want to, anyway. It gives me hope that there is something more for my mind, for the essential part of me, than just the short span of the existence of the body which is often so unsatisfactory.'

'Are you a spiritualist, Felix?'

'I don't know. Am I? Perhaps it is only wishful thinking, the hope of being able to get, in some other existence, some things that I have missed in this life.'

'Do you believe in prayer?'

'Not for myself, no.'

'For blessings for others?'

'Possibly, if there is no personal motive. I'm rather like my cowman's little girl whom I met the other day when she should have been at Sunday School. When I asked her why she wasn't, she said, "I asked and asked God not to send Mummy another baby, but last week she had one and so God and me's fallen out and we're not friends any more."'

Eve laughed, glad that he had lightened the conversation which was taking her further than she wanted to go in her thoughts.

She moved her hands as they lay in her lap, and he caught the glint of her ring.

'So you're wearing it again?' he asked, a note of acceptance in his voice.

She covered it with her other hand and nodded.

'Why are you going to marry Lewis, Eve? You're not in love with him.'

'How do you know that?'

'Because you're essentially honest and it doesn't ring true. Why, Eve?'

She longed to tell him the truth, but would it be more palatable to him than what he thought now?

Again she was on the brink of telling him when they heard footsteps and Lewis's voice calling for her querulously.

'Her master's voice!' said Felix, and turned to her, caught her in his arms and kissed her full on the lips, just once and fiercely.

'That's in case I never get another opportunity, and to remind you, in case you don't know it, that there's something in life you may be missing,' he said, and let her go and left her abruptly.

By the time Lewis found her, he was gone and she was left shaken and trembling.

'Oh, there you are, Eve! I wondered where on earth you'd got to,' he said irritably. 'Myrtle's making up the list for the cars and—'

'I'm sure she can make it up without my help,' snapped Eve. 'What do I know about your family and friends? I'm tired. I'm going to bed,' and she brushed past him and fled into the house and the small room that had been allotted to her.

Felix's kiss still burned on her lips and the memory of his arms was still about her, fierce arms that had held no tenderness, savage lips that had bruised her own.

'Something in life that she might be missing,' he had said.

Yes, Felix, you – you! Or was this love, this wild desire to be absorbed and possessed by him, this passionate hunger of body and mind which would give her no rest, no peace?

She must get over it. She would, once she was away from him where she could no longer see him, no longer listen for his voice or his step.

During the next few days of hushed activity, the house filling with relations from a distance who may or may not have known who Felix Welby really was, he and Eve met seldom and never alone and he did not appear at meals. When they did meet for a few moments, she avoided his eyes, though once she caught them, his look half-mocking, half-tender. He was busy, much in request, given innumerable problems to settle since he knew more about the affairs of Weir House and the estate than either Victor or Lewis, but at last the long, tiring ceremony was over, the long drive to and from the cemetery where Mrs Belamie had already arranged to be buried, the irksome necessity for the change of cars following the velvet-draped coffin which had to be carried to the spot beyond which the hearse could not go, the loads of flowers on farm carts, the long procession of 'mourners' in their own cars, or horse-drawn traps, even on foot.

They were making a gala day of it, thought Eve, as she listened to the subdued chatter, even little bursts of quickly-hushed laughter when the guests (she could not think of them as mourners) were being transferred from the fleet of small cars running a shuttle service to the larger ones. Then she checked her thoughts, remembering the dead woman and her love of display, the way she had enjoyed the 'ball' she had arranged, insisting that everyone else should enjoy it. Perhaps she would not have minded, since all these people had come to do her honour.

Felix was thinking the same thing, for whilst he was putting her into the car she was to share with the two brothers and Myrtle, he bent his head to whisper to her.

'The old lady would have enjoyed all this, wouldn't she?' and Eve responded with a nod and a furtive smile.

Finally, when all but the relations and close friends had gone, regaled with what Felix called 'the funeral baked meats', a loaded buffet set in the huge dining-hall and on the terrace, those who had contrived to remain crowded into the library, a room that had rarely been used during Eve's stay. Mr Pawnsford was to read the Will, or at least such portions of it as would interest the assembled company. Victor and his fiancée and his brother were well to the fore, but Eve had refused to be drawn forward by Lewis. Felix had taken up a position near the door amongst the humblest and least expectant of such of the servants as had managed to get into the room.

The Will, even cut down by the lawyer's dry, unemotional voice, was wordy and at its conclusion, there were a good many puzzled glances from one to another.

There was a long list of bequests, amongst them a stupifying one of five hundred pounds to 'my young friend Evelyn Brayle' with the strange proviso that she should remain in residence at Weir House for the six months immediately following Mrs Belamie's death. There were generous annuities to Emma Ford and to Corke, who broke down and wept openly; every servant on the huge staff, including the farm workers, had been remembered and mentioned by name, a month's rent had been remitted to all the tenants, large and small, and Felix's cottage was given to him freehold with a bequest of five hundred pounds. Each of the grandsons was also left five hundred pounds and (with what everybody knew to be an intended insult) Myrtle was left ten pounds 'to buy a mourning brooch'.

The Weir House estate, and the residue of what was probably a large fortune, were left in trust, to be dealt with in such fashion as a secret clause provided.

Everybody was bewildered except the grave-faced lawyer, and the family, all but Felix, dismayed and furious. Which of them was to get the estate and the money after all? Were they to be made fools of, in the end, by the old woman after whom they had dallied hopefully all these years? Even Felix had been left more than they had, for he had been given his cottage, and Eve, whom Mrs Belamie had known only a few weeks, was to receive the same amount and to live in the house for the duration of this extraordinary provision, whilst nothing at all had been left to the other relations.

Questions and angry comments were poured out to Mr

Pawnsford, who brushed them aside as if they had been merely annoying flies, calling the two grandsons and Felix aside.

'I've got something to say to you three in strictest privacy,' he said. 'It concerns the secret clause in the Will. Where can we go? I suggest Mrs Belamie's bedroom with Miss Ford outside the door to ensure our privacy.'

They trooped out, the rest of the company making way for them curiously, but outside the library door, the solicitor turned to Myrtle, who had accompanied them.

'I am sorry, Miss Mellor,' he said, 'but my instructions were explicit. Nobody but these three gentlemen' and she was obliged to stay behind in impotent anger which was not made less by coming face to face with Eve.

'You managed to do very nicely for yourself, didn't you?' she said, beside herself with rage. 'Of course, the Will will be contested. Everybody knows the old woman was mental. I wouldn't begin to spend that five hundred pounds, if I were you.'

'I'm sorry, Myrtle,' began Eve, for she really was, but Myrtle cut her short.

'Sorry? You needn't be. The Will won't stand, of course. Leaving Victor, her own grandson, a miserable five hundred and leaving you, a nobody, exactly the same! Of course she was mad. I shall see Mr Pawnsford about it myself. Felix too! Everybody knows who *he* is, the illegitimate child of her daughter with no right to anything at all. It's disgusting, flaunting it instead of being ashamed of it.'

'You can't exactly blame Felix for his parentage, can you? And after all, he did work here,' murmured Eve, but Myrtle, with a final snort of fury, flounced off, leaving Eve to see to the rapidly departing guests in consultation with Corke and Mrs Hodd, who were pleased to be relieved of Myrtle's presence.

As soon as she could, Eve escaped to her room.

She felt stunned by the Will, and particularly the bequest to herself. Five hundred pounds! It was amazing, incredulous wealth though at one time it would have meant nothing to her. For one thing, she could pay Lewis back his hated hundred pounds. She could scarcely bear to wait to get her hands on the money in order to do that.

Then she thought of the extraordinary condition that Mrs Belamie had laid down in requiring her to remain in the house for six months.

Well, she wouldn't mind that. Probably Mr Pawnsford would be able to tell her why she was to remain. There would be a lot of things to do, she supposed, though she did not know exactly what.

And, deep down in her mind, was the knowledge that for six months she would remain in touch with Felix. It was madness to prolong it, but the memory of his arms and his lips would not be denied, and who could tell what might happen?

8

Mr PAWNSFORD, inscrutable as ever, seated himself at a table which had been cleared of the dead woman's books and papers, and, having seen to it that Emma Ford was mounting guard outside the door, signed to the three men to be seated, fidgeted with his documents for a few moments and cleared his throat.

'As you know, gentlemen, my late client, Mrs Belamie, was in many ways a peculiar woman,' he began, 'but I want to make it quite clear to you at the outset that she was perfectly in possession of her faculties, perfectly competent to devise and execute this Will. She did, in fact, obtain a certificate of her complete sanity from her doctor, no doubt anticipating that an attempt might be made by some person or persons to overthrow the Will, which would make her intestate and entirely alter her wishes. Inevitably the Will will be administered – in due course.'

'Well, get on with it, Pawnsford,' said Victor irritably. 'No one wants to contest the Will. Of course she was sane, though a damned difficult old witch. Get on with it, man. Who's going to get the money?'

Mr Pawnsford looked at them, at the two brothers who were obviously angry and perturbed, and at Felix who sat in a relaxed attitude and with no expression on his face save that of a faintly interested outsider with nothing personal at stake.

'This private provision of Mrs Belamie's Will concerns all three of you and is specifically addressed to you,' said the lawyer in his unemotional, legal voice, though he knew he was about to electrify them. 'My late client herself dictated the superscription, which reads, "Personal and private to my three grandsons, Victor and Lewis Belamie, the sons of my son Louis, and Felix Belamie, known as Felix Welby, the son of my daughter, whom I hereby acknowledge to be my grandson."'

The two brothers gave snorts of indignation and outrage, looking at Felix as if they could not believe their ears, but he neither heard them nor saw their faces. He stared past them at the bed with its satin cover folded over the pillow where that bedizened, grotesque head would never lie again, but he could almost believe that he could see her there still, her bright blue eyes so like his own snapping fire, her little wizened body shaking with mischievous, fiendish laughter.

'So you did it at last, old girl?' he asked silently. 'You named me as your grandson. Thank you – grandmother.'

'Mr Welby, are you paying attention? *Mr Welby.*'

Mr Pawnsford's voice recalled him with a jolt, but he could not believe what he was hearing. He must surely still be in that dream?

' – house and all the moneys and possessions outside my specific bequests to whichever of my said grandsons shall marry within one year of the date of my death the said Evelyn Brayle. Further if it can be proved that she has any knowledge of this provision before such marriage, I revoke this clause and the entire estate and moneys shall go to the specific charities listed hereunder. If no such marriage takes place in the specified time, this clause revoking the bequest shall come into operation and the said charities shall become entitled to receive the estate and all moneys pertaining thereto.'

There was a stunned silence in the room, a silence which Felix broke at last with a chuckle. He seemed to hear the eldritch laughter of the old woman whose brain had conceived this extraordinary device for the disposal of her wealth.

Lewis found his voice first.

'Well, as Eve and I are already engaged, that presents no problem,' he said with smug satisfaction, a satisfaction which did not find a complete echo in his mind.

Then Victor burst out angrily.

'What about Myrtle and me? The thing's preposterous! The old woman was mad. That's proof of it.'

Mr Pawnsford's eyes turned to the two brothers. For once they were bright with amusement. He had argued ineffectually with his client when she had propounded her extraordinary suggestion and tried in vain to make her change her mind. She had told him flatly that if he were not prepared to draw up the Will as she wanted it, she would find some other lawyer who would, and it was she herself who insisted on the doctor's certificate of sanity before completing the Will.

'I know my grandsons, Victor and Lewis, and have no doubt that they will try to make out that I have lost my senses. I'll have that certificate from the doctor, from a dozen doctors if need be, but that's how I want my Will to be and that's how it's going to be,' she had said, and, remembering the occasion, Mr. Pawnsford also remembered the malicious laughter that had accompanied it.

'The only thing I'm sorry about,' she had gone on, 'is that I shan't be there to see their faces when you tell 'em. You'll get all the fun.'

Now, seeing those three faces, he was not laughing for it would not have become him, but his eyes were twinkling in spite of his still strong disapproval of the clause he had just read out. For one thing, who could ever prove that Eve Brayle knew or did not know of it? He had formed a high opinion of her during the past few days, but with so much money involved, who could tell?

'My client had anticipated such a claim being made and had amply provided for it. I assure you that she was entirely sane, extraordinary though this provision is. I may say that I disapproved of it and raised every possible objection to it on both legal and ethical grounds.'

'B – b – but—' stammered Victor in fury.

Felix's voice broke in, cool and undisturbed except by his cynical amusement. Not one of them could have guessed what were his own reactions to that scandalous provision.

'My dear Victor, it's quite simple really. Eve with the money or Myrtle without it. You can both scramble for it. A pretty problem for you both, a very pretty problem,' with a chuckle so reminiscent of the old lady's that instinctively the other three men looked round as if she might indeed have been there.

'You seem to have overlooked the fact that you, too, are involved,' said Victor nastily.

Felix shrugged his shoulders.

'Oh, you can count me out. I have no aspirations to the lady's hand. I am quite content with my cottage and my five hundred. It's between the two of you, and I wish you luck.'

'I would remind you again that I am already engaged to Eve,' put in Lewis with an air of superiority, 'and you, Victor, are engaged to Myrtle.'

Victor did not reply save by a glare at his brother, but Felix remarked in his lazy fashion 'Don't forget that you've got to get the girl to the altar within a year!'

'I ought to remind you, gentlemen, that Miss Brayle is to have no knowledge of this provision,'' said Mr Pawnsford, knowing that here lay both the weakness and the strength of the position.

If Eve married in ignorance of this secret provision, it could only be for love, whereas if she discovered beforehand what she stood to gain by her marriage to one of these three (and presumably it would be Lewis), the others would leave no stone unturned to prove that she knew of it. Henceforth, they would be implacable enemies, ever on the watch against the others. It was a diabolical scheme which surely could have been conceived by no other brain than that of the dead woman.

But did Felix Welby even come into it? His calm indifference suggested that he had no interest in it or in Eve Brayle, and Mr Pawnsford had had little opportunity of observing these two together. He had known Felix well ever since this hitherto unacknowledged grandson had come to Weir House, and his attitude had always been one of acceptance of his position and indifference to it. The solicitor felt that Felix would consider himself well rewarded by being at last recognised by Mrs Belamie as her grandson. He was a hard worker and contented with the job he carried through so successfully, was universally liked and respected by those he considered his own sort, his workers, the villagers, other farmers, and it was Mr Pawnsford's belief that he would have no use for life as a rich man, owner of the Weir estate and the 'lord of the manor'.

'I therefore advise you most earnestly to tell no one, no one at all, about this provision of your grandmother's Will,' he added as they rose to break up the meeting.

The brothers' faces were a study in consternation and uncertainty. Lewis, in spite of his bold declaration that as Eve was already engaged to him and Myrtle to Victor, knew that he had a long way to go before he could induce her to marry him, whilst Victor was uncomfortably aware of the difficulty of apparently transferring his affections from Myrtle to Eve if the former were not to know the reason. His mind was weaving through the devious paths of possible ways and means, but he already saw that, in spite of Mr Pawnsford's warnings, he would have to tell Myrtle. He was uncomfortably aware that she could, and would, bring an action for breach of promise against him if he broke off the engagement, for though neither of them had that passionate strain in them which could make it difficult to resist anticipating the married state, there had been several occasions on which they had not resisted it and Myrtle would have no difficulty in proving it. It was a measure of his real feeling for Myrtle that he was wondering now whether it had not been her intention to make it impossible, save at the cost of a public scandal, for him to break off the engagement.

He gnawed his fingers in his impotent fury, conscious of Lewis's air of superiority of position and Felix's look of derisive amusement as a mere onlooker.

As the four of them trooped out of the room, Felix turned to the solicitor.

'If you've a moment to spare, Mr Pawnsford, I'd like to go into those figures you wanted. Come into my office, will you?' leading him to the small, business-like room, with its desk and files, where he did his accounts and interviewed callers.

'I wish I could have persuaded the old lady to leave you better provided for, Felix. She wouldn't listen, but you've never had a square deal from her. It's a poor recompense that she has at last recognised you as her own kith and kin.'

'It's quite enough recompense, and it must have cost a lot to her pride to do it even in this way.'

'Er – what will you do now? Sell the cottage? Let it? Find a new job? I could put you in touch with several men who would be glad enough to have you.'

'Good for you, Mr Pawnsford, but at the moment I have not made up my mind. Mrs Belamie always said she intended to leave me the cottage, but I never really reckoned on it, and I imagine that for the present, for possibly the first year, it will be necessary for me to stay on to keep things going. After that – well, who knows?' with a momentary grin as he thought of that year and its possibilities. 'Now, what about these figures?' and the two men became immersed in the details of the big estate now to be wound up.

Mr Pawnsford wondered what Felix really thought about that extraordinary Will. He certainly did not appear to be interested at all in the fortunes of either his cousins or Eve Brayle.

Lewis, full of a mixture of jubilation and apprehension, went to find Eve. Myrtle, in high dudgeon, had retired to her bedroom, abandoning the position she had assumed as the hostess and leaving everything to Eve. She was still furious about her ten-pound legacy and in no condition to meet the eyes, sympathetic or spiteful, of the relatives who had received not even that. All she wanted was to clear the house of them with all speed so that she and Victor and Lewis could be alone again. Surely Eve Brayle would not remain here? Though, of course, she would forfeit that absurdly unjust legacy if she did not.

Both Mrs Hodd and Emma Ford showed their approbation of the transfer of the arrangements for the house and remaining guests from Myrtle to Eve, and she had two willing helpers.

'Will any of them want to stay over tonight, Mrs Hodd, do you suppose?' she asked. 'Have we got enough food if they do?'

'Some of them will have to stay till tomorrow, Miss Eve, but don't worry about food. Though they fell on it like a flock of cormorants, there's plenty left, though you might ask Mr Felix when you see him if he'll send up some more eggs.'

When Lewis came to find her, Eve and Emma Ford were busy with the list of wreaths which had to be suitably acknowledged, and she looked up as his approach, not pleased at the interruption.

'Can I speak to you for a moment, Eve? In private,' with a meaning glance at the nurse.

'Oh, not now, please, Lewis. We're so busy, and there are still a few aunts and uncles and cousins and what-have-you left over to be entertained. Can't you see to them?'

'Where's Myrtle?'

Eve could not resist a slight smile.

'Retired to her room. Exhausted. By grief, I imagine.'

'Well, I'd like a word with you as soon as you are free,' and she gave a little sigh of impatience as he went reluctantly away.

'Men!' said Emma Ford. 'When there are jobs to be done, they just litter up the place and get under your feet.'

Eve laughed.

'You haven't much use for them, have you, Emma?' for during the last few harassed days, she had slipped into the habit of calling the friendly woman by her Christian name.

'Not me. I had a father and two brothers and a brother-in-law and they were all the same. Hanging about the place whilst you were cooking and never on hand when the meal was ready. Like as not just gone round to the local to have one, and not content with one, of course, with the dinner on the table getting cold. And when the woman of the house is sick, and she has to be almost dead on her feet before she gives in, the next thing you know is that *they* are sick, they don't feel very well, and they must either go to bed or lie down and the wife or the mother or whoever it is has to crawl out of bed in self-defence. And when the poor men take to their beds, if you don't go near them you're neglecting them and they may die for all you care, and if you do go, they were just dropping off to sleep and you've disturbed them! Men! Give me women every time, even my cantankerous old darling, God rest her soul,' and she wiped away a tear.

'You were fond of her, weren't you?' asked Eve softly.

'I loved her, for all her sharp tongue and funny ways. She didn't mean anything by them. You know that, and she was fond of you, Eve. She never liked Myrtle, with her smarmy ways. I could have split my sides laughing when she was only left ten pounds for a mourning brooch! And you five hundred. I'm glad she left you that.'

'I wonder why she did?' asked Eve uncomfortably. 'She didn't really know me at all, did she?'

Emma nodded her head.

'Enough to know that you were the genuine article, my dear, and were not hanging round her for what you could get. Eve—'

The girl did not reply. The words had dug deep into her conscience. If she had felt badly about her deception of Mrs Belamie before, she felt a thousand times worse when she knew that she had left her this money, once the initial shock of surprise was over. She would have liked to refuse it, but it would not only release her from her hated obligation to Lewis but, if Mrs Belamie really wanted her to remain at Weir House for the six months, the least she could do was to respect her wishes, whatever might be the reason.

'Eve – it's none of my business but – why are you going to marry Lewis Belamie? You can't be in love with him, not a girl like you.'

The girl's suddenly frozen look told her that she had encroached too far on their growing friendship and she spoke again quickly.

'All right. Consider that not said. I'd no right to say it. Here's another without an address. How the heck are we expected to know who May and Lucy are, even if they do feel deepest sympathy for us? Pass me the address book, dear, will you?'

It was not until late that evening that Lewis, who had been haunting her, found an opportunity of being alone with Eve.

'I must speak to you,' he said.

'Tonight? I'm dead tired, Lewis. Can't you wait till the morning?'

154

'No. I won't keep you long. Come in here,' opening the door of the library.

She went with a bad grace, and he shut the door.

'Eve, what about our engagement?' he asked.

'Well, what about it? Surely that's off? Thanks to Mrs Belamie's legacy, I shall be able to pay you back your money, and I suppose we can concoct some likely tale to account for breaking it?'

'I don't want to break it. You know that. I want to marry you. I want it more than anything in the world,' he said and there was a look of desperate resolve on his face.

'I've already told you I don't want to marry you, Lewis, so please don't ask me again. We're not in the least in love with each other, and I can only imagine that you're asking me because you feel you ought to, but I assure you there isn't the slightest need. You don't have to save my face or anything. Engagements are broken every day and people don't have to tell the world their reasons. I can't think why Mrs Belamie wanted me to stay on here for six months, but I want to do as she wished and also I badly need that legacy – to pay you back, for one thing.'

'Oh, forget the money! It doesn't matter. I – I'm in love with you, Eve,' desperation in his voice.

She was still incredulous, but her face softened.

'I'm sorry, Lewis, if you are because I'm not in the least in love with you and never could be. Please find some other girl, won't you?'

'Is that final?' he asked bleakly.

She nodded.

'I'm afraid so. Please don't mind about it too much.'

She hated having men propose to her because she had to hurt them.

'I'm not going to give up,' he said, dogged determination in his voice. 'You're still wearing my ring, anyway.'

She was wearing it only because it explained her presence there, but now she slipped it off and tried to give it back to him.

'It's only an empty symbol,' she said as gently as she could.

'Please go on wearing it, at least whilst the rest of these people are here. It's the least you can do,' and at that moment Felix opened the door and looked in.

Whether he saw her with the ring in her hand instead of on her finger she could not tell, but with an air of defiance, she put it on again.

'Sorry. Have I interrupted something?' he asked with a look of cynical amusement from one to the other. 'I wanted to get some papers I left here.'

Lewis turned and marched out of the room, flinging a look of dislike at his cousin, realising when it was too late he was giving him a chance of succeeding where he had failed. Felix's indifference might well be a pose and in spite of it he might be after the prize himself.

'What was that? Surely not a lovers' quarrel?' asked Felix when they were alone. He sounded amused.

'I don't see what business it is of yours,' she replied tartly.

'None at all, but I am naturally interested in my cousin's fortunes,' the note of amusement deepening. 'By the way, at long last my grandmother has acknowledged the relationship, so I suppose I can call him that. Born on the wrong side of the blanket, of course!'

'Is that supposed to interest me?' she asked witheringly.

'No, I don't imagine that anything about me interests you, but as we are going to spend the next six months in fairly close proximity to each other, I thought you might as well know that I have been given some status.'

'Please let me pass. I – I'm very tired,' for suddenly she felt at the point of exhaustion, with no more strength for quarrel or argument.

His face softened.

'Yes, I'm sure you must be. It's been a hard day for you,' and at his tone her eyes filled with the tears she had not shed all the day.

'It's over at last. I – I was very fond of Mrs Belamie. It's been beastly to watch everybody crowding round to see what they had got out of her.'

'I agree. I told you the vultures would gather, didn't I? I

know you were fond of her and she of you. So was I, though we fought like cat and dog. I'm glad she left you that money, Eve.'

'And she left you your cottage. I'm glad of that. Except for the servants, and perhaps in his own way Mr Pawnsford, I think you and I were the only two who really cared. It's sad, after that long life and with all that money. It wasn't any good to her, was it?'

'Its power, which is what she enjoyed. Is it what you would enjoy, Eve?' looking at her speculatively.

'No. I didn't think much about money when we had it but now I see that it puts a false value on everything. You don't know who your friends are.'

She drew a deep breath. After tomorrow she would be alone with Felix. Did she really want to be? Was this strange man in love with her, or could he ever be?

Warmth stole into her heart. Once she was free of Lewis and this absurd 'engagement', might not things be very different between her and Felix?

'I – I'm really very tired,' she said.

'I know you are. I won't keep you any longer,' he said, and opened the door for her and watched her go wearily up the stairs.

But Lewis did not go the next day nor the next nor the day after. Neither did Victor nor Myrtle. Eve had been perfectly willing to regard Myrtle as still the hostess, but she rather elaborately declined the position.

'It's for you to decide such things, Eve,' she said with the distant air she had always adopted towards her supposed future sister-in-law. 'I am merely a visitor in this house where I have always been a welcome guest. You can see how you like running such an establishment without any experience.'

If she were chagrined to find that Eve, with the willing co-operation of Corke and Mrs Hodd and the servants, managed to run it very well, she did not show it.

By the third day, Victor had made up his mind and had asked Myrtle to go with him to the little erection in the grounds known as 'the Italian Pavilion'. It consisted of marble pillars and a stone roof and was open on all sides, with marble slabs for seats and a fountain is the middle.

'I can't imagine why you have to bring me to this dreary place with only cold slabs to sit on merely to talk to me, Victor,' she said pettishly. 'I don't know even why we're still staying here. Why can't we get back to town?'

'I've got to tell you something, though Mr Pawnsford said I ought not to.'

There was a desparate note in Victor's voice and he was fidgeting nervously with his hands. As far as was possible to his temperament, he was in love with Myrtle, but he hoped she would be persuaded to see eye to eye with him. He knew she had boundless ambitions.

'Mr Pawnsford? Is it about the Will?' she asked sharply, all attention now.

'Yes. That secret clause. I've made up my mind to tell you about it, dear,' looking at her apprehensively. 'We always thought the old girl would do something ridiculous in the end. Well, she did. She – she's left the estate and the residue to – to whichever of us – marries within a year.'

Myrtle heaved a sigh of relief.

'Well, that's simple enough, and why are we hanging about? All we've got to do is to go back to town, get a special licence and get married straight away. You mean married first, I suppose?'

'It isn't quite that. You see – one of us has got to marry Eve. Otherwise, and also if Eve finds out about it, everything goes to charity.'

She stared at him open-mouthed, her eyes horrified and incredulous.

'But – she must have been mad!'

'Pawnsford says she was quite sane and competent to make a Will. She got the certificate of two doctors to say so. Whichever of us marries Eve within twelve months gets the money, the Weir estate, everything.'

She was still staring unbelievingly at him.

'You can't mean that! Actually she's left it to Eve!'

'Only if she marries one of us.'

'But she's going to marry Lewis!'

'One can't be sure. They haven't been hitting it off, and she's not been wearing her engagement ring, not until just before the funeral. They don't act like an engaged couple. Eve doesn't, anyway.'

'Perhaps she knows?'

'Even if we knew that and could prove it, it won't do us any good because *if* she knows, the whole amount goes to charity.'

'I've never heard anything so ridiculous in my life! How could Mr Pawnsford ever have allowed her to make such a Will?' cried Myrtle angrily.

'Can you imagine anyone ever *not* allowing her to do anything she meant to do? And she has provided that if anyone tries to contest the Will, the same thing happens; everything to charity. I'm not supposed to tell you, dear, but – well – I had to, hadn't I?'

'I don't see what it has to do with us,' she said bitterly.

'Well, you see, I thought that if – if I married Eve and got the money, I could pay her handsomely to give me a divorce so that you and I could marry afterwards.'

He mumbled over the speech and did not look at her as he spoke. He knew as well as she did that it was a despicable suggestion, but when a great deal of money is at stake, morals are inclined to become earth-bound.

She was silent, staring out between the marble pillars without seeing the enchanting view they framed.

She, too, was as much in love with Victor as her nature allowed, even though their quarrels were frequent and bitter and she had become his mistress with but little persuasion, only part of her surrender to him occasioned by her desire to tie him to her. But she *had* surrendered and, having done so, had perhaps spoiled herself for him, men being men. Once married to a girl with Eve's undoubted charms, a girl younger than she was and infinitely more attractive, would he ever want to give her up to return to a mistress already superseded, if not actually discarded?

But she had a burning desire for all that money could bring her, and to be mistress of Weir House. How far could she trust

Victor if she let him go? Though he had no idea of it, she had already passed the rubicon of thirty. She was, in fact, almost thirty-eight and admitted to thirty, whilst Victor was only twenty-eight. In two years' time she would be forty, and there had been no other man in her life but Victor and she would have little chance of finding one.

His voice broke in on her bitter thoughts, apologetically and hopefully.

'Of course, it wouldn't mean anything – darling. It would never be real marriage, not – not in *that* way.'

She looked at him with curling lip.

'You don't expect me to believe that, surely? A man married to a girl like Eve Brayle?'

He flushed uncomfortably.

'I mean – no children, or – or anything.'

She was visualising it actually happening, Victor coming out of church (it would be a church wedding, of course!) with a white-clad, starry-eyed Eve on his arm, smiling his way through the reception with her, going off in a car with her to some unknown destination, arriving at the other end alone with her, and then nothing happening 'in that way'.

He was a man, wasn't he?

'When we were actually married, the condition laid down by the Will would have been fulfilled and then I could tell her. I doubt if *she* would have anything to do with *me* after that!'

'You'd feel proud of yourself when the moment came to tell her, wouldn't you?'

'She might not have me in the first place,' he suggested mildly.

Myrtle looked at him critically. No, she might not, but her eyes were partially blinded by her love for him, and she saw him as a desirable *parti* for even a much younger woman than herself who was looking for a man to support her. Victor might not be a glamour boy, but he was steady and reliable, made a good living and would not expect his wife to help to support the home. A girl without money, which she knew Eve to be, might she not jump at the chance of Victor, since obviously she had accepted his (to Myrtle) much less desirable brother?

'I think she would,' she replied at length. And then, throwing discretion to the winds, she agreed to the shabby scheme.

'We can't lose it all, Victor. We simply can't. You'll have to do it.'

He looked at her for a moment and then away again.

'I thought you'd see it that way, after the first natural reaction. Of course, I'm not going to enjoy the performance.'

'I'd like to be sure of that,' she retorted. 'She's pretty and she has good clothes and knows how to wear them and how to attract a man. Look at Lewis! He fell for her, didn't he? And without the spur of this ridiculous Will.'

'Not my style,' he replied gallantly, now that he was safely over that difficult hurdle. 'And not at all the right type to be mistress of Weir House.'

She put her arms about him and kissed him with an unusual fervour, conscious that she had already lost him and terrified of what she had done.

'Darling, you do love me, don't you? And you won't let it make any real difference? I mean – we can go on seeing each other?'

'Of course we can. I'll arrange something. We'll have to – quarrel or something so that you can go back to town in a huff and leave me after breaking off the engagement.'

'Leave you? Down here, do you mean?'

'But of course. I can't just go off and leave her to Lewis though I'll have to get back to my job, for a time, anyway. It's a confounded nuisance her staying on here, but at least Lewis won't be able to be here any more than I shall. I'll have to think of something, arrange something—'

It did not occur to him to tell her that Felix too was involved. He was older than either brother and was regarded as a confirmed bachelor at thirty-two; nor could his position as the farm manager, working at a small salary and living in a cottage, be supposed to offer any attraction to a girl who, in getting herself engaged to Lewis, was evidently looking for something better.

'We'd better be getting back to the house,' said Myrtle. 'It's beginning to rain. You – you'll get it over quickly, darling?'

'As soon as possible. Of course, I've got to lead up to it a bit, get her interested in me and show that I'm attracted to her and all that. I can't just rush into the house and propose to her. Besides, we've got to have an official breaking-off of our own engagement first. You'd better give me back the ring.'

She drew it slowly off her finger, gave it to him and then threw her arms round his neck again.

'It will be all right, darling, won't it? Promise me that it will!' and now the tears were running down her cheeks. It was such an awful thing to do, to give up the man she loved, the man who was so nearly her husband, so that he could marry this younger and more attractive girl.

He kissed her and patted her consolingly.

'Of course it will be all right. It just means that we shall have to wait a bit, a year, two years perhaps.'

Two years! In two years she would be forty!

Already she regretted it.

'Have we got to, Victor?' she asked in sudden desperation. 'Does it matter all that much? We've got each other, and you're doing well and in time you'll get your partnership—'

He disengaged her arms, gently but firmly.

'Of course it matters. You know that as well as I do. Nobody knows what *Grand-mère* left, but it may run into millions. Now we've quite decided, haven't we? And the rain's really coming down now. We shall be soaked,' and he started to run for the house, followed by a quickly bedraggled Myrtle.

He heaved a sigh of relief as he ran. Of course he was fond of Myrtle and still wanted to marry her. In fact, he felt himself in honour bound to do so, which was a curious state of mind for a man to be in whilst he was contemplating getting married as quickly as possible to someone else!

Even the most reluctant of the funeral guests, reluctant because of the luxury of staying in a well-run, well-staffed house after their own servantless homes, had departed. Eve was getting worried about how long the brothers and Myrtle intended to stay. It was an uncomfortable situation, for everyone looked to her for directions in small matters whilst she felt that Myrtle had more right to consultation and she was being forced into the position of hostess which she had no wish to occupy. Also Lewis was becoming more and more lover-like in his attitude, though she had insisted on his taking his ring back and told him in no uncertain terms that she no longer recognised their 'engagement'; and that afternoon, before Victor and Myrtle had gone to the Italian Pavilion, she had made the position so clear, without actually declaring it publicly, that Lewis had gone off in high dudgeon and secret alarm, and Felix, who had come into the room whilst they were speaking, whistled softly and dropped into a chair, regarding her with amused interest.

'The birds in their little nest seem to have fallen out,' he said, offering her his packet of cigarettes and a light.

'You weren't supposed to have heard that,' she said, 'but I may as well tell you, and everybody else, that I am no longer engaged to Lewis.'

His eyebrows lifted and he gave an amused chuckle.

'Well, well, well,' was his only comment.

'How long do you think they're going to stay, Felix?' she asked, a desperate note in her voice, 'and what am I supposed to do here? I'm in a completely false position, living in a house that doesn't belong to me, having the servants coming to me for orders I haven't any right to give and treating me as if I belonged here. I'm not sure that I shall stay.'

'If you don't, you're going to lose your five hundred pounds.'

'I know, and I need it badly and even without it I feel I'd like to do what dear Mrs Belamie wanted me to do, but why did she want me to? I can't see any point in it.'

'You've been kept pretty busy so far,' he reminded her.

'For three days, but now we've answered all the letters, acknowledged all the flowers and sorted out all the private papers and turned them over to Mr Pawnsford. The only thing left now is to decide what to do with the clothes.'

'Emma's been talking to me about her legacy and the annuity. She wants me to find her a cottage in the village.'

'Oh, surely she's going to stay with me, Felix!'

'You can hardly expect her to, can you? She's a worker, and wants to act as a sort of district nurse to the village and estate. Why not come with me tomorrow to look for a suitable place? There are one or two vacant cottages which could be made habitable and Pawnsford will empower me to spend the money.'

'Emma's the right person to go with you,' said Eve, but it gave her a little thrill of anticipation when he had made his suggestion.

'She'll be sorting out the clothes, and you can't help much with them. A few hours away from this house would be good for you, especially when you have just broken off your engagement. The only decent thing for your late beloved to do now is to go back to London, so he may have cleared out by the time you get in – and persuaded Victor and *his* beloved to go back with him.'

She could not know why there was a slightly amused sound in his voice, nor that he did not actually believe either brother would go and leave the field clear for him.

She flushed a little at his tone and the look of interested speculation which accompanied it, but that was the way he had always regarded her relations with Lewis and she badly wanted to go with him the next day.

'Well, if I can be any help—' she said hesitantly.

'Even if you can't, it will get you away from the house, and you might as well make the acquaintance of the village people if you're to live here for six months. You'll find them on the whole friendly folk, but they'll regard you as a visiting foreigner, English rather than Cornish. Even I am not accepted as anything but a foreigner,' with a little chuckle of affectionate amusement.

He stayed and talked to her as he had not done before, with a complete freedom from the antagonism which would always have been liable to spring up between them at his cynical gibes over her relations with Lewis, nor did he make any further reference to the broken engagement. Released from the certainty he had felt that her only object in accepting Lewis's proposal was that of his expectation of getting his grandmother's estate, or at least a share in it, he saw her in a different light. He felt without any justification for the belief that there had been more in it than that, and before he dismissed it from his mind, he came very close to the truth. Could Lewis possibly have lent her money and could she, until she received her legacy, see no other way of paying the loan save by agreeing to this ridiculous engagement?

Well, anyway she was free of that now, though she was no more accessible to him than she had been whilst she was engaged to his cousin; in fact, she was less so, for the terms of that fantastic secret clause in the Will had made it impossible for him, Felix, to ask her to marry him and by so doing become, through her, the owner of the Weir estate. It was an impassable barrier between them, according to his inflexible code, and for the first time in his life he felt bitter towards the old woman who had raised that barrier. Could she have known that he was in love with Eve and raised it deliberately?

Nothing of this bitterness and frustration appeared, however, as he sat and talked to Eve with a freedom he had not known before.

He was telling her various bits of Cornish history, particularly of Weir House, parts of which had stood for three hundred years of storm and stress.

'There's an old book in the library, begun in the lifetime of the son of the original owner and continued spasmodically, most of it in manuscript difficult to read, over the years. When Mr Belamie bought the place, he added a lot to it and after his death, my grandmother added some more. There was a curse laid on the house during the seventeen hundreds which said that no direct heir should ever inherit, and actually none ever has. When Louis, the old lady's son, died, people said that the curse was still working, and she herself more than half believed in it. It's always been an indirect heir, a nephew or a distant cousin, until the Tregeans, as a family, died out altogether and the place came into the market and Mr Belamie bought it.'

'Surely the curse would have been lifted when there were no more Tregeans?'

'One would have thought so, and yet the only son met his death before he could inherit.'

'Is that why Mrs Belamie did not leave it to Victor or Lewis?'

He gave a shrug.

'Possibly.'

'Wasn't there some mysterious clause in her Will about the estate? I was so staggered at learning that she had left five hundred to *me* that I didn't really listen to the rest.'

'Some special provision, I believe,' he said but saw that she was not really interested and was glad to change the subject. 'When we are in the church, have a look at the various Tregean monuments which you hadn't a chance of seeing when we went there for the funeral. I'll get the vicar to bring out some old manuscripts and records if you're interested?'

'Oh, I am! I've always led such a wandering life, living for the most part in posh hotels, or in some very modern rented house and recently in a London flat, that I've never met up with real history before, lived amongst things that have endured through hundreds of years, and it does something to me! I want to be a part of it all, though I know I never can be. I'd like to be able to go on with that history of the house, write something in it that I've contributed to it – but I don't imagine that in six months I shall have a chance!'

The excuse of looking for a cottage for Emma proved to be no more than that, for he had already found one which Emma approved, but he showed it to her and then took her on to make the acquaintance of the villagers, with all of whom he appeared to be on the best of terms. Almost the whole of South Cawer belonged to the Weir estate and as such came under his control. She was amazed at the amount of work he did in addition to running the farm, and said so.

'But you ought to be paid the earth for looking after all this!'

He gave a shrug.

'I've never had a yen for money and I get along,' he said. 'What more can a man ask of life than to be allowed to do the one job in the world he enjoys doing so long as it provides for his needs? Mine are few. Now I'm going to take you to visit old

Ben Tremarth, who is a potter and makes some of the finest pottery in the country. Some of it is sold in London, but it's the devil of a job to get him to part with anything even to make a living. He's a real character and nobody knows how old he is. If he doesn't like you on sight, he won't even open his door to you. When the Belamies first came to live here, he refused them entry though he rents his ramshackle cottage from them, and he never let them in. You can imagine how that annoyed Mrs Belamie! She gave him notice to quit many times but he would not go, said she was a foreigner with no right to Weir House, and there is a rumour that is not very well founded that he might be able to prove his own right to the whole estate through a long-dead Tregean. He has never done so, though. Like me, he is perfectly content to live as he does. He has never had a wife or anyone to look after him, but lives quite alone. This is his cottage. He's never let me do anything to it, and I suppose that in a more enlightened part of the country, it would be condemned as unfit for human habitation.'

It was certainly in a ramshackle state, the roof roughly patched where the original thatch had gone, the thick walls of grey local stone pitted by the many storms it had withstood, some of the windows boarded up, only one at the left of the battered door kept bright and shining in contrast to the dilapidated condition of the rest.

Felix rapped on this, and after a time it was opened and the hoary, shaggy head of an incredibly old man appeared at it.

'Ben! I've brought a visitor to see you.'

'Oh, it be you, Felix, m'dear. Who you brought along o' you this day?' peering suspiciously at Eve.

She came forward rather shyly and smiled at the old man, who seemed to study her closely for a minute and then his wrinkled, leathery face returned her smile toothlessly.

He nodded and shut the window again to reappear a moment later at the opened door.

'We're in, Meredith, we're in,' said Felix in a whisper to Eve, and slid a hand under her arm to bring her forward.

'This is Miss Brayle, Ben, and she's going to live for a few months at the big house to look after it.'

'Huh,' grunted the old man. 'I heard tell as the old woman is dead. So you be the young mistress?'

'Oh no, I'm only going to stay there as a sort of – well, caretaker, I suppose. It's nice of you to let me come in and see some of your wonderful work, Mr Tremarth.'

'Eh? What's that? I be called Ben. Most forgot any other name. They boys be plaguing me again, Felix, throwing stones and such. I'll have the law on them, that I will, though my stick round their backsides is what them'll get once I catch they. Come you in, missie, though there beant much to see,' his tone seeking to deprecate the pride with which he surveyed his work.

In a corner of the one room, which with the bedroom above it and a tumbledown shed outside it comprised the whole of the cottage, stood an ancient potting wheel, foot-driven by the huge stone in which it was set, and on rough shelves, on a big table and on every available place on the floor, stood pieces of his work in varying states of completion, from the most delicate figures to pots of all sizes and shapes, some left in their native clay, red or white, others glowing with colour worked in the most intricate designs.

Eve was fascinated, and so obviously interested that presently the old man, with a deceptively grudging air, showed her his kiln, hand-fired with charcoal, in the shed at the back, and explained to her in a dialect which she could not always understand the various processes that went into the making of the pots. He even 'wedged' a lump of the clay which he dug with his own hands from a pit somewhere on the open moorland, and set it up on the wheel so that she could try her hand, with little success, at throwing a pot. He showed her with pride the various glazes he used, though he was very secretive about the sources of them.

'Come you again, missie, any time so be you like,' he told her at parting, and he even gave her a small pot, exquisitely fashioned and with an intricate design of reds and blues and greens, the inside finished in a delicate duck-egg blue and showing the authentic whorls of the hand-made pot.

'You've certainly made a hit there,' laughed Felix when

they had left, the pot carefully held in her hands. 'He's never even given me so much as a saucer! And if you're seriously interested in the history of the Tregeans, old Ben could tell you more about them than you'll find in any writings on the subject, much of it scurrilous and probably libellous! Now we're going to drink dandelion wine with another of the oldest inhabitants, on a somewhat different scale. Here, take this,' giving her his handkerchief. 'I'll stop at the village pump so that you can get the clay off your hands. I'll look after your precious pot.'

By the time he took her back to Weir House, she felt that she had entered a different world and also that she knew a lot more about Felix, who had shown her a different side to his character when he had been amongst the simple, friendly if slightly suspicious people who were his real friends. There was a warmth and sincerity about him which was lacking in his dealings with his cousins and their kind and a complete absence of the cynical attitude towards them.

There had not been time for the promised visit to the church which he proposed for another day and she felt a warm glow that stayed with her even when she found that her three 'guests' were still at the house.

'You're coming to dinner tonight, aren't you, Felix?' she asked him at parting, and he caught the note in her voice and answered it recklessly.

'If you're inviting me, yes,' he said.

And at dinner that night, Myrtle and Victor broke the news that their engagement was at an end.

Eve looked from one to the other in amazed concern.

'You surely don't mean it?' she asked, for though they had frequent and open quarrels, they always made them up and appeared to be a normally happy pair if not in love in the way she would want to be.

'It's quite definite, I'm afraid,' said Victor, avoiding the eyes of Lewis and Felix, the former's filled with a startled apprehension, the latter's with amusement. 'We decided to tell you when we were all here together, and that it's entirely mutual.'

Eve looked again at Myrtle and saw that she had recently

169

been crying, for her eyelids were red beneath the make-up. It could not have been she who had broken off the engagement then, she thought, and felt a surge of indignation towards Victor which she could not very well at the moment express.

'I'm sorry,' she said. 'I'm really terribly sorry,' and her indignation increased when Felix laughed – actually laughed!

She gave him a withering look.

'I don't know how you can see anything funny in it,' she said. 'Come along, Myrtle. Let's have our coffee in the little sitting-room and leave the men to themselves. Perhaps Felix will be able to explain the joke to Victor, or at least apologise to him.'

'Oh, I do, I do!' said Felix. 'I apologise most abjectly, Victor,' but his tone and the expression on his face, still twisted into a sardonic grin, negated the apology and Eve, with another look of indignation and affront, stalked out of the room followed by Myrtle.

But when they were alone in the small sitting-room used by the family as an alternative to the terrace in good weather, or the big drawing-room in the evening, and she turned to Myrtle in friendly concern, she stopped short at the look of concentrated hatred on the older girl's face.

'You! It's all your fault! Why did you have to come here in the first place, worming your way in where you were not wanted—'

She stopped herself just in time before blurting out the real reason for the breaking off of her engagement. What good would that do any of them?

Eve's face was a study, its chief expression being of utter consternation.

'Whatever do you mean? What can it possibly be to me – how can it be my fault if Victor's broken off your engagement? It's nothing to do with me!'

'I can't discuss it with you. I'm too upset, but I hate you. I hate you!' and Myrtle turned and rushed out of the room and up the stairs, leaving Eve utterly amazed. As she had said, what on earth had it to do with her?

In her bedroom, with the door locked, Myrtle lay on her

bed and cried again, the hard, bitter tears of one to whom weeping was an unaccustomed thing.

Was she a fool ever to have become a party to this, for all Mrs Belamie's wealth? Supposing she really lost Victor to this blonde siren? What hope had she of ever getting him back once he had succeeded in marrying her? Seeing in him everything that was desirable, she could not conceive of any girl in Eve Brayle's position turning down such a chance, and in any case it might take two years for Victor to get free again, and the dreaded prospect of being forty loomed over her. What wonder that she felt as if she were crying tears of blood?

Eve, once she had recovered from the shock of Myrtle's behaviour, went slowly back to the room where the three men sat at the table still, glaring at one another.

'Victor, I'm so very sorry about all this,' she said in a troubled voice. 'Poor Myrtle's terribly upset and she seems to think it's my fault, something to do with my coming here, but of course that's absurd. I'm sure she only said it because she's so unhappy. She's gone up to her room. Can't you go up to her? Can't you make it up with her? I mean – the best of friends fall out at times – lovers' quarrels—'

He raised an authoritative hand to check her, his face unmoved by her appeal.

'Please, Eve, not any more. Believe me, Myrtle and I have discussed the situation fully and we are entirely agreed that there is no alternative but to end our engagement.'

'What a heart-burning interview that must have been!' put in Felix and Eve looked at him indignantly.

'That's utterly beastly of you, Felix. Haven't you any decent feelings at all? If you haven't, the commonest courtesy might keep you quiet.'

He laughed.

'My dear Eve, don't you know me well enough yet to realise that I have neither decent feelings nor common courtesy? For one thing, it didn't surprise me in the least to hear that the engagement has come to an abrupt ending. Better luck next time, eh, Victor?'

Victor glared at him.

'That's just the sort of thing one would expect you to say, Felix,' he snarled.

'Then neither of us has done anything unexpected, but it beats me how you, Lewis, can have allowed Eve to escape from you as she appears to have done.'

'I don't see that it has anything to do with you,' said Lewis.

'Oh, it hasn't. It hasn't. I'm merely an interested spectator of your love affairs. Well, as I, unlike the pair of you, have work to do, I'll get on with it,' and without another glance at any of them, strolled out of the room.

Eve was both furious and nonplussed. Was this the same man with whom she had spent the happy hours of the afternoon? This the man who had been so kind to old Ben, so sympathetic to the small troubles of Miss Trimble at the post office, had listened with such patience and sympathy to the worries of Mrs Carter about her children, to whom he had promised help?

He had been perfectly beastly to Victor and had laughed, actually *laughed*, when he told him in front of poor Myrtle that they had broken off their engagement.

She felt furiously that she never wanted to see him or speak to him again, and yet knew in her heart that she would want both by the next day or the day after. What a maddening hold a man could have on the girl who was fool enough to love him!

9

EARLY on the following morning, Myrtle returned to London and the job she now hated, wondering desolately whether it would henceforth be her whole life.

She had tried to have a last interview with Victor, but he had escaped from it, turning his eyes from the sight of her white face and tear-reddened eyes which made him uncomfortably aware how changed she appeared from her normal, hard-eyed composure. Spurred on by his greed for wealth, he ignored it.

'Don't make a scene now, Myrtle,' he told her. 'I've promised you it will be all right. I'll see you in town.'

When she had gone, refusing to speak to Eve again, he had a few bad moments with his conscience but soothed it by the thought of his freedom to court the youthful attractions of Eve.

He was not long in preparing the ground, and dogged her footsteps for several days, vying with Lewis in paying her small attentions and in devising things for her entertainment and pleasure until she began to feel that possibly Myrtle had had some justification for her attack on her, a troublesome and even slightly nauseating idea. Was Victor falling in love with her as well as Lewis? She was by no means the sort of girl who imagines that every man is in love with her, but the attentions of the two brothers were becoming embarrassing, and as Felix kept away from her she had no relief or escape. She wished fervently that they would go back to London, but both of them had asked for extended leave, urging the business of settling their grandmother's estate, which of course neither of them was called upon to do.

After a day of intermittent rain when she had been confined to the house, Eve saw Felix in the distance and pushed open the french window with the thought that even in his most cynical humour, he would be a relief from the cloying attentions of Victor and Lewis, but she had reckoned without the latter.

'Let me get you a coat, Eve. It will be cool outside,' he offered, his gallantry still reminiscent of long-unused wheels that squeaked a little from rust.

'I don't want a coat' she said, but he went with her into the garden and she missed her chance of following Felix, though angry with herself at permitting herself to be the follower.

'I'm afraid we're letting you do too much,' began Lewis. 'You must be tired.'

'Tired? With doing nothing? Don't be absurd,' she said irritably. 'I only wish I had something to do, if only out of gratitude to Mrs Belamie for leaving me the money out of which I can pay you back, as soon as I get it.'

'I wish you wouldn't, Eve. It was a gift, not a loan.'

'Thank you, but I prefer to regard it as a loan. Can't you understand that I want to be free of the obligation?' her irritation growing.

'You know how I feel about that – that I'd rather you felt you could be under a still greater obligation – or rather, put me under one by saying you will marry me. Won't you, Eve?'

'Oh, please, Lewis! Must you ask me that again? I've said no, and I mean it. I'm not in the least in love with you. I wish you'd go back to London and forget about me.'

'I shall never be able to do that. I – I really do love you, Eve. Couldn't you—'

'No, Lewis, I couldn't. Please take that as final, and don't ask me again,' and though she really wanted a walk after having been shut up in the house for most of the day, she turned to enter it again.

Hell's bells! Would he never take no for an answer and realise that she meant it? Was she to have no peace?

Victor was lying in wait for her.

'Too cold for you?' he asked.

174

'No. I wanted a walk but Lewis really is making himself a nuisance, wanting me to be engaged to him again.'

'Someone else?' he asked with an attempt at playfulness which did not suit his rather heavy style.

'No,' she said sharply. 'Victor, couldn't you persuade Lewis to go back to town with you when you go?'

'I'm not sure that I want to go back yet, but there's no reason why he shouldn't. After all, as the elder grandson, things naturally devolve on me.'

'I thought Felix was doing everything?' she asked pointedly.

'Not everything. After all, Felix is only a sort of bailiff. All the decisions have to be made by the family,' said Victor pompously.

'I wonder how Mrs Belamie really did dispose of the house and the estate in her Will? Wasn't there a secret clause or something? Not that it matters to me, of course.'

'No one exactly knows what will happen – yet. There will be a lot of settling up to do, valuing and so on, and the specific bequests to pay – but let's not talk about things like death and Wills,' with a determined cheerfulness. 'I believe you play, don't you? The piano, I mean?'

'After a fashion. Why?'

'Well – as a matter of fact, I sing a bit and I wondered if you'd like to try over one or two songs for me? Mustn't get too rusty, you know!'

The idea amused her, child of the modern age of canned music and jazzy lyrics, but she went with him to the music gallery where she saw, to her further amusement, that he had been raking out some sheet music, yellowed with age, and that some old-fashioned songs have been placed on the rack of the piano.

'Oh, Victor, surely nobody sings things like these nowadays?' she said, turning through them.

'I like the old songs though you never hear them now, or anything that has a real tune in it. I used to get Myrtle to play for me—'

He broke off, wishing he had not introduced her name and Eve caught at it at once.

'I'm sorry about you and Myrtle,' she said sincerely. 'Isn't there anything you can do about it?'

'No. It was quite mutual.'

'Are you sure? She seemed to take it very badly. Can't you—'

'I'm sorry, Eve. Sorry for Myrtle, I mean, if she is really feeling badly about it, but it was the only way. You see – I don't care in that way for Myrtle any more and the only fair and kind thing was to tell her so frankly, wasn't it? A marriage without love must be a failure from the start, and you see – there's someone else, someone I'm desperately in love with.'

Eve took fright from the way he was looking at her. She had had a moment of pure horror. There was a fatuous look in his eyes and he moved nearer to her, breathing heavily over the piano.

Surely he wasn't going to try to make love to her?

She sat down on the stool and opened the first of the songs placed for her and began to play loudly, crashing down on the introductory passage and cutting short anything he might have been going to say.

It was Tosti's 'Good-bye'!

He cleared his throat and began to sing. Surprisingly enough, he had a pleasant light baritone and though he made the sentimental ballad unnecessarily dramatic so that it was all she could do to resist a burble of laughter, she persevered to the end and then closed the piano.

'I think that's enough for tonight,' she said. 'I'm not feeling like "Good-bye, summer" just yet, are you?'

'We could try another?'

'Another day, perhaps, if you're still here,' and he went off in a huff, leaving her there.

How stupid he had been, he thought, to encourage any talk of Myrtle.

Eve sat where he had left her, staring out between the two lighted candles across the dim length of the room towards the long, unshuttered windows which opened on to an iron-railed balcony and gave access to the garden below.

The sickly sentiments of the song persisted in her mind.

> 'Back to the joyless duties,
> Back to the fruitless tears,
> Loving and yet divided
> All through the empty years.'

The joyless duties, yes, and perhaps the empty years, but not – oh heavens! *not* to the fruitless tears! No tears for her. She did not belong to a tearful generation.

Yet suddenly she bent her head over the closed keyboard and held her eyelids down and simply forced back those tears, those idotic, fruitless tears!

What had she to cry for? A man who didn't want her and whom she didn't even *like*!

The man who had been standing on the balcony, ready to be amused by the sight of Victor pouring out his heart in song whilst Eve played for him, saw her bend her head when she had been left alone, and hesitated. He longed to go in to her, and at that moment there was no laughter in his face, no mockery in his eyes.

Then he turned and went softly away.

The flowers are not for you to pick, he quoted to himself savagely.

Once Myrtle had gone, there was open rivalry between the two men for Eve's favours, and to do them justice, both were more than a little in love with her. In this old grey house, rid of the dominating presence of Mrs Belamie whom no one had ever been able to forget whilst she was still alive, Eve was like a shaft of sunlight. The servants, as many as still stayed on, adored her and she seemed to collect smiles wherever she went.

'You know, Emma, I'm getting terribly spoilt here!' she said one day. 'When I go back to London and have to find myself a job of work, I'm not going to like it one bit.'

'Oh well, no need to think about that just yet, my dear. You're only young once. Enjoy it whilst you can. Is that Victor or Lewis bobbing about outside waiting for you?'

'I wish to heaven they'd go back to their jobs of work and leave me to enjoy the rest of this heavenly summer!' sighed Eve, but Emma only laughed.

'Get along with you! Go out and play with your two nice young men. A good many girls would give their eye teeth for the opportunity!'

Eve could no longer close her eyes to the fact that they were both angling for her, and if it had not been that she was sick at heart for Felix, she might have enjoyed it, especially as she was having this free holiday with nothing to do and no worries about the immediate future.

Lewis even got up early one morning and was waiting for her, a meagre figure in swim trunks and a new beach wrap, when she ran down for the before-breakfast swim which she had made into a habit, though since the death and funeral of Mrs Belamie, Felix had never joined her.

'Good gracious, Lewis, what's happened to you?' she asked at sight of him, for he was never keen on swimming except in the hottest part of the day and even then he went blue with cold.

'I thought it was too bad to let you go alone every day, and I rather fancied a dip this morning,' looking round at the slightly misty patch over the sea and trying to appear more enthusiastic than he felt.

'Well, all right,' said Eve ungraciously, 'but don't expect me to revive you if you're dying of cold,' which, of course, she would have at least to try to do.

They were not even going to let her have the sea to herself now!

She did not enjoy the swim, and went deliberately too far out for him to be able to follow her, ignoring his shouts to her 'not to take foolish risks'. When at last she came back to the shore, she found him blue and shivering on the rocks.

'You shouldn't have come,' she told him impatiently. 'It's quite unnecessary for you to make a martyr of yourself for me. What's the big idea? I've come alone ever since I've been here.'

'I don't think you ought to,' said Lewis between pale, shivering lips, dragging the gaudy beach wrap about him and wishing he could feel like a Roman in a toga rather than a worm in a peeling skin. 'Think how awful it would be if anything happened to you!'

178

He was not thinking just of all that money going to charity, either. He was thinking of that bright young life with all its potentialities cut off, and something of this showed in his face for her laughter was gentle.

'You're getting quite human, Lewis,' she said.

'It's because I'm so fond of you. You know that.'

She had to keep her eyes off him. He looked such a figure of fun, so utterly unromantic, with his lank ends of wet hair over his eyes, his teeth chattering and a dewdrop at the end of his long nose. Even when she kept her eyes on the ground, she could see his feet in a pair of old sandals padding along beside her own bare ones and tripping every now and then over the trailing ends of his gown.

'I don't think this is quite the time or the place for a declaration of passion,' she laughed. 'You'd better hurry indoors and get dressed before you catch cold, and I really wouldn't do this again if I were you!'

When they reached the house, it was to find Victor already dressed, immaculate in white flannels and blazer, a white silk cravat at his throat, spotless white shoes on his feet, presenting a contrast to Lewis's dejected appearance.

Eve was right. She never seemed to feel the cold, whereas he caught cold under the slightest provocation and if he had caught one now, he would have to stay in bed and leave the field open to Victor.

To his horror, he sneezed.

'You see, you've caught a cold already. For goodness sake go and put on something warm, and a thick sweater, and if you've got any quinine, take some of that,' and he had no option but to slink away and do as she told him.

Decidedly that adventure had not been a success, he reflected miserably.

'Good swim?' asked Victor in the slightly paternal manner he had begun to take towards her.

'No. Deadly. I was bothering all the time about Lewis. I can't imagine why he decided to go in before breakfast. He can't take it, you know, and I'm sure he hated it.'

'Poor Lewis. I'm afraid he's never been very strong,' he said, flexing his superior muscles under his superbly tailored whites.

Eve suppressed a grin.

'Let's have breakfast, shall we? I've ravenous. Do you mind if I sit down as I am?'

'I should love you to do so. You look charming,' he said, casting an eye over her *ensemble* of white swim suit and gay little jacket.

Her damp hair had tightened into little curls, her face glowed with a becoming tan and she looked enchanting.

His eyes gleamed. He was more worldly wise than his brother, who, he said half jokingly, half disparagingly, knew a good deal more about 'stars and stinks' than about women. Victor had had a good many affairs with the other sex, though until he met Eve he had decided to settle down with Myrtle, who would make a good wife, had her head screwed on the right way and would be careful with his money, even if he inherited a goodly share of his grandmother's fortune.

Now, freed of the watchful surveillance of Myrtle, he could allow himself thoughts of Eve, entrancing thoughts.

He set a chair for her, waited on her, began to fancy his chances with her. Lewis? Pff!

'You look very resplendent this morning,'' she said, helping herself from the dish of kidneys and bacon which he had brought from the hot plate on the sideboard. She, thank goodness, was not always thinking about her figure but appeased the healthy appetite of the young and slim.

'I have asked some people over for tennis this afternoon. I think it's time we had a little fun again, and I propose a few sets this morning to get us into trim.'

He played a good game and showed to advantage on the tennis court, though he was running to fat and told himself he must watch it.

'Singles? Against you? You'll beat me, of course, but a man loves to have his ego boosted by exhibiting his superiority to what he calls the weaker sex,' she said, but laughingly agreed to take him on, and when he was waiting for her to dress, Lewis appeared for breakfast.

'My dear old boy,' said Victor gaily, 'you should never have revealed yourself to her as you looked this morning! You looked shocking. How could you ever have hoped to capture her in that get-up? And if you do go down with one of your bad colds, don't blame anyone but yourself.'

'You don't look so picturesque yourself chasing about a tennis court with your tummy sticking out,' returned his brother sourly.

'I hope you're not suggesting that I'm fat? Perhaps a bit overweight from too much office life and driving my car, but a bit of exercise will soon get that down. I've asked the Millen-Hayes and the Trebennans for tennis this afternoon, by the way, and Eve and I are going to get a bit of practice in this morning.'

'You know I don't play.'

'Oh, that's all right, old boy. There'll be six of us, enough for a four and a single unless two people want to sit out. Oh, there you are, Eve. And looking delightful, if I may say so,' as she appeared in white blouse and shorts, very trim and business-like.

If she had hoped that Felix, who loved a game and played equally as well as Victor, would join them at the party that afternoon, she was disappointed, for there was no sign of him, and after a hard set in which she had partnered Victor against Nan Trebennan and Toby Millen-Hayes, she threw herself down in a deck-chair in the shade.

'I need a rest,' she said, 'and a long, cold drink. Get one for me, Toby, will you?'

'No, I'll get it,' said Victor.

She lay back in her chair when the new set had been made up and looked dreamily at the back of the old house showing grey through the trees. How much she had come to love its age-old ruggedness and its air of timeless peace! And in six months, less than six now, she would have left it, never to return. It was small wonder that Lewis and Victor longed for possession of it, though neither of them had the deep feeling for it that Felix had. Why could not Mrs Belamie have left it to him since she had to leave it to somebody?

Then she caught sight of a tall figure coming round a corner of the house and entering it by a side door without a glance towards the tennis courts, and, knowing that he was going to his office, she watched for him at one of the windows and presently saw his dark head as he sat down at his desk.

He was always so busy nowadays. Had he really no time for play, or was he deliberately avoiding her? The sweet memories she had of him, memories of his arms and his lips, had the power to wipe out those other moods of his as if they had never been, and she knew she was wanting him desperately. Had those kisses really meant nothing to him? Did she mean nothing?

On a sudden impulse, she got up from her chair and ran through a shrubbery to the house, choosing a path which would not cross Victor's or the maid's carrying the tray of drinks. In a few moments, slightly out of breath, she was at the door of Felix's office.

'May I come in?' she asked.

He looked up, surprised.

'You? What brings you here? I thought you were having a tennis party,' but he smiled and she saw that she was welcome.

'Why didn't you come? It's such a lovely day. Do you have to stay here working?'

'It's not my party. I wasn't invited.'

'Silly! As if you needed to be!'

He made a grimace.

'I didn't think I'd be very welcome. Besides, I've got a heck of a lot to do,' indicating the books and papers by which he was surrounded.

'Can't I help you? I can read and write and add up two and two and can usually make it four.'

He smiled and there was a suspicion of tenderness in the smile that made her heart suddenly race. He was an unpredictable man, you never knew what mood you would find him in but when he smiled like that, you'd go through fire and water for him.

But before he could reply, a maid appeared at the open door behind Eve.

'Mr Felix, there's a – a person wanting to see you,' she said.

'What sort of a person, Annie?'

'A – a peculiar sort, an old man, a dirty old man,' said the girl, her nose wrinkling in disgust. 'He'm a furriner, Mr Felix. He do talk funny like.'

'All right. I'll come. Where is he?'

'At the back door. Cook said not to let he in.'

Annie scuttled away and as Felix went down the back stairs, Eve followed him.

At the back door stood an old man, his face leathery and furrowed, his clothes in rags and consisting of a dirty, much-patched shirt, a pair of disreputable shorts and one bare foot wearing a boot with the toe out. The other leg was a wooden stump strapped on at the knee.

'Oh, Granfer, you old rascal,' began Felix. 'I somehow felt it would be you. Where are you out from this time?'

'Cardiff, my boy. A trifling peccadillo, the matter of a few shillings at a time of acute financial embarrassment – oh!' breaking off as he caught sight of Eve and snatching off a battered straw hat which might have been discarded by Bud Flannagan and made her a low bow.

For all his disreputable appearance, he spoke with a cultured accent and his bow was one of old-fashioned courtesy.

'I did not see that you had a lady with you,' he said.

Felix laughed and moved for Eve to stand beside him.

'This character is Jervis Clane, *Mr* Jervis Clane, Eve. Miss Brayle,' and the old man acknowledged the introduction with another bow. 'Well, Granfer, I suppose it's the same tale? Dead broke and with nowhere to go, and you want me to do something about it?'

Eve had the odd impression that there was friendship, even affection, between this most unlikely pair. The old man's keen blue eyes were twinkling and Felix was smiling as he rubbed his chin ruefully.

'Well, you'd better get along to the cottage and find yourself something to eat and I'll be there as soon as I can.'

'Oh, Felix, all that way and only one leg!' cried Eve.

'My dear, he tramps miles and has walked or scrounged a few lifts all the way from Cardiff.'

'Let me take him in the staff car. He's an old man and must be all in,' she urged. 'I can bring it back.'

Felix chuckled.

'They'll probably want it disinfected afterwards, though I assure you he's much cleaner than he looks. They couldn't have turned you loose like that, Granfer?'

'No, they presented me with what they called decent clothes, but I gave them away in exchange for these somewhat well-worn garments.'

'Gave them away?'

'What else could I do? The poor fellow could get a job fruit-picking if he had better garments, whereas no one would employ me even if I were wearing them. I assured him that I had a friend who would help me,' his eyes twinkling again amidst their innumerable wrinkles.

'You old reprobate! Well, if you will run him down to my cottage, Eve, I'll make my peace with the staff. I haven't got my own car here. You know where they keep the keys?'

She nodded and smiled and set off with the old man beside her, and Felix could imagine that he would entertain her with small talk about the beauty of the countryside and would usher her into the car with the most exquisite courtesy.

When they had started and were bumping along the uneven road, Eve glanced at her companion with a curious smile.

'You know Felix well?' she asked.

'Like my own son, and that's what he's been to me. More than a son. A friend, good and faithful. He's saved me from going inside many times, but what's the good? And I'd rather die on the open road than enter one of these homes they have. I'll have a bite to eat, and perhaps a bed for the night in one of the out-houses, and borrow a little money from my good friend and maybe an old suit he's finished with, and get on my way again,' but she thought there was a sound of weariness which was rather defeat than bodily tiredness.

What had he got to live for, and why must people go on living when they are old and finished with life?

At Felix's cottage, he got out of the car with surprising agility in spite of his wooden leg, opened the door for her and gave her his hand, a quite clean one, and walked up the garden path with her, pausing to comment knowledgeably on some of the plants in the roughly-tended border.

'I'll get you a meal, Mr. Clane,' she said.

'I shouldn't dream of putting you to the trouble, Miss Brayle. By the way, Felix always calls me Granfer. I should be honoured if you would do the same.'

'May I? I should like to, but you look very tired, so you sit down and rest whilst I see what's in the larder.'

'Thank you, my dear, but do you mind if I have a wash first? At the sink, of course. I'm a little dusty, though I fear there is nothing I can do about these clothes until Felix finds me something else. I don't think I've had the pleasure of meeting you before. Are you Felix's young lady?'

She coloured a little under her tan.

'Oh no, nothing like that. Just a friend. I – I'm staying at Weir House,' and as she spoke she suddenly remembered the tennis party. They would be wondering where she was. Then she gave a little shrug. After all, she was not really the hostess and it was Victor who had invited the guests. She could leave the old man and be back almost before she was missed, but she knew she was not going to. Felix would not be long, especially when he saw that the car had not returned.

She found a home-cured ham, home-made bread and butter from the farm and set it on the kitchen table with a pot of strong tea, sharing the tea with him, and when Felix joined them, he found them sitting at the table in animated conversation. Jervis Clane, during his long life, had been in many of the countries which she herself knew and they exchanged descriptions of places as they had been sixty years ago and at the present day.

'Well, you two seem to have found something to talk about,' Felix said, looking at them with what she felt was affection. It warmed her heart. 'I see that you found something to eat. Will you stay for a bit, Eve, or have you to get back to the tennis party?'

She laughed.

'It's a bit too late for that already, and what excuse could I

185

give other than urgent private affairs? I think I'll wait now until Lewis and Victor have made up some excuse and their guests have gone. After all, they weren't my guests. I wouldn't have presumed to invite any.'

'You have a perfect right to, you know. Anyway, I'll ring up the house and leave a message that you are here and safe so that they won't call up the police. Will you stay for a meal?'

'For this meal, yes. I've been looking droolingly at that ham. I'll get some more plates.'

'When I've telephoned, I'll go out and cut a fresh lettuce and there are plenty of tomatoes ripe.'

'Let me get them,' said Eve, and it was a rare delight to be doing things for him and playing at being the housewife, bringing in the lettuce and washing it at the sink, finding a dish for the tomatoes and making fresh tea.

'I left a message with Sarah,' he said, coming back with a grin. 'I wasn't going to risk an altercation and explanation!' and Eve smiled serenely. At the moment nothing mattered but the fact that she was here in his home and that they were on friendly terms.

The old man was plainly very tired, almost too tired to puff at the pipeful of tobacco which Felix had offered him, and he rose thankfully at the first suggestion of bed.

'In the barn or anywhere,' he said. 'Just give me a bundle of hay and a blanket and I'll be as right as rain,' but Felix would not hear of it, taking him upstairs into his small guest room and giving him a pair of his own pyjamas in spite of the old man's protests that he was used to sleeping 'raw'.

When Felix came down again, Eve had washed up and was putting the dishes away.

'You needn't have done that,' he protested.

'I like doing it. Suppose you sit down and let me wait on you for a change. Slippers? Cigarettes, or will you have a pipe?'

'In the other room, then. I only have my meals in the kitchen, though my guests ought to have had theirs in state. Poor old Granfer! How much did he tell you about himself?'

'Well, he made no secret of the fact that he has been in and out of prison for a good many years, but he merely mentioned it as one of the unavoidable and not really regrettable things. Who is he, Felix, and how did he get like this? He must have had a public-school education and been somebody at one time?'

'He's really *Sir* Jervis Clane, though he won't let anybody know it, and he was the Governor of one of our small colonies some forty years ago. Then he got into a scrape, something to do with his wife, I believe, though he's never told me the whole story, was brought home in disgrace, went from bad to worse, was disowned by his wife and children – and well, that's all there is to it. He's an old rascal in many ways, lives by picking up this and that but does it so openly that he's usually caught and sent for another spell of prison. I helped him once when he was trying to steal from me and he's never forgotten it and never stolen from me again. I'd trust him with my life. I trusted him with more than that when I let you go off with him.'

She was silent. She could not speak. Her whole being was filled with a surge of happiness. She could only sit there, her mouth quivering, her eyes soft, her heart in them, but he did not look at her as he spoke, his voice not quite steady.

When he spoke again, it was in his normal tone and with perfect control.

'Everything about here and on the whole estate is perfectly safe. He wouldn't even steal an egg or poach a rabbit. He says himself that a bird doesn't foul its nest or a fox his hole, and he regards this as the only nest he has, or the only hole. I'm careless with money and often leave loose change about, but he'd never take a half-penny, not even a piece of bread without being invited to do so. Poor old Grandfer. What am I to do with him? He's evidently on his last legs – or on the one he's got left. I've been thinking about him, and I think I'll keep him here now that the cottage is mine. Would you think that a mad thing to do?'   . .

'No, a very kind one,' she said softly. 'Would he stay, do you think?'

'I think so, though for years he's been tramping the country-side, comes to me for a good meal and a night's rest now and then but disappears again and won't even accept a shilling from me, only the occasional suit of old clothes. You heard what he said about having given away the things they provided him with when he left the prison?'

'You think he did? He didn't sell them?'

'No. He's got a queer code of honour, wouldn't take money for anything that's been given to him, and never tells a lie – and that's landed him in prison a good many times! I think that having tried to serve his country well and failed (I shall always believe through no fault of his own), he feels that that country owes him a living and that's why he's lived off it, but he won't let them put him into a home and take care of him.'

'And you say that his wife and children disowned him, though you think it was her fault?'

'Yes. His name's not really Clane, though he was knighted when he became Governor. He surrendered even his name to them and his private fortune, which I believe was considerable, and vanished from the sight of the world, their world. He's never told me this. I gathered it, piecing it together, when he came to me once so ill that he was delirious and I looked after him. He never knew what he had told me, but – well, his wife was a lot younger than he was and is still alive and queening it in London society and his children are all married well, having managed to live down the name he gave them.'

'Poor old Granfer,' said Eve softly. 'What a beast she must be, not even troubling to find out what had happened to him!'

'There are plenty of women like that. For better, for worse, but not many of them can accept a turn for the worse,' he said grimly.

'You don't think much of our sex, do you, Felix? Is that why you've never married?'

'Partly. But also – I've never met the right woman, one whom I feel I could trust to the end of time, for better or worse.'

She caught her breath in an inaudible sob, for the atmosphere between them had changed abruptly and he had become hard and cynical again, his mouth tight, his eyes when they met hers wearing a defiant challenge in them.

She rose to go. What could she say when he was like that? He was an enigma to her, for only a few minutes ago he had spoken of her as being 'more than his life'.

'I'd better go now. I must take the car back,' and he made no attempt to detain her.

But after she had gone, he seemed to see her there still in her brief white tennis dress, her warm, bright hair against the high, cushioned back of the old settle, her presence making sunshine in the room from which the daylight was already beginning to fade.

He had told her that he had never found a woman whom he could trust to the end of time, but had he found her? He wanted her desperately, with body and mind, but he could not forget that she had engaged herself to Lewis Belamie without loving him. Why? Was it because she had hoped to marry a rich man and had broken her engagement because she could no longer feel sure that he was going to be rich?

Whatever there had been between her and Lewis, he must put her out of his mind. If she were ever going to be rich, it should not be through marrying him, Felix Welby, who had no right to anything, not even his name, except this cottage and his ability to work.

Eve, having replaced the staff car without its having been missed, went straight up to her room, telling Sarah that she had had a meal and did not want dinner. She had no intention of seeing either of the Belamies and having to explain her actions, though when they sat at dinner, there was an uncomfortable silence between the two brothers until the maids had left the room.

Corke had left the house and gone to live on his substantial pension with a married daughter.

'Funny thing her going off like that in the middle of the tennis party, and with Felix,' said Victor. 'You don't think—?'

'That Felix is trying to get his hand in? After all, he was included, you know.'

'Yes, but – he's never shown any sign of being interested.'

'And surely she wouldn't consider *him*?'

'You never know,' said Victor glumly.

'But a man like Felix? A bastard without even a name of his own?'

'Does she know, do you think?'

'I daresay she does. Everybody else does. I don't suppose it would matter to her much, though, if she got the money with him.'

'Yes, but how would she know about that, unless he told her? And how would we know if he had?' argued Victor bitterly. 'That's the most insane part of the whole lunatic thing. How would any of us know she had not been tipped off about it?'

Lewis's thin lips curled.

'Your efforts have not been marked by any sign of success so far, have they? You don't imagine I shouldn't know why she suddenly changed her tune towards you, if she did? Actually, I don't believe she is a gold-digger at all but a really decent girl who'd refuse to sell herself even for this place.'

His brother stared at him.

'You're really in love with the girl, aren't you? Well,' as Lewis did not answer, 'all I can say is that, having once become engaged to her, you were every kind of a fool to let her go.'

'What would you have done if she gave you back your ring and practically told you to your face that she never wanted to see you again?'

Not for anything would he have admitted even to his brother how he had induced Eve to pretend she was engaged to him.

'My dear fellow, I know my way about amongst women a bit better than you do and I'd have paid her a bit more attention in the first place if I'd wanted to stay engaged to her. And, by the way, hadn't she met Felix by the time she decided to break it off with you?'

'Yes, I suppose she had,' admitted Lewis with a frown. 'What are we going to do about it now, if anything? Go back to London and leave the coast clear for him? And I can't stay here much longer. Had a letter only this morning asking me when I am returning.'

'I'll have to go back as well if I'm still reckoning on that partnership.'

With the issue still undecided, it was agreed between them that they would return to London together the next day but would contrive to spend the next week-end and probably every week-end at Weir House. Their only hope lay in the fact that Felix and Eve had shown no sign of any mutual interest and did, in fact, appear to be actually antagonistic towards each other.

The next day, to her infinite relief, they left together, promising to return for the week-end. As this was only Tuesday, it was too far away for her to worry about at the moment, and in the meantime she would be alone with Felix and anything might happen.

She was not one to wait for things to happen; she went out of her way to encourage them, and presented herself in his office when Victor and Lewis had gone and she had seen him return to it.

'I've come to help,' she said. 'There's nothing for me to do about the house as Mr Pawnsford says all the servants who have not been pensioned off are to remain, and I'm bored and must have something to do.'

'What makes you think you can help me?' with a half-smile.

'Well, I can, can't I? Please let me.'

He agreed after a show of reluctance and soon they were working together on the huge mass of data needed for the settlement of the estate.

In an hour's time, he called a halt.

'Let's have tea, or something long and cool. Which would you prefer?'

'Long and cool, I think,' she said, stretching her arms.

He pressed the bell and lit a cigarette for her.

'I don't know why you should imprison yourself in here like this just to help me, but I must admit that I'm getting on faster.'

The sunshine was on her bright hair, or perhaps she had brought it with her, and as he lit her cigarette, he saw an engaging little smudge on her cheek where she had pushed back a stray curl with inky fingers.

'Why are you looking at me like that?' she asked.

'You've got a smear on your cheek,' was the disappointing reply.

'Is that all?' and she took out her handkerchief and dabbed at the wrong place with it.

He took it from her and wiped off the smudge and then, on an uncontrollable impulse, bent over her and framed her face in his hands. She sat quite still, her lips parting, her eyes soft and bright, her whole expression an invitation.

But he did not kiss her. His hands dropped and he turned away.

'Why didn't you?' she asked softly. 'You wanted to, didn't you?'

'Like hell I did!'

'Then—'

And at that precise moment, Annie appeared at the door.

'You rang, Mr Felix?'

'Something cold to drink, Annie, please. What will you have, Eve? Orange? Grapefruit?'

'Anything but passion-fruit,' she said with a wry little smile, but though he gave her the same little smile, he did not return to the subject of the kiss he had not given her.

'Cook wants to know if you will be lunching here, Mr Felix,' said Annie when she returned with the tray of drinks.

'Yes, I'd better. I've got to go to Petterton this afternoon – that is, if I may stay, Eve?'

'Of course.'

'My car's developed a more fiendish squeak than usual and until I have time to find out what's the matter, I can't trust it.'

'Can I come with you to Petterton?'

It was the first time she had asked deliberately for his company, and to her chagrin he did not at once jump at it and she was quick to withdraw the suggestion.

'Never mind. I don't really want to go,' she said.

'Please come, Eve. I want you to.'

'You didn't exactly rush at the idea, did you?'

'Perhaps because – I want it too much,' he said in a low

192

voice, and once again the atmosphere of the room had changed and had become charged with the gold and blue of dreams.

'Felix, why are you like this? Treating me sometimes as if you hated the sight of me and at others almost as if—'

She could not finish the sentence. She was not going to ask him to love her.

'Haven't you learned yet that I'm a moody fellow, and that there's no accounting for my moods?' he said lightly. 'Annie's brought orange and lime. Which will you have?'

'Oh – either. It doesn't matter. I don't think I'll come with you this afternoon, after all. Perhaps I'll walk over and see Granfer, if he's still there. Is he?'

'Yes. Rather to my surprise, he was delighted with my invitation to him to remain, though he'll probably be off again in a few days. It would be very nice of you if you'd go and see him – and you wouldn't enjoy going to Petterton. There's nothing there but some cottages and a few old boats.'

She did not tell him that she would not have cared if even they had not been there. He had accepted her change of mind without comment. He was probably relieved to be rid of her company, she thought bitterly. Well, it would be a long time before she made any advances again!

10

THE summer, lingering late in Cornwall, was over, and it was autumn.

Nothing very much had happened, except that with every fresh day some new link had been forged, the old strengthened, between the girl who loved so deeply and seemed to make her love so plain, and the man who hardened his mind but not his heart against the temptation of her.

Old Granfer had settled down in his last home, the only home he had known for nearly forty years, a reformed character but only because now his code prevented him from being anything else; but he entertained Eve greatly by tales of his felonious exploits, chuckling over the times he had not been found out but having no regret or sense of injustice over the many times he had had a prison sentence.

She felt she had no pride left where Felix was concerned, and paid frequent visits to his cottage on one excuse or another until she ceased to make any.

The old man was not idle, and whenever the weather made outside work possible, was to be found in the garden, which he transformed into neat borders and well-cut grass and rows of vegetables which no longer straggled untidily and unprofitably. He now grew more than the requirements of the house, and Felix insisted on his keeping for himself any money he could make by selling outside it. Eve drove a small van to the village on market days and, with Granfer delighted to be beside her, set up a stall for him in the market place and helped him to sell his produce. By so doing, she came to know and be known by the villagers and her appearance was greeted with smiles that were no longer guarded and suspicious, and she took part in and enjoyed all the local gossip.

At other times in the week, Granfer cut and stacked logs for the winter fires whilst she sat beside him, entertained by his reminiscences, or collected and sorted, ready for him to cart away, the logs he had cut.

When the autumn had really set in, with its rain and mist, and there were little more than the brassicas and a few root crops in the garden, and the logs cut and stacked, she would have fewer reasons for spending so much time at the cottage. Felix had completed the accounts and statements which Mr Pawnsford required for the settlement of the estate and was busy on the farm and superintending repairs to the cottages, and she rarely saw him except in his own home. Once he had finished the work in his office in Weir House, he never went there for meals even at her express invitation, deliberately keeping away from her though she was eating her heart out for him.

'What are you going to do all the winter, Granfer?' she asked him one wild day of wind and rain when, almost blown off her feet, she had helped him to stack the last of the logs in the out-house for immediate use, for now there was a big fire in the living-room which the old man, who had been homeless for so long, had made more homelike and comfortable.

'Well, I thought I could start on the house,' he said, looking round. 'There's plenty to do, white-washing, painting and so on, things Felix never has time for. I thought we could start on this room.'

'We? You mean you're going to let me help?'

'I'm not very good on a ladder, so if you could do the high part of the walls, I could do the rest, and we could do the ceilings with a brush fastened to a pole. What do you think?'

She was delighted if not very experienced. Granfer stumped down to the farm buildings for white-wash, and by the time Felix came home that evening, they had made a reasonably good job of the kitchen ceiling and Eve, mounted on the top of a ladder, was starting on the walls.

'Good heavens! What on earth——?' he began.

She looked down on him saucily.

'Granfer and Eve, interior decorators,' she said. 'Sorry about the mess on the floor. Perhaps if we'd started to white-wash that instead of the ceiling, we should have got more on the ceiling and less on the floor. When we do the living-room, we shall need a different colour, not just white.'

'Eve thinks yellow would be nice,' said Granfer, who plainly adored her.

'You'd make it bright green with red spots if she wanted it like that, wouldn't you, you old rascal? You know, there's no earthly need for you to be doing this, Eve.'

She ignored the faint annoyance in his voice.

'But I love it. I'm beginning to fancy myself as a white-washer, but they'd have a fit if I started on Weir House,' she said, applying her brush with vigour.

'Perhaps it has got a bit dingy, but you know we've got a staff of painters and I could have taken them off some of their other work to do this.'

'Why, when we're happy, even if we are making a mess?' but in looking round at him, her foot slipped on the ladder and he was just in time to catch her as she fell.

For a long moment he held her, gripped closely in his arms and her laughter died, her face pressed against him.

Then he released her abruptly.

'You haven't got the right equipment,' he said. 'You need two pairs of steps and a board. I'll have them brought up in the morning.'

'Then you're going to let me help Granfer?' she asked, a little breathless after that moment in his arms.

He gave a rather wry smile.

'With both of you against me, I don't see what else I can do. Do I get any tea, by the way?'

'The kettle's on, sir, and there's a cottage pie in the oven – and we didn't mix it with white-wash either,' she said. 'Go and sit down in the other room and we'll bring it in to you. You look tired, Felix,' her tone and her bright face softening.

Granfer looked at them with the twinkle in his eyes. These two were his family, his children, all he had in the world. Why were they wasting the precious time of their youth when they were so plainly in love?

'I've had a long day,' said Felix, looking for a chair to sit on whilst he pulled off his boots. 'The Yeo's want a new thatch, but since old Jenner died, I haven't a thatcher and it's the devil of a job to find one. The roof ought to be stripped and tiled.'

'Oh no, Felix! That lovely old cottage! Bill Mayo was telling me the other day that he knows someone in Petterton who can thatch. Shall I ask him who it is?'

Felix smiled.

'Don't mean to say you've got round old Mayo as well? I'm always having rows with him about the way he neglects his place and he wouldn't do a thing to help me, but perhaps if you asked him—' His smile turning into a chuckle. 'I don't know how I've managed so long without you!'

'Nor do I,' she retorted, but flung him a saucy smile as she went to wash her hands at the sink.

'Are you going to stay and share the cottage pie? Is it big enough?' he asked.

'Enormous. We thought it would save us cooking tomorrow. I suppose I could stay, though. I'll give Mrs Hodd a ring.'

She did not tell him that she had already arranged matters with Mrs Hodd, who, like the rest of the staff, was observing 'what was going on between Miss Eve and our Mr Felix' and strongly approved of it, giving no indication to either of the two concerned that they saw through the subterfuges which Eve thought she was making so cleverly. They did not like either Victor or Lewis and were keenly interested in the way one or both of them managed to turn up nearly every week-end, but thought very little of their chances.

Many were the discussions and speculations 'below stairs' as to what was going to happen eventually to Weir House, but the most popular opinion was that it had been left to Eve Brayle. In their view, nothing could be more satisfactory than that she should marry Felix Welby and that they should live in the house together.

Later that evening, when it was time for Eve to go home,

Felix said, as she had known he must do, that he would drive her home as she had walked down rather than use the staff car.

The rain had stopped though it was still a blustery night with a high sea running, and she said she would like to go by the cliff road so that she might see it.

'You won't be able to scramble up the cliff path. It's too slippery and also you'd be blown off.'

She persisted.

'I want to see the sea. I've never seen it in a real fury before.'

'You'll see it many times. However, if you insist, I'll take you first and drive you back to the house afterwards.'

He did not want to be alone with her just then amidst the wildness of nature in the raw. He was afraid of what it might do to him, afraid of the unleashing of passions as savage and undisciplined as that of the sea, but if he did not take her, she would go alone, perhaps be blown off the cliff— He shivered and turned the car on to the lower road that led to the sea.

'Don't get out of the car,' he said. 'It isn't safe,' but she laughed and opened the door and got out, driven back at once against the car by the fury of the wind.

She laughed again, battling to keep her feet, and the next moment he was beside her, his arm about her to steady her.

'You know—' he began.

Against his arm, she turned her face up to his, still laughing, her lovely face glowing from the wind, her hair blown by it, her face—

'Yes? What do I know?' she asked, her mouth so close to his that he could hear her voice above the storm.

His other arm came about her, gripping her to him, holding her tightly.

'That I love you, that I have from the beginning, that I always shall,' he said, and his lips came down on hers, bruising them, forcing them open. She had never been kissed like that, his tongue thrust into her mouth, but it was what she herself wanted instinctively, and more than that – more—

When their mouths parted, he held his head back from her without letting her go from his arms.

198

'Well, now you know,' he said, with almost a groan.

'Yes, now I know. You know too, don't you, my darling. I love you, and it isn't just one of those things, is it? Don't let's talk. Not yet. Kiss me again,' and she closed her eyes and he took her lips again more gently and with a kind of desperate tenderness, smoothing back the wind-blown hair and feeling its warm vitality beneath his hand.

'Oh, Eve, my little love, my sweet. You don't know how much I've wanted to do this, to say all sorts of foolish things to you and to let you know that I mean them.'

'Is it for ever, Felix?'

'Yes, for ever, my love.'

'Me, too,' she whispered and laid her head against him and knew boundless, unutterable peace and yet an affinity with the storm that raged about them.

'Isn't it a wonderful night, all this?' she said after a pause. 'All this wildness and commotion? Look at the sea and how it lashes against the rocks, trying to destroy them though it never can. They've been here since the beginning of time and they'll still be here at the end of it. That's how I love you and have always loved you, from the beginning of time to the end of it. Isn't it wonderful to be in love?'

He held her closer.

'Yes, wonderful. Eve – I'll never let you regret it. I swear it. I'll make up to you for everything you have lost.'

She twisted back her head so that she could look into his face. Her eyes were sweet with love, her mouth trembled with it. There was nothing more she wanted in the world.

'How could I lose anything if I have you?' she asked. 'Why have you fought me for so long? You must have known.'

He kissed her again.

How could he tell her what she was going to lose by loving him? For he was still determined that she must lose it. He would not take a price with her. She must come to him with nothing, or not at all.

But this was their perfect hour. He would not spoil it.

They got back into the car and he drove her round to the other side and back to the house.

He took her into his arms again in the car.

'Darling, shall we keep this to ourselves for a little while?' he asked her not quite steadily.

She nodded at once and joyfully.

'Yes, let's. Oh heavens, it's Friday and one of them is sure to come down, probably both,' making a grimace of distaste.

'Victor and Lewis? Are they worrying you?'

'And how! Lewis proposes to me every week-end, and though so far I have been able to fend Victor off, I shan't be able to much longer. Do you realise that you've secured for yourself a positive siren who is quite irresistible to men?'

He frowned and did not echo her laughter.

'You did once promise to marry Lewis,' he said shortly.

'Dear heart, forget it. I've never been in love with anyone but you.'

'You must have made him believe you loved him or you would not have been engaged to him.'

Some day, perhaps when they were married, she would tell him about that, but just now she was too ashamed of it. It had been such a mean, paltry thing to do. She could not believe that she was the same girl; in fact, she was not the same. Loving Felix had transformed her.

She linked her arms about his neck.

'Darling, I believe you're jealous!' she told him laughingly.

'I don't think it's that, but I wish you hadn't been engaged to him first.'

'If I hadn't been, we should never have met. Isn't it worth it?'

'Worth everything in the world,' he agreed, 'but don't let me catch you even looking at Lewis Belamie again, that's all! Lewis Belamie!' he repeated with such scorn and disgust in his voice that her laughter broke out again and she hid the sound of it against him.

'If we're not going to tell them about us just yet, we shall have to make up our minds to let Victor propose to me. I can't ward him off much longer, but perhaps when I've turned him down, he'll go back to poor Myrtle. I never did understand how that came to grief. They'd been engaged for ages.'

'Well, let him propose and get it over – so long as you're not tempted to accept him.'

She gurgled with happy laughter.

'I really don't see what the Belamie men see in me that they want to marry me because I'm sure they disapprove of everything I am and do. Anyway, don't let's talk about them any more. They don't matter two hoots to us – though I suppose if we go on living at South Cawer after we're married, and I'd like to, we shan't be able to help seeing them. Do *you* know which of them is getting Weir House, Felix?'

'No,' he said abruptly and she misinterpreted his manner.

'You ought to have had it, Felix. You care for it a lot more than they do. I do wish she'd left it to you.'

'For your sake?' he asked quickly.

'Only for yours, darling, because you really do love the place, don't you?'

'I love *you*.'

She nodded blissfully.

'Thank heaven for that. I must go in, darling. I'm soaking wet. Do you know your roof leaks and it's raining again?'

'Sorry, sweet. I'll really have to get another car.'

She kissed him swiftly and ran indoors.

'Tell Granfer I may not be down in the morning if *they* come, but I'll be down on Monday,' she called out as she ran.

Victor came down alone the next day, brought her a great sheaf of flowers, though the greenhouses provided all she could possibly desire in that line, and an enormous box of chocolates though she seldom ate sweets, and, safe in her own secret knowledge of the love she shared with Felix, she resigned herself to getting over Victor's proposal of marriage with the greatest possible speed and the least hurt to him.

She received his rather pompous words with sincere regret but told him frankly that she did not love him.

'But you've let me come down here week after week, knowing what I had in mind,' he complained, disappointed and affronted, for in her new happiness she had received him even joyfully. All life was bathed in a golden light for her.

'I couldn't very well keep you out of what is much more your home than mine,' she told him.

'I suppose there's some other man?' he flung at her suspiciously.

'Why should you come to that conclusion merely because I don't want to marry you?' she asked coldly.

'Is it Felix Welby? It's the sort of sneaky, underhand thing he would do, but let me warn you about something. Do you know about Ellice Grant?'

He was beside himself with frustration and anger.

'No, who is she?'

Her heart had missed a beat but her voice was calm and controlled.

'Only the girl he's engaged to. Some people say they're actually married though he would never have admitted it whilst *Grand-mère* was alive because she did not approve of her. If you don't believe me, ask him.'

'It's nothing to do with me, so why should I ask him? Anyway, I prefer not to discuss Felix's affairs. I've got some letters to write,' and she went up to her room and sat down, heartsick, to think over what Victor had told her.

It was hard to believe, yet why had Felix fought so long against his love for her when she had made hers only too plain? And why had he asked her to keep their engagement secret? She herself was prepared to admit it at once.

Ellice Grant. The name meant nothing to her. If there were anything for her to know, she must wait for Felix to tell her. She remembered the spite in Victor's voice. Probably it was only that, the poisoned dart of a man with a mean mind. Yes, it must be that.

She could scarcely bear to wait until Victor had gone back to London so that she could rush down to the cottage to see Felix, not to ask him questions about this woman but to be assured of his love. She did not expect to see him during the week-end as he preferred to keep clear of the house when either of his cousins was there, but as soon as Victor had left on the Sunday night, she slipped out and ran like a homing bird to the cottage.

Granfer was sitting dozing in front of the television set which Felix had bought for his benefit. He was alone but woke with a start when she let a blast of cold air in at the door.

'Did I wake you, Granfer?' she asked.

'No – no, my dear,' he said, getting up with his unfailing courtesy and setting a chair for her. 'I was watching the programme. Most interesting.'

She laughed.

'You're an old fraud. The screen was blank. There's nothing on at this time on Sunday nights! Where's Felix?'

'He's not back yet. He said he'd be back tonight, though. Can I get you a cup of tea or coffee?'

'Not back? You mean he's gone away?'

'Only for the week-end. He went yesterday morning, to London or somewhere. Private business, I think, though of course he does not tell me. Why should he? Do let me get you some tea,' stumping to the cupboard where the 'best' china was kept and beginning to set it out on a tray.

The old man was so pleased to be playing host to her that she could not immediately leave him, but after she had shared the pot of tea with him and there was still no sign of Felix, she made an excuse to slip away, refusing the old man's escort.

She went by the cliff path and stood where she and Felix had stood two nights ago. Was it only two nights since her whole world had changed? She tried to recapture the glory, but it eluded her. Even the sea looked different, grey and sullen and menacing.

Ellice Grant.

She could not get the name out of her mind. What had she to do with Felix? And why had he made this sudden journey, 'to London or somewhere' on private business without telling her? Surely in this new and sweet relationship with him he would have told her, even if he had gone on private business?

Instead of going to his cottage the next morning, she took the car and drove down to the village to do some of the household shopping, and stopped for a word with old Ben, the potter.

His wrinkled face creased into a smile at sight of her, and she sat down to have a gossip with him.

'You must have known everybody in the village for a great many years, Ben,' she said presently.

'Ah, I did that, m'dear. There's none that comes and goes without old Ben knows, furriners an' all,' with a wheezy chuckle that was reminiscent of a rusty gate.

'Did you know anybody called – Ellice Grant?' she asked, ashamed of the impulse to put the question but unable to stop herself from doing so.

His face changed oddly and his toothless mouth drew in.

'Ah, I knowed 'un, but better you ask Felix,' he muttered. 'Don't live hereabouts no more,' and she saw from his expression that she was not likely to get any further information from him.

But he has said 'Ask Felix'!

Could she do that? And if she did not, would he tell her?

But when she got back to the house for lunch, she found him there waiting for her and joy rushed back to her heart at sight of him.

'Oh – darling!' she cried and was crushed in his arms and kissed until she fought him off with breathless laughter.

'You got rid of Victor all right, then?' he asked her. 'The rejected suitor, I hope?'

She nodded.

'Poor Victor. I hate refusing proposals, but I really didn't give him any encouragement. Not like I did you!' with a laugh. 'I thought that in the end I should have to propose to you! Felix—'

Her face had grown grave again, almost wistful.

'What is it, my sweet?'

'You – you do really love me, don't you? I mean – just me, myself.'

In her ignorance of the facts, she could not have worded her question worse, and she saw him flinch and his mouth harden.

'What has Victor been saying to you about me?' he asked.

'Why – nothing. Nothing at all. I was just asking a silly question. I know you love me.'

He held her against him and kissed her eyelids and her lips, her hair, her throat.

204

'You ask me that? You dare to ask me that? Can't you believe me even now? Is it so difficult to believe?'

'Have you ever loved anyone before me, Felix?' she asked him, so ready to believe him, so desperate never to doubt him again.

'Never, Eve.'

'Haven't you ever – kissed anyone before?'

He threw back his head and laughed.

'Darling, I'm a man and I'm nearly thirty-three and you ask me a question like that? Of course I have. Haven't you?'

She smiled unwillingly.

'You know I have. But – I've never loved anyone before.'

'Not even Lewis?'

She flinched but held his eyes steadily. There was perfect candour in them.

'No, not even Lewis.'

Again she had the urge to tell him of that disgraceful pact she had made with Lewis Belamie, but again her courage failed her and she remained silent. If only he would tell her about Ellice Grant, she would tell him about Lewis, she thought, frantically seeking an excuse for not telling him, but he too was silent until Sarah came into the room to summon them to lunch and by tacit consent the subject was dropped though now and then he caught a look in her eyes that was speculative, almost appealing.

He had spent a good deal of time during the week-end thinking about her and their future and had finally reached a decision, though not without apprehension. He could not bring himself to rob her of her inheritance; he could not see the Weir House as other than that, since for himself he wanted nothing, and certainly no share in Mrs Belamie's fortune. He would have been happy to work for Eve and knew that by his work he could have given her reasonable comfort in a small home, but had he the right to deny her the wealth which would come to him by their marriage within the stipulated time?

He cursed the old woman who, with fiendish glee, had put him in this position, knowing, as he had felt sure she had known, what his feelings for Eve were.

There was no third course; he must either marry her within the year or lose the estate, and would she, could she, believe that he only wanted it for her sake? It was a bitter problem to solve and the only possible way was to marry her without letting her know what was involved and to trust in his power to make her so happy, so sure of his love, that when the truth was revealed to her, she would accept it and *know* that he had had no ulterior motive. Would she, would any girl, believe it?

Yes, Eve would. She must, if they were to have any happiness.

He felt that the secret marriage was essential, but how could he explain it to her?

Eve, of course, did not understand.

'Darling,' he asked her with all the earnestness in his power, 'will you trust me? Can you? I know it's a lot to ask, far too much, and you'll be quite justified in refusing. But if you can accept my solemn assurance that this secret marriage is essential to our happiness – if you love me enough – if you are quite certain of my love for you – then, will you, Eve?'

She was so much in love, wildly, blindly, passionately and for the first time. All she desired in life was to be his wife and share whatever of good or ill should come to them. Whatever lay in his past, she wanted to forget it so long as the future was hers.

'Will it be – for long, Felix?' she asked in a whisper.

'A year. Not so long as that now.'

'Then – yes, I love you and trust you, and isn't that all that matters? Yes, my darling – yes.'

Tears were running down her cheeks, though she did not know why, except that she was divinely happy. He kissed them away.

'I'll never let you shed any more,' he promised her. 'We're going to be happy,' and she dashed the last of them away and smiled into his eyes with perfect trust in the future.

'It will be best to wait until you are free to go from here,' he said. 'Then we'll go to London and get married quietly and have a honeymoon, just the two of us.'

She laughed.

'I'd always imagined that when two people had a honeymoon, they had it alone. What then?'

'Then I'm afraid it means parting, more or less, though I'll be with you as much as I can. Have you anyone you can trust, really trust? To live with, I mean. I couldn't bear you to be alone.'

'There's Marcia, the girl I lived with before I came here. She's sweet and understanding. I can trust her utterly.'

'Then when we're married, we'll tell her. It'll make things easier for you. But no one else, no one at all, though I'll be ready to murder anyone else who casts eyes of love on you!'

'Don't worry. No one will,' she said happily. 'I'll be a positive hermit!'

In the weeks that followed, they were supremely happy, and though the servants knew what was in the wind (for how could they disguise their happiness from them?), no one spoke of it to them. Victor and Lewis, undaunted and still hoping, came down at most week-ends, and these were blank spots of separation, Eve rather enjoying the secrecy now that she was so blissfully sure of Felix, and at length the time came when she could go back to London and to Marcia.

The house was to be closed, with only a skeleton staff remaining, though still no one knew what was going to happen to it, and on her last night, she and Felix went round it, hand in hand, bidding good-bye to all the places which had shared with them their happiness and memories.

'You're sorry to leave it, aren't you, darling?' he asked.

'Yes. I love the old place, and the people, and the village folk. Also it's where I met you,' pressing her head against his shoulder. 'Shall we ever be able to come back to it? When we're married, I mean? I'd love to live in your cottage. Could we, do you think? Might the new owner, whoever he is, not keep you on? He'll surely need someone like you?'

'Perhaps. Who can tell? I'll be here for a year, anyway.'

Marcia was delighted to have her back, and on their very first evening together, Eve told her about Felix.

Marcia frowned a little.

'I don't like all this secrecy, Eve. What's the point of it? Even when you're married, it's still to be a secret. Why?'

'I don't know, but I don't really care now. Wait till you meet him. Then you'll understand why I'm so crazy about him. He's not keen on my getting a job again, but I shall have to. You see, he's not rich or anything, though he's paid properly for his work now,' and she told her about Mrs Belamie and who Felix was, adding to Marcia's apprehension, for Felix Welby had not even a name of his own to give this girl who had fallen so deeply in love with him that she did not care.

When she met Felix, she was obliged to re-adjust her opinion of him, but was still not sure that he was all Eve believed. She tried to persuade her to wait a bit longer, say a year at least, but in spite of her entreaties and vague forbodings, they were married one blustery March morning, and set off for their secret honeymoon in Majorca, where Eve had once stayed briefly and wanted to stay again.

It was a time of feverish happiness, of snatching at each hour as if Fate yielded them up reluctantly and they must last them for all the memories of happiness they would ever have.

'Live for the day,' had been her father's happy-go-lucky advice to her, which in the end had proved his own downfall. 'If you worry about anything, you worry three times, once for the past which you can't alter, once for the present when you've got it and once for the future which may never happen.'

Only on the last night of their honeymoon did she refer to the need for secrecy to which she had so blithely and, without understanding it, agreed.

'Darling, can't I go on being your wife when we get home?' she asked, clinging to him desperately as their separation loomed near. 'Tell me. Whatever it is, I shall understand. Is it because you don't want to take me back to the cottage? Because you want to get another job and have more money, a bigger house, a better position, before we let people know? Because I don't care. All I want is to be with you, to make do on so little, to live in the cottage, to live anywhere and anyhow rather than be separated from you.'

It was the only reason she had been able to think of, and it

208

was a poor one. It was either that – or the ever-nagging thought of Ellice Grant.

But he caught at it.

'My dearest love, believe me that this is the only way – at present. I've got to stay in my job and at the cottage for the time being, and you couldn't live there, you really couldn't. You know what it's like, those two little bedrooms and no proper bathroom, only a tin bath in the shed and not even any electricity. It's been all right for me. I've managed and I haven't really cared for myself, and if I'd tried to do anything about it, the whole place might have tumbled down.'

'It was disgraceful of Mrs Belamie to let you live like that,' she said heatedly.

'She rather enjoyed it, felt, I suppose, that I was paying both for what she had spent on me and for my mother's sin. My pride would never let me ask her for anything and I never wanted to go anywhere else, as I could have done. It will only be for a little while longer. Trust me, darling. Please trust me. I couldn't bear you to live like that – and then there's Granfer. If he knew we were married, he would just walk out and leave the place to us, and you wouldn't want that to happen, would you? He would just die on the road if he took to it again. As soon as I am free to leave there, we'll find somewhere to live where he can come with us to end his days, but until things are settled, I can't pack up the job and go somewhere else.'

It was such a poor excuse and he knew it, but his introduction of Granfer into the argument made her accept it, for she knew that it was true. The old man would just wander away and die, for there was not room for three in those tiny bedrooms, where a big bed would take up all the space in either of them and she would be acutely uncomfortable. The cottage had been built at a time when nobody cared how the poor lived.

'I wouldn't mind,' she said mutinously, but she knew she would, and Felix knew it too. She had never lived like that and even the happiness of being with him would soon have its brightness dimmed by the make-shift discomforts of every-day life.

'Soon, darling. I promise you,' he told her and wondered

if he were a fool to wait, not to tell her the truth, and that there was nothing to prevent them from living in luxury in Weir House.

But he could not bring himself to tell her yet, not until he had made her sure of him. It was a curious hangover from the days of his childhood and young manhood that he found it so hard to believe that he was of paramount importance to anyone, that he really belonged to anyone, even to Eve. He had been a solitary boy, voluntarily cutting himself off and standing apart from boys who liked him and would have invited him to their homes. He was alone, without even a name.

Many times already, in this brief fortnight, he had blamed himself for marrying her. The thought of the inheritance which would come to him had become an intolerable burden to him. He dared not put her to the test by telling her about it. Would she believe him? Would she not, remembering the efforts made by Victor and Lewis to persuade her to marry one of them, put him in the same category as a fortune-hunter?

So it was almost with relief that he took her back to London and to Marcia, who fortunately looked at things from a more practical viewpoint and agreed with him that Eve could not live in the primitive conditions at the cottage which he made clear to her, even exaggerating them.

He did not want Eve to take a job, saying that he could maintain her, but she insisted and Marcia thought it would be better for her to be occupied. She found work in a small draper's shop near the flat, kept by two maiden ladies who were struggling to keep the business in spite of ill health, and Eve's bright presence and her willingness to work for what they could afford to pay her brought new life to them and new customers to the shop, which she soon transformed and, with their approval, got rid of much of the old, unsaleable stock by organising an out-of-season sale.

Every Saturday she either went half-way to meet Felix and spend the night with him at some tiny country inn, or on occasion he came to the flat, and she felt she merely existed from one Saturday to the next.

It was on one of his visits to London that by mere chance

Victor saw them together. His car had been held up behind a bus at a stop, and they had got off it together and, with her arm tucked in his, they had gone off in animated conversation.

Both he and Lewis had seen her in London and taken her out on several occasions, though she had given them no encouragement to do so, but to neither of them had she ever mentioned Felix. Yet here she was, in London with him and obviously on very friendly terms with him.

Though their hopes of marrying her had by now faded and they had made up their minds that she, and the Weir money were lost to them, the thought that Felix might succeed where they had failed was unendurable and Victor cast about in his mind for any means that might discredit his cousin in Eve's eyes.

Then what seemed to him a gift from the gods appeared. He heard that Ellice Grant had returned to South Cawer! How could he bring them together? And before the year in which Eve could inherit by marrying Felix was up? Would he be able to persuade her to go to Weir House again? Though shut up and maintained only by Hodd and his wife, it would not be impossible to re-open it, for as Mrs Belamie's grandsons they might be expected still to take an interest in it until it passed into other hands.

Reluctantly he told Lewis of the friendship between Eve and Felix, and his plan for bringing her face to face with Ellice Grant.

'What if Ellice won't agree?'

Victor gave a snort of scorn.

'She'll do anything if it's made worth her while. A five-pound note would probably be enough, and if she produces the child – ? Don't forget that it was Felix who saw her through that and everybody in the village knows it. I think it's worth a trial, if we can persuade Eve to go down there with us. She probably wouldn't go alone with one of us, but she might if we both went.'

Eve proved unexpectedly co-operative. It was a week-end when she had not expected to see Felix, for it was the time of the spring sowing and he had told her that after the wet winter it was imperative for him to take advantage of the fine spell to get long-delayed work done. It would be the first week-end since their marriage that they had not met, but if she were at Weir House, they could at least see each other even if they could not spend the night together.

So, keeping it from Felix as a surprise, she jumped at the chance.

Someone else was to be given a surprise, too; Victor.

He and Myrtle had not renewed their engagement, though they still met. For one thing she had a room in a flat which was in the same block as Victor's, having taken it for the convenience of being near enough to him to be able to slip into his flat at such times as the man with whom he shared it happened to be away.

Alec Emett, the friend with whom he shared the flat, was a kindly soul, genuinely sorry about the broken engagement, and when he met Myrtle in the lift on Saturday morning, he chatted with her and invited her in for a pre-lunch drink.

When she hesitated, he hastened to assure her that Victor would not be there.

'He's gone down to Cornwall for the week-end,' he said.

'Alone?' she asked, surprised.

'No, Lewis has gone with him and I believe they've taken that girl Lewis was supposed to be engaged to, though I fancy that romance came to an end. Perhaps it hasn't, though, because she rang Victor up this morning to confirm the time of the train, but he'd already left, so I told her the time of it. She sounds a nice girl and was evidently quite excited about going, so perhaps she and Lewis are going to make it up? Now what will you have? I'm afraid there's only beer or Scotch.'

'I don't think I'll come in, Alec, after all,' she said. 'I don't really like drinking at this time, though it was very nice of you to ask me. I think I'll just go on up to my room, if you don't mind.'

When she reached it, she paced the floor, sick with anger. Though Victor had not referred to their broken engagement again, she had believed that all this nonsense about Eve was over and that in due course she and Victor would be married.

It came as a shock to her that he was still seeing Eve and that moreover they were going to Weir House together. Did he still hope to marry her? She did not believe, had in fact never believed, that Eve's sole attraction for him was the eventual inheritance of the Weir estate. He was in love with her and his promise to get a divorce from her and marry her, Myrtle, was just a fantastic scheme to keep her quiet. In these months since their engagement had been broken, she had become convinced of it.

And now they had gone down there together! Would he tell her what she stood to gain by marrying him? Had Lewis insisted on going with them for that reason?

Resolved to throw everything to the winds rather than let him marry the girl she hated with a bitter hatred, she packed into a case the bare necessities and caught the next train to Cornwall.

Eve had gone with the two brothers in high spirits, and though they more than suspected that the thought of meeting Felix might be the cause, they could not but relax under the spell of her gaiety and charm. Lewis had long ago decided that it was not worth getting married, even to Eve, and had left the field to Victor on the other's assurance that he should share the proceeds of his own success. The younger brother had no love for Weir House as a home, but merely what it would mean to him in terms of cash which he could use for the only thing dear to his heart and set up his own laboratory for research. He would much prefer a substantial sum in cash to Eve and Weir House, and, having failed to get the top prize himself, was only too willing to further his brother's plans.

As soon as she was able to do so in private, Eve rang up the cottage, but Felix was not in.

'Don't tell him I'm here, Granfer,' she said, a little burble of happy laughter in her voice. 'It'll be a surprise. Just tell him that Victor and Lewis are here and that he's wanted at the house. He won't expect to see me!'

They had arrived in time for a late lunch, for she had asked for the morning off, and she still had the hours of the afternoon to fill in so rather than spend them in the house with the Belamies, she went for a walk, renewing her acquaintance with many loved spots, timing her return to be there when she might expect Felix to call.

Lewis met her in the hall.

'Where have you been?' he asked angrily.

'For a walk. Why? Am I a prisoner here?'

'You haven't been with Welby?' he demanded.

She was on her guard at once, for she had not even mentioned him.

'Why on earth should I? Don't be absurd, Lewis.'

'There's someone I think you ought to see,' he said and turned back into the room from which he had just come.

Victor was there with a perfect stranger, a woman of about thirty, dressed in a rather flamboyant style and with a face that might have been pretty but for its hard features and bold eyes.

Eve looked enquiringly at the two brothers. Why should she be interested?

Then Victor introduced the stranger.

'This is Miss Ellice Grant – Miss Brayle.'

Ellice Grant!

The name had remained in Eve's memory though she had tried to forget it, a little stinging fly buzzing about her. Now it had pounced. She knew it from the look of triumph in the girl's hard eyes and the smile that flickered about her mouth.

'How do you do?' asked Eve perfunctorily and neither of them held out a hand.

'Miss Grant has something to tell you which we think you should know,' said Victor.

'Why?' asked Eve.

'Because I've just come back to South Cawer after being away for some time, and I'm told that you and Felix Welby became very friendly whilst I was away.'

Ellice Grant's voice was as hard as her face, with the faint burr of the Cornish speech underlying it.

The blood rushed to Eve's face, but she spoke calmly and coolly.

'I do not understand why you should be interested, Miss Grant.'

'You will. I am engaged to Felix Welby, or I was, and he is the father of my child. I came back after I had had it, expecting him to marry me. If you have any doubts about it, here are his letters enclosing the payments he has been making me whilst he carried on with you.'

She had taken some folded sheets of paper from her bag and now laid them open on the table beside Eve. Involuntarily she glanced at the top one. It was typewritten and it read:

Dear Ellice,

Herewith the money as usual. I hope you are getting on all right.

Yours sincerely,
Felix.

She felt sick. There could be no doubt that he had written the letter, and the others were probably like it. His signature was too familiar to her for there to be any mistake. Her face was quite white now, and she put out her hand to steady herself by the back of a chair. Victor, suddenly alarmed, moved as if to help her, but she drew back and shook him off.

'Don't – touch me,' she said in a queer, strained voice which did not seem to belong to her. 'I suppose this is your doing?'

'I – I had no idea – of course when she – when Miss Grant—' he spluttered, and at that moment there was an unexpected diversion, for Myrtle walked into the room.

'Myrtle! You here?' he asked, dumbfounded.

'Yes. At a rather crucial moment, I think. You didn't expect me, did you? If it was private, you shouldn't have left the door open.'

None of them saw the tall figure of a man who was still standing in the passage behind her.

Felix had been at Helston station enquiring about some bags of seed which had gone astray when Myrtle's train arrived, and he had been amazed to see her and had at once offered her a lift.

'You're on your way to Weir House, I suppose?' he asked.

'Yes. Seeing that they're all there, Victor and Lewis *and* Eve Brayle, I thought I might complete the party,' she said, evidently very angry, and he could find nothing to say as he took her to the car.

Why had they come, and brought Eve with them? He was greatly perturbed, wondering what they had found out, if anything, but feeling that whatever had happened, his place was at Eve's side.

When he attempted to talk, avoiding the topic which was exercising both their minds, she had shut him up brusquely.

'I'd rather not talk. Just take me to the house,' she said and had not troubled whether he followed her into it or not.

Now she was looking from one to another, her head high, her eyes blazing, two spots of colour bright in her pale cheeks.

Then she ignored the two men and Ellice Grant, and centred her attention on Eve.

'You might as well know what this precious family has been up to, why Felix left this woman in the lurch when it seems she was going to have his child, why Victor broke off his engagement to me and why Lewis did his best to get you to marry him. It was because whichever of them married you got this house and the money. I don't care, Victor,' turning on him like a tigress as he attempted to interrupt her. 'I don't care if she does know. Now none of you will get it. You've got the truth at last, Eve, and I imagine you'll send the lot of them packing. I don't care about the money, I never have. It's – Victor I wanted–' and she burst into angry tears and rushed out of the room.

Felix stood aside to make way for her and then strode in, his face grim and set.

He looked at no one but Eve, who had crumpled into a chair and sat there, staring at nothing, her world in ruins. It had all happened so suddenly that she could not even begin to think. Everything was chaos.

'Eve – my darling,' he said in a low, gentle voice, the grimness leaving his face for a moment.

She shivered away from him though he had made no attempt to touch her.

'No,' she said, 'no.'

Ellice kept silent. This was more than she had bargained for, and certainly she had not expected to see Felix.

Victor interposed. It shook him to see Eve so crushed. All he had expected of her was anger and disgust. For the moment he had almost forgotten Myrtle's outburst and that she had revealed the closely-guarded secret.

'The best thing you can do is to clear out, Welby, and take that woman with you. We'll look after Eve.'

Felix gave him an icy stare.

'You'll pardon me if I look on that as my job. Eve is my wife. We were married three months ago. As for you, Ellice, words fail me—'

Eve rose precipitately from her chair.

'I don't want to see any of you again, ever,' she said chokingly. 'I'm going back. Don't any of you take me to the station. I'll ask Hodd,' and she went stumblingly from the room.

Not even Felix dared to go with her at that moment.

II

'I'm going to Cornwall tomorrow, to Weir House.'

Marcia looked up sharply, but Eve's face expressed nothing of what she must be feeling at that moment. It was calm and her voice perfectly controlled. It did not seem possible that she was the same gay, pleasure-loving girl she had been only a year ago though Marcia had gradually grown used in the last six months to the change in her. She had become quiet and reserved, but though there was often a look of brooding sadness in her eyes, she now never spoke of either the past or the future.

She had arrived back at the flat very late on the night when Marcia had believed her to be in Cornwall, and the two girls had talked until the early hours of the morning, when Eve had poured out the whole tale, refusing comfort or consolation or to believe in Felix any more.

'I can see it all now,' she had said furiously, white-faced, hard-eyed, tight-lipped. 'What a fool I was to imagine they were all after me for myself! Victor broke off his engagement, Lewis grew suddenly maudlin, and Felix – I suppose Felix would have married this Ellice Grant but for the fortune I was trailing behind me! And all this talk about loving me! Now I've told you the whole thing and after tonight, I don't want to talk about it any more or hear any of their names.'

'Darling, you and Felix are married.'

'Then we can get unmarried just as soon as he likes. He's got what he wanted, hasn't he?' bitterly.

'I'm sure it's not what you think, Eve. Felix *loves* you.'

'Me, or a fortune? It's no good, Marcia. My eyes are wide open at last, and they'll never be blind again. Can't you laugh at me, seeing myself as a *femme fatale*, with all of them falling for me?' and Marcia felt that she would never be able to forget the bitterness of Eve's laughter.

'I'm never going back,' she said. 'I'll never willingly see any of them again, especially Felix. He can do what he likes about the marriage. I've finished with him, with all men.'

Yet now, after six months during which time she had never mentioned him, she was going to Cornwall again. Why?

'You'll see Felix?' asked Marcia.

'Yes. Don't ask me any more, Marcia. You've been an angel to me, putting up with my bad temper and – all the time when I haven't been able to talk to you. I've been trying to make up my mind what to do, and I'm still not sure. It will depend on Felix. I've sent all his letters back unopened. I didn't want to hear what he had to say. I was too heart-broken, or perhaps it was my pride that was broken and not a matter of hearts at all! I've been trying to pick up the pieces and fit them to-gether to make some sort of pattern for my life again. That's why I am going to see him,' and she gave a little shiver which told Marcia something of the strain which she was putting on herself by the coming interview.

There was no word or sign of love for Felix, no softening of eyes or voice, and Marcia sighed.

'It's not going to be easy for you, is it?' she asked gently.

'No.'

Just the one unequivocal word. How far, how very far, Eve had gone from the light-hearted girl to whom life had been fun! Marcia could not bring herself to ask the question that burned in her mind. What was Eve going to do when she was face to face with the man she had loved and married and since hated?

She still had no answer to that unasked question when she saw her off the next morning. Eve's eyes were still remote and her smile of farewell did not reach them.

She had asked Marcia for a picnic lunch so that she would not have to leave the compartment, and she sat stony-faced throughout the long journey. One word, one name, beat into her brain remorselessly.

Felix. Felix.

Though she thought she had schooled herself to withstand any emotion, the sight of the old grey house tore at the shreds of her heart. Though she had lived in it for less than a year, it was the only real home she had ever had. In it she had known great happiness and deep sorrow. How many other women had worked out their destinies in it, for good or ill? She remembered that old history, written by many hands over many generations of people to whom it had been home, only so very few of the writers women. Some day she would read it again, but possibly now with more understanding, but she would never write in it. Why reveal to future generations, which would not stem from her, the bitterness of her heart?

The place had that indefinable air of not being lived in, though the lawns had been tended and the flower beds, naked now, stood waiting for the coming of their spring glory. The early bulbs were already pushing through the earth and in a sheltered corner snowdrops bravely swung their white bells in the misty rain.

The outer door had always stood open, but now it presented a blank, forbidding face to the girl who had returned unannounced. She thought, with a sense of unfamiliarity, of the one who had left it only six months ago in anger and humiliation. Could she have been that same girl?

There was a rattling of chains, the sound of heavy bolts being withdrawn, the turning of keys, and she was face to face with Mrs Hodd.

'Oh – oh, Miss Eve! Dear life, you've come back!' and arms went out to clasp and hold her whilst tears ran down the cheeks that were like a rosy apple.

Then the arms set her free and the woman stood back in smiling, tearful apology.

'Excuse me, Miss Eve – ma'am – but I were that glad to see you—'

'It's all right, Mrs Hodd. It was a nice welcome. I wondered if you were still here or if I should have to explain myself to a stranger.'

'Come you in, my dear – ma'am. You won't find a fire except

in our quarters, as we only light them once a week to keep the place aired, but if so be you don't mind coming to our room, me and Hodd will get fires in no time.'

'Of course I don't mind, Mrs Hodd, but the house doesn't strike cold. Quite warm, in fact.'

'That's that there central heating as Mr Felix had put in. Me and Hodd, we don't like it much, but then we're used to the cold. Come right in, ma'am,' opening the baize door which led to the servants' quarters and the housekeeper's room. 'I'll get Hodd to light the fires whilst I make you a cup of tea. Hodd, look who's here! Miss Eve – at least—' giving her a slightly apprehensive look.

Eve had already realised that they knew her new name to which she must begin to accustom herself. Except on her honeymoon and during those secret week-ends, she had never been called by it.

She held out her hand to Hodd, who was vainly trying to conceal the fact that he was in shirt-sleeves and braces and without a collar.

'It's nice to see you again,' she said with a smile. 'I didn't know if you'd be here, so I got a taxi from Helston. By the way, I see that the road has been widened. I suppose Mr Welby had it done?' introducing his name deliberately. 'I think you know that I'm Mrs Welby?'

'Yes, ma'am. Mr Felix told us and we're main glad to see you, Mrs Hodd and I.

Mrs Hodd set the most comfortable chair for her and enquired about her luggage, evidently assuming that she was staying.

'Just a small case. The man put it on the step. Perhaps you'll bring it in, Hodd.'

'Yes, and light some fires,' ordered his wife. 'I'll get you some tea, ma'am. Sit you here and rest a bit,' and she hustled him out of the room, evidently needing some private consultation with him as to the accommodation of the guest who was now the mistress of the house.

To forestall them, whilst Mrs Hodd was preparing her tea (probably a real Cornish tea, she thought, with scones quickly made and hot from the oven, and with home-made jam and a great bowl of cream!) she slipped out of the room and up the stairs.

Perhaps Felix was not even living in the house? Though as he had been to so much trouble to get it, it would be strange if he weren't.

But she opened the doors cautiously and found his room, a small one on the first floor intended as a dressing-room and communicating with a large double room which, with tightened lips, she ignored, closing the door behind her firmly.

Opposite was the room which she always thought of as hers, the Queen's Room, and as she stood in its open doorway she heard Hodd coming up the stairs with her case.

'I'll have my old room, Hodd, this one,' she said. 'I'd really love the luxury of a fire. Do you think I could have one?'

'Of course, madam. We're that glad to have you back. There's a plenty of hot water if so be you'd like a bath. Mrs Hodd will have your tea pretty nearly ready, but I'll have a good fire burning by the time you come up again. I'm afraid there's no one here to look after you but Mrs Hodd and me. We look after the master, but he'll maybe get a girl in from the village tomorrow.'

He looked expectantly at her, no doubt hoping to hear that she was staying in spite of the smallness of her luggage, but she said nothing except to thank him and go down the stairs again.

Tomorrow?

Well, that would look after itself.

To her surprise, she found that she was hungry, but she had not been able to eat her lunch and had had only the sketchiest of breakfasts.

'Mrs Hodd, I've eaten an enormous meal,' she said. 'I'd forgotten how wonderful your scones are. I doubt if I'll be able to eat another thing tonight. What time are you expecting Mr Felix?' nerving herself to ask the question calmly.

'He's usually in about half past six these dark evenings, ma'am. I expect you'd rather have your dinner in the breakfast-room as there will only be you and the master?'

The master. So he had turned from Mr Felix into that? Hodd had called him that as well.

She was in her room when she heard him come up the stairs. They would have told him, of course, that she was here and she moved swiftly across to the door and locked it, but there had been no need. He did not even try the handle but spoke to her from the passage.

'Eve?'

'Yes, Felix.'

The sound of his voice saying her name sent her into a wild tumult, and she put her hand to her throat as if something were choking her, but her own voice sounded calm and controlled.

'Mrs Hodd told me you were here. Have you everything you want?'

'Yes, thank you.'

'Dinner will be at half past seven, unless you would like it earlier or later?'

'Thank you. I'll be down by then,' she said and after a pause in which each could feel the other's nearness, she heard his door open and close again.

She had chosen her dress carefully for that night, not an evening gown nor even a cocktail dress, for it was to be no gala occasion, not white like a bride nor black which might conceivably be mourning for lost happiness, but honey-brown, and round her throat the string of pearls given her by her father; and on her finger she wore her wedding-ring. It was loose for she had lost a good deal of weight. It would slip off easily.

Then, pale and wraith-like, with only her bright hair to give her colour, perfectly composed, though she was conscious of a pulse throbbing at her neck, she went down the stairs to meet Felix.

He was waiting at the bottom of them and the quick look of anticipation went from his eyes as they met the calm gaze of her own.

'Hullo, Felix,' she said without warmth.

'My dear,' he murmured, hesitated and then held open the door of the big living-room for her, a room filled with memories.

'It was nice of you to come, Eve. I was afraid I was never going to see you again. There's time for a drink before dinner,' and he mixed the one she usually chose, a little gin and a lot of tonic.

'You wouldn't rather have something stronger tonight?' he asked as he gave it to her.

She shook her head, unable to command her voice at the moment, and took a gulp of the weak drink which helped to restore her confidence. He talked easily about impersonal things that did not matter, and presently she asked him about Granfer.

'The poor old chap died some weeks ago. I told you about it in the last letter you sent back to me. He was disappointed not to see you again, but he sent his love.'

That shook her a little. Perhaps she would have come – but she had not been ready to come then.

'I'm sorry,' she said on a softer note.

'I knew you would be. He was very fond of you.'

'Was he ill? In pain?'

'No. He just said "I'll be taking to the road again", and when I went to call him in the morning, he was dead. Then I moved in here. There didn't seem much point in keeping on the cottage, but he wouldn't have been happy here. Too many things to remind him of the past. Are they reminding you, Eve?'

'Shall we talk about that afterwards, Felix?'

'As you like. The main thing is that you've come back. Are you going to stay?'

'I don't know. That's what we've got to decide. Shall we go in now?'

Conversation over dinner was not easy.

'I see that you've had central heating put in,' she said during a pause which threatened to become painful.

'Yes. It's such an old house that it was a risk, but in these days it would be difficult to sell the place without it.'

'Are you going to sell it, Felix?'

'Possibly. That is for you to decide,' and they were back to the personal and painful again, but when they had finished

224

their meal and were back in the living-room, where now a great log fire blazed on dogs under the vast chimney, he turned to her.

'Now, Eve?' he asked determinedly.

'We've got a lot of things to say to each other, but the first thing to be settled is the question you asked before dinner, which is whether I'm going to stay.'

'Are you?'

'That depends. I don't want to mess up our lives more than they are already. I want to make the best of a bad job, but if I stay, if we try to make a home together – it won't be as your wife, Felix.'

He drew a long breath. He had been prepared for almost anything, but not that.

'You really mean that, don't you?'

'Yes. I've thought about it a lot. I hate divorce and perhaps there's no reason in law for one. I shall never want to marry again, but if you do, I daresay it could be arranged.'

'I don't,' he said shortly.

'Then we can't go on leading this sort of semi-detached life for ever. I don't want it and probably you don't either. I thought we could agree to make some sort of life together. We both love this house, and I am ready and willing to live here with you, to be – friends and companions, sharing our interests, building up something—'

'A façade for the outside world?' he put in bitterly, when she paused.

'You don't want to?'

'I want you back on any terms. I don't want a divorce and I don't want to go on living alone, but what you propose would still give us a semi-detached life. I take it that we are not to be – lovers any more. Is that it? You in your room and I in mine?'

She nodded without speaking. It had been unbelievably difficult, but the place where she kept her heart now housed only a hard, cold stone.

He got up and walked across the room and stood staring out of the window, the prospect no more bleak than his mind.

Did he want her back on those terms? Would it be a life at all?

Then he turned back to her.

'You've changed a lot, Eve. I would not have believed that you could be so unforgiving, so lacking in understanding. After all we've been to each other, can you still believe that I married you for the sake of the money?'

'Why not? The other two would have done.'

'But I *loved* you. I still do.'

She shrugged off his protest with a gesture.

'Love? Don't let's talk of that. I don't feel that way any longer. It all – died, and it won't live again.'

'You're not still thinking of Ellice Grant?'

'No, not now, though I did at first. I know that men are different from women and that that sort of thing is, I suppose, necessary to them. And that is why I want to say something else. If – if I come back on my terms, I want you to feel that – you don't owe me anything in that way so long as you – you don't make it – public.'

'What you are saying is that so long as I leave you alone, I am at liberty to take a mistress, or a succession of them?'

She flushed, flinching at his tone.

'I wanted to – be fair to you,' she said in a low voice, not looking at him, and he gave a short laugh.

'You don't know me very well, do you? Still, I thank you for your permission, and your consideration. I suppose it is what I deserve since you know of the Ellice Grant episode, but that was before I met you. I think, by the way, that it is a fallacy to regard men as different from women, especially nowadays when two world wars and the march of time have taken the shackles off. However, there's no point in pursuing that – or in pursuing this conversation at all at the moment. I did not know why you had come back to me nor that anything of this sort was in your mind, but may I take the night to think it over? I may not want you back in any other capacity but as a wife in every sense of the word. Do you mind if I leave you now? I have several matters which need my attention, but don't be afraid. I shall not attempt to see you again tonight and you need not even lock your door. Good night,' and he walked out of the room without another word or glance.

Eve sat quite still where he had left her. She did not know quite what she had expected, arguments perhaps, attempts to make love to her, expressions of remorse, anything but this cold, calm attitude of needing time to give her proposal consideration. True, he had said that he still loved her, but when she had brushed that aside with scorn, he had not renewed it. He had not even been angry! She had been so sure that he would want her back on any terms, but it seemed that he might not, and yet surely it was she who was guiltless and could dictate the terms? He wouldn't even be living in this house if it had not been for her!

Presently she went up to bed but could not sleep. She heard Felix come up, very late, but he did not even pause at her door, which she had locked.

She was beginning to regret bitterly that she had come. Though she told herself that she had no love left for him and would never live as his wife again, she had not been prepared for him calmly to accept it, if that was what he meant to do.

She had planned it all so differently. Though she had brought with her only the one small case, she had left everything packed up ready to be sent to her. She was prepared to establish herself at Weir House as its mistress, as Felix's wife in every other way but the one thing. She would open the house again, entertain there, make a good life for them both and spend his money wisely and without reckless extravagance. She would help him in his plans for the development of the village for the betterment of its people, and she knew that those plans had included the building of a small factory, suitably sited, to provide work and to stem the drift of the young people away into the overcrowded towns. He had spoken of such things whilst Mrs Belamie had been alive and before there was any thought of his being in a position to carry them out.

It had all seemed so easy and practicable when, through her, he was in that position, and surely he owed her something?

She slept at last and woke late so that on going downstairs, she was told that he had gone out and would not be back until the evening. He was evidently giving her the opportunity of going back to London if she wished. Had he then made up his mind to refuse her offer? It galled and humiliated her.

He came back in time for dinner, after she had spent a lonely day with her own thoughts. He apologised for not having had time to change.

'Not that I've ever troubled about that since I've been alone,' he added.

'I've been thinking over your proposition, Eve, and decided to accept it,' he went on after a pause. 'After all, this is as much your house as mine, perhaps more so, and you have a right to live in it but you could hardly live here by yourself. Also I have my uses and shall continue to look after the estate and your interests. Have you any ideas as to what you want to do? Or want me to do?'

She fought down the lump in her throat which threatened to choke her. Was this Felix talking to her like this, to her, Eve, who had lain in his arms through magical nights, Eve whom he had vowed to love and cherish all their days?

But her pride sustained her now that he had accepted her terms and she could not go back on them.

'I thought we might open the house, entertain perhaps, make new friends.'

'And do a bit of explaining to the old ones? No doubt your fruitful brain will be equal to that. I'll have a hard court laid down in addition to the grass one. You saw that I had had the road widened? We could make it good so that larger cars can use it in comfort, but I'm afraid there is nothing to be done about the cliff path.'

'Oh, don't alter that, Felix!'

She was thinking of the first time she had come to Weir House and had climbed up on a donkey. She had not known any of them then, not Mrs Belamie nor Victor nor Myrtle – nor Felix.

'Just as you like,' he said. 'It's quite picturesque. I had to take down some of the rhododendrons to widen the other road, and shall have to take a few more to have it made good. I have the plan here,' and he took it from his pocket and invited her with a gesture to study it.

228

She bent over it with him.

The new way of life had begun.

From then on, it became possible to live together, sharing the things that did not matter, leaving a world between the things that did. If Felix resented the isolation into which she had thrust him, he never showed it; if Eve found her life unsatisfactory, robbed of everything that had for a brief time made it heaven, she never let him see it. To their small world they were a companionable couple who never quarrelled as all their married friends did at times; but also they never knew the joy of making up.

Eve started entertaining on a small scale but quickly, as the number of their friends grew, on a more lavish scale.

'Can we afford it, Felix?' she asked as her first big dance was mooted.

'Yes, go ahead. It brings in business too. I've got Elling interested in the plans for the factory and he is talking of extending it off his own bat. That means a lot more work for people, and we shall need houses and if we can guarantee the work, we can get help from the council.'

He was indefatigable, working early and late, putting into operation his various schemes for providing work for a village that had been slowly dying under the feudal system imposed on it in Mrs Belamie's time. He spent money on enlarging and improving the farm and put in a capable young man to run it, keeping the main control in his own hands. If he became hard and relentless over the bargains he drove, and insisted on an honest day's work for good pay, he still took time to investigate grievances which, if they proved to be genuine, he was quick to set right. Ruthlessly he condemned and pulled down insanitary and tumble-down cottages and re-housed the occupants, whilst taking care not to destroy the age-old charm of the village, and if the tenants grumbled, as many of them did, they either had to get used to being better housed or they moved out, if they could, to villages where there was neither electricity nor water and they could live in insanitary conditions again.

They were getting richer, but all Eve could do was to spend

the money he made, though he always made a pretence of showing her the plans and consulting her.

Occasionally she raised a protest, as for instance when he said that old Ben Tremarth's cottage would have to come down.

'Oh, Felix, it'll break his heart. Leave him where he is. He can't have long to live.'

'He'll have a lot longer with water out of a tap instead of coming through the roof, and electricity to heat his kiln instead of having to get up two or three times a night to fire it with wood. He'll sell more too.'

'But he doesn't want to. When I tried to buy those beautiful salad bowls the other day, he wouldn't either sell them or give them to me.'

'That's his look-out. The place is infested with rats and all sorts of vermin and it's coming down.'

Eve would not argue with him. She, as well as other people, realized that when he had made up his mind to a course, his will was inflexible.

On the day that the workmen came to Ben's cottage to pull down his kiln and remove his potting wheel, they found the old man lying dead on the pile of old clothes and tattered blankets which he called a bed, and round him were scattered the remains of broken pots, bowls, vessels of every kind, the purpose of many of them being only beauty. Even the delicate little figurines lay smashed to atoms.

The doctor could find that he had died only of senility; the villagers said he had died of a broken heart, and for a time they turned their faces away from Felix when they met him.

Eve did not speak of old Ben to Felix, but when he was buried she sent the most rare and beautiful flowers in the hot-houses for his grave, putting them in a jar which he had given her so that one thing of perfect beauty should remain to his memory. It might well be smashed by hooligans or stolen, but at least she had given what she could.

Felix had nothing to say about Ben's death though it hit him hard. The old man had always been one of his special friends, but he did not feel responsible for what had happened to him. He was only doing his duty, as he saw it, in trying to get him properly and comfortably housed, but he longed for Eve to say something about it, even if she blamed him, so that he could talk about it and justify himself. The episode, small in itself, seemed to have widened the gulf between them and he drew further and further into himself and his narrowing world.

On the very evening of the day when old Ben was buried, they were giving a dance, and the death of an obscure, dirty old villager was not sufficient reason for cancelling it so Eve, sore at heart because Ben had died and, before dying, had destroyed all the beauty he had created, stood to receive her guests as if life were a song.

She was always beautifully gowned, for that was part of what she felt to be her duty to Felix, and tonight she was in a formal dress of apricot brocade, fitted to her slender figure and flowing out in graceful folds to her feet. Diamonds, Mrs Belamie's diamonds, sparkled at her throat and in her ears, encircled her arms and her fingers. She was *en règle*, beautiful, poised, mistress of this great house and hostess to her friends and her husband's. Envious eyes were cast at her. She had everything – youth, beauty, wealth and Felix. What more could heart of woman desire?

She would have liked to wear black, oddly affected by old Ben's death, but Felix did not like her in black and she was always meticulous about yielding to him in things which did not matter.

He had the first dance with her, and then, his duty done, drifted away and presently she saw that he was dancing with Jane Millen-Hayes and had danced with her more than once. Jane had recently come home from her finishing school in Switzerland and was paying a long visit to her brother and sister-in-law, a dainty sprite of a girl with dark, flashing eyes and black hair dressed in the untidy fashion of the day – or Eve imagined she had had it dressed like that though it looked as if she had just come from her bath and had not troubled to do it at all. She was dancing with verve and abandon, at one moment at arm's length from her partner, at the next pressed closely against him and looking up at him with those saucy, provocative eyes.

Eve turned away. She felt slightly sick. Did Felix really like that sort of thing? But he looked as if he did, and he danced again and again with her and he was laughing as her straggling ends of hair were blown across his face by the uninhibited zest of her dancing. He tucked them back behind her ears and said something to her which made them both laugh.

Felix and that girl?

Later in the evening, doing another 'duty' dance with his wife, he told her casually that he had asked people for tennis the next day.

'We might as well take advantage of a probably fine day, though there is always the hard court. That is, if you don't mind, Eve?'

The question was merely perfunctory and polite. When did she ever mind? She was always there, playing the hostess to perfection.

'Who is coming? How many will there be to provide for?' was all she asked.

He told her a few names.

'And the Millen-Hayes, of course, though I don't suppose Freda will play.'

Freda was expecting a baby.

'They will bring Jane, I suppose?'

She watched his face with jealous eyes but it expressed nothing.

'Yes. She plays a rattling good game.'

So he knew at first hand? The girl had never played at Weir House, and he must have played with her, or seen her, at the Millen-Hayes'.

The next day Eve found herself watching them, a perfectly matched pair, Jane as quick as lightning about the court, retrieving seemingly impossible balls, smashing them back into the far corners of the court and drawing from him cries of 'Oh, well played, partner!'

A tournament was hastily arranged which Jane and Felix, playing together, won, and Eve presented them with absurd

232

prizes which he had collected on the spur of the moment, the remains of a cooked duck for Jane, done up with blue ribbons, a large cabbage for him.

'I shall keep it all my life,' she said with a mock-theatrical gesture, pressing it against her heart to the detriment of her white tennis dress.

'In a day or two you won't be nice to know,' he told her, trying to tuck the cabbage into the top of his trousers. 'What about staying to dinner, everybody? Can we rustle something up, Eve?'

There was always plenty of food in the house.

'You're not going to eat my duck,' declared Jane. 'I shall have to go home and change. Look at me! Couldn't you have presented me with a live duck, or at least an uncooked one?'

'I'll run you back and wait for you,' offered Felix. 'What about you, Freda?'

'I should look the same in anything – a lady about to produce an elephant! I'll just put my feet up somewhere if I may, Eve.'

As they were going into the house together, Eve heard Felix's car start. It had a distinctive note. She had not realised until now that she had come to recognise it amidst all the others.

She had not played today, choosing to look after her guests instead, but out of deference to the men who would be in flannels and the women who could not change, all she did when she had conferred with Mrs Hodd was to go to her room to wash and renew her make-up. There was ample provision for guests in the downstairs cloak-rooms.

She stared at her reflection in the glass. Her hair, still in short, burnished curls, had remained neat and unruffled, her skin, faintly tanned after a cold, wet summer, was well cared for, for what else had she to do but look after herself? Her figure had matured a little, but it was to her advantage and her white dress fitted it sleekly.

What could Felix see in that girl with her bunched, untidy hair, her pert face red and perspiring from her exertions, and her shirt and shorts parting company here and there, though she had carelessly dragged them together?

She pulled herself up with a jerk. Surely she couldn't be *jealous*?

It was an unpleasant thought, and unworthy of one who had re-made her life and Felix's to a definite plan, a plan which was working out well and with which she was satisfied.

But as the days went on, and the weeks, and still Jane Millen-Hayes showed no sign of wanting to return to her own home, she knew she could not dismiss this new and growing relationship between Jane and Felix. The Millen-Hayes were frequent visitors to Weir House and numbered amongst their closest friends and Jane came with them, but when she did not, Felix was missing as well. Of course, his work kept him out of the house a great deal, but once, when Eve had gone into the village for a last-minute purchase of something Mrs Hodd needed, she saw them together, Jane getting into his car in which he had obviously been waiting for her. Later they had come back together, Jane explaining gaily that she had happened to see him and had asked for a lift so that she could collect a book which Freda wanted to borrow, a thin excuse and one which she scarcely troubled to make.

What, if anything, was Eve prepared to do about it?

She told herself that she wanted to be fair to Felix, and if he had fallen in love with Jane and wanted to marry her, she could not stand in his way. It seemed incredible now that they had once been passionate lovers, counting the hours to the time when they could be together again. They were now so far apart, not feeling even the warmth of enmity. They were just friends, mere acquaintances almost, each going their separate ways though they shared in the hospitality of the house which was no longer a home, meticulously consulting each other's wishes, always considerate, always polite.

Always *horribly* polite, she thought fiercely.

At last she could bear it no longer. She would give them all the chances they wanted, the chance to become lovers if that was what they wanted, and she felt that she would know if that had happened, though she was sure it had not happened yet in spite of Jane's brazen way of laying claim to him.

'Felix, would you mind if I go up and stay with Marcia for a few days? A week or so perhaps?' she asked him one day.

'No, of course not. It'll do you good – if you don't run into the London fogs at this time of year. Wouldn't it be better for you to take her away somewhere into the sun, if she can get the time off for a holiday?'

'I don't suppose she could,' said Eve and he did not pursue the subject.

'I may be away for a week at least,' she told him when he took her to the station to see her off.

'Stay as long as you like. We've nothing fixed down here which could not be altered. Good-bye. Give Marcia my love,' and as the train left the platform, he turned away.

'To go back to Jane,' she thought bitterly.

When, if ever, would she see him again? She lay back and closed her eyes as if to shut out the thought.

Why should she mind? They had become nothing to each other, less than nothing.

12

Mr pawnsford was in London, and Eve had asked him to come to see her.

'They told me at your office that you were on holiday, but I should be most grateful if you would see me,' she said.

He liked both of the Welbys, but felt that all was not well with them, but when by arrangement he called at Marcia's flat, he was deeply shocked by her statement, made without preamble.

'Mr Pawnsford, I want a divorce.'

'My dear young lady – my dear Eve—' he said.

'You sound surprised, but I think you must have known that Felix and I were not getting on together. The fact is that – we have not been living together as man and wife since I came back to live at Weir House and – I feel it is not fair to him, though he has accepted the position and is no more interested in me, in that way, than I am with him. Our marriage was a mistake and it was too much bound up with money ever to be a real success. You see, he only married me to get the estate and – I was young and silly and fancied I was in love with him, but I wasn't. I want him to be free so that he can marry someone else.'

'Is there someone else? Has he told you so?'

'Not in so many words, but there is. How can I get a divorce? I'm afraid I don't know much about it.'

He frowned and looked distressed. Knowing Felix, he felt pretty sure that there had been no thought of the money in his mind when he married Eve. If ever there had been a man in love, Felix was that man, so what had gone wrong?

'You didn't know, before you married Felix, that he would inherit the Weir estate, did you?'

'No. I was absolutely astounded when I found out. That was some time after we were married. But don't let's go into all that now. What I want is to get a divorce in the easiest and quickest way.'

He wondered if it were she and not Felix who had found someone else.

'Well,' he said slowly. 'The easiest and quickest way, as you put it, is to prove adultery in a case which is not defended, though of course if either of you has refused – er – marital relations—'

'It was mutual,' she put in quickly.

'In these cases, one has to avoid any appearance of collusion you know.'

'You mean that if both of you are unhappy and want a divorce, you can't get one?'

'Yes, I'm afraid that is what it amounts to.'

'How unfair and stupid! That should be the chief reason for granting a divorce.'

'I'm inclined to agree, but I don't make the laws,' he said drily.

'And one of us has got to commit adultery? How – utterly beastly and degrading.'

'You see, divorce is supposed to be a punishment meted out to the wrong-doer, not a reward. You could get it for desertion, of course, if you were prepared to wait for three years.'

'No, I wouldn't want to do that. Neither would Felix.'

'I take it that you have discussed it with him?'

'No, but I know he would agree. We just want to be rid of each other.'

He rose to go.

'Well, think it over again and of course you'll talk to Felix about it before you go any further, which I very much hope you won't. Is your marriage really past mending? Can't you do anything to put matters right? It seems to me you have everything that should make you happy.'

'Except love,' she said bleakly.

'Think it well over, my dear, and come to see me again, or I will come to you, either of you, but don't, I beg of you, do anything precipitate. Time heals most things, you know.'

After he had gone, Eve sat hunched up before the fire, thinking over what he had said.

Adultery! A beastly word, and a beastly thing to do. Would Jane, a modern of the moderns, go through with it? Or would Felix have to do some other even more beastly thing to provide 'evidence', dragging himself through the mud to satisfy some predatory old judge.

Unless she provided the 'evidence' herself?

The thought sent her cringing even lower into her chair, and at that moment the telephone bell rang and she dragged herself up wearily to answer it.

'Eve?'

'Yes.'

'It's Phillip. I happened to run into Marcia this morning and she told me you were staying here, and alone. Could we meet? Perhaps have dinner together for old times' sake?'

Phillip Shawn. It was a long time since she had seen him, but he was the one link with the past and in her increasing loneliness, neither loved nor loving, her mind had gone back many times to the old life, happy and carefree and cherished. Phillip was a part of that life, and the little warmth that crept into her heart sounded in her voice.

'Oh, Phillip, yes. I'd love to!'

'I know you're married, but I don't even know your name.'

She laughed and told him.

'When, Eve? Tonight?'

'Yes, if you like. I'll meet you somewhere. Dress up?'

'Yes, please. I could pick you up, though.'

'No, tell me where to meet you and I'll be reasonably on time.'

She was remembering, with a slight stab of conscience, that Marcia had been in love with Phillip for a long time.

He appointed a time and place, and she left the flat before Marcia came home.

It was a nostalgic evening, with Phillip still obviously in love

238

with her though he did not say so in so many words. She was softer and kinder than she had been, warming her frozen heart at the fire that still burnt for her, though now across the barrier of her marriage.

'Don't come in,' she said when he had brought her to the door. 'Marcia will be asleep,' but she suddenly clung to his hand as if it were a life-line and he bent and kissed her.

'Eve, are you happy?' he asked.

'So-so,' she said, trying to infuse a little gaiety into her tone but without much success. 'I'm an old married woman now, you know. Transports over and all that.'

He was not deceived. To think of Eve not being happy! He had suspected it all the evening. Now he was sure.

'Am I going to see you again? Soon?' he asked.

'I'm a lady of complete leisure.'

'Then – tomorrow for lunch? We could drive out somewhere in the afternoon, unless you have already had too much of the country?'

'How will the stocks and shares get on without you?'

'They'll manage. I have very efficient clerks. One o'clock? May I call for you?'

She nodded and ran up the stairs.

Her week lengthened into a month, then six weeks, and soon it would be Christmas and she would have to say something about her return. Felix had written to her each week, on the same day, and she could imagine that he had a note on his engagement pad, 'Write to Eve', for the letters sounded like a record of business, one partner keeping the other up to date with current affairs, or perhaps even a manager to an employer!

She replied in kind, commenting on the various things he had in hand, the new houses, the purchase of the piece of land for the extension to the factory, the delay in having the new pedigree cattle delivered because of the fear of foot-and-mouth disease.

Factories and foot-and-mouth disease when she was starving for something human and kind! She would not admit to herself that it was Felix for whom she was starving, not the cold, hard man he seemed to have become but the Felix of her honeymoon and of those secret week-ends when she had flown to his arms like a homing bird, sure of her welcome.

Then his letters began to mention Jane. She was evidently still there. He spoke of her only briefly, saying that she wanted him to enter with her for the county hard-court championship, but that he could not find the time. But he would find it, thought Eve jealously, for Freda, writing to her after her baby had been born, said that Jane and Felix were making the most of the weather to get in a lot of practice on the hard court at Weir House. Freda's letter seemed to convey a subtle warning to her to come back, but if Felix wanted Jane, as he certainly did not want her, Eve, then he could have her.

She was adrift in a boat without a pilot and without rudder or anchor.

She turned to Phillip Shawn.

'Phillip, are you still in love with me?' she asked in a strained voice one evening when he had called to take her to a concert, but, not feeling that she could bear the music she loved because it would tear her heart out, she had asked him if he would take her to his house instead.

He had been surprised at the request, for they had never been there since she had returned to London. It was a small, comfortable house and he had an elderly housekeeper to look after him.

'You know I am, Eve,' he said soberly.

'You asked me once if I were happy. You know I'm not, don't you? I – well, I suppose I've left Felix.'

'I'm terribly sorry, dear.'

He would never have spoken of his love for her had she not asked him that direct question. She was married and the daughter of a man he had liked and respected, and as such was sacrosanct to him.

'Do you want me, Phillip? Enough to – marry me eventually?'

'I'd have done anything in the world to be able to do that,' he said very gravely.

'I don't think I'm in love with you. I was with Felix, but now that is all over. I may not be able ever to feel like that

240

again. I don't think you do more than once. "The first, fine, careless rapture" and all that,' with a bitter smile. 'But I'm very fond of you, Phillip, and I think I could make you a good wife, I know all the answers now.'

'But – Eve darling – you are married—'

'I know, but I may as well tell you the whole story now, humiliating though it is. Felix married me because under the terms of his grandmother's Will, if he did, he would inherit the Weir estate. He married me for *money*, Phillip. Now I want to get free from a marriage which, though I did not know it, was sordid from the start.'

Not for the world would she have told him about Jane.

'Oh, Eve, my dear!' he said, shocked and distressed.

'There's only one way. I've seen the lawyer about it. If I am away from Felix for three years, he could divorce me for desertion, but I don't want to wait three years. I'm lonely, Phillip. I want someone to take care of me, to love me. Please – Phillip!'

He could not mistake her meaning and he put his arms about her and held her closely, and when she lifted her face he kissed her lips. Her mouth was unresponsive and she closed her eyes so that he should not read what was in them; but deep in his heart, he knew.

'Darling Eve,' he said shakily, 'I'd do anything in the world to make you happy. You know that. But – is this what you really want?'

She clung to him, hiding her face against him. It was not what she wanted and they both knew it, knew that she could never bring herself to do what was cheap and nasty, betraying all that was finest and best in her. Her silence had answered him, and after a while he gently set her free.

'Let me take you back, darling,' he said, and she nodded but could not look at him.

How many men would have refused what she had offered, refused it for her sake and not for his own? Oh, why, why could she not have loved Phillip rather than Felix? Yet there her heart was fixed and there it would remain.

They were silent until he stood with her at the foot of

Marcia's stairs and then he asked her when he should see her again.

'I don't know. Tomorrow perhaps. I'll ring you,' she said and turned and left him.

Marcia's door was open and the light showing but she felt she could not face her tonight and murmured a good night to her and shut herself in her own room. The reaction had set in and she was between shame of what she had meant to do and relief, in spite of the humiliation of his refusal, that Phillip was the kind of man he was and that he knew her better than she knew herself. Yet how was she to set Felix free as she was determined to do?

In the morning she rang up Phillip as she had promised, but told him she could not meet him that day. Her voice was strained and uncomfortable but when he agreed at once, she felt again that she did not deserve his love and wished with all her heart that she could accept it.

Then she asked Mr Pawnsford to come to London and see her, though she did not know what she was going to say to him. He thought she looked ill but his eyes were remote and stern.

'I want a divorce from Felix as soon as possible,' she told him. 'If necessary, I will provide the evidence, but I don't want to wait the three years unless I must. Is there no other way?'

'I'm afraid not,' he told her shortly, giving her a coldly accusing look. So it was she who wanted to be free for her own purposes? Well, unless she had the courage to incriminate herself, it would not hurt her to have to wait for the statutory period of desertion, and in the meantime she might have learned a bit of sense. All his sympathies were with Felix and after a pause for consideration, he decided that frankness was the best course to pursue. Also Felix had not bound him to secrecy.

'I may be violating a confidence, Mrs Welby, but there is something I think you ought to know. Your husband did not want you to be told until it became necessary. Now I think it is. Immediately after your marriage, even before it became publicly known, Mr Welby came to see me and told me of it and said that he wanted to make a Deed of Gift to you of the entire estate to which he had become entitled by the Will of the late Mrs Belamie.'

She stared at him, bewildered.

'But – but he couldn't do that!'

'He could, and in fact, did. He kept nothing for himself but the cottage which was willed separately, and he has taken only his salary as manager and that, in my opinion, a much smaller one than what he was entitled to in the circumstances.'

'You can't mean that! He – he couldn't possibly—'

She could not go on. She was dumbfounded. Felix had done that! Handed over to her everything that he had stood to gain by the marriage? Robbed himself of the very reason for it? Left himself with nothing in his own right?

'I assure you that he did, Mrs Welby.'

It was 'Mrs Welby' now, not the friendly 'Eve' which she had been to him since her return to Weir House.

'In effect, your husband has been merely your employee, and I need hardly point out to you that he has improved and added considerably to the value of the estate during his stewardship, acting under the Power of Attorney which you signed.'

She remembered that. He had asked her to do it so that she need not be troubled with small affairs and she had laughed and agreed and had thought no more about it.

'So it all belongs to me?'

'Everything.'

They had been standing, but now she dropped down into a chair and sat staring at him in bewilderment.

'But I don't want it,' she cried passionately. 'It belongs to Felix. He must take it back!'

'I suppose it could be done, but it would be very difficult. Felix would certainly not be willing to accept it, especially if you intend to go through with this divorce. I am afraid I cannot advise you on that, as Felix is my client. You understand that if he does not wish to divorce you, there is nothing I can do about it.'

'But he will, he must!'

243

'That is between you and him. I could not possibly step in. I advise you to see him, or at least to write to him. If that is all, I will take my departure, Mrs Welby. I am extremely sorry that this situation has arisen and I can only hope that better counsels will prevail. I wish you good-day.'

After he had gone, Eve sat on bemused, bewildered, angry. How could Felix have put her in this position? How *could* he? It altered the whole circumstances, and did Jane know that if she married him, she would be marrying a poor man? She knew nothing about Deeds of Gift, whether she could have refused it, whether Felix could.

She started to write to Felix, but put all her efforts into the fire. She was not a good letter-writer at the best of times, and now her mind was so muddled that nothing she wrote made sense. She would have to go and see him. Only by talking to him would she ever straighten things out.

The thought of seeing Felix frightened her, and yet, deep down in her mind and unacknowledged, she knew that she wanted to. She could not part from him like that.

Would Mr Pawnsford tell him that she wanted a divorce? That she wanted to give the estate back to him? That she refused to accept it?

Marcia knew that she was desperately unhappy, but had not asked for her confidence and since it was all mixed up with Phillip, she could not tell her. She felt more alone than she had ever been in her life. She did not even tell her the next day that she was going to Weir House, but caught a train soon after Marcia left for her office in the morning.

It was a miserable journey, the tiny stream of comfort being that she was going to see Felix again, even if it were for the last time.

At Helston station, she ran into Toby Millen-Hayes, almost the last person she wanted to see, but it was too late to avoid him.

'Eve!' he said, when she would have slipped by him.

They both felt uncomfortable and he wished he had not stopped her, but it was too late and he made the best of the unfortunate meeting.

244

'You going to the house?' he asked, as if this were an ordinary occasion and he did not know she had been away for weeks. 'Can I give you a lift? I've just been seeing Jane off.'

'Jane? You mean – she's gone away?'

'Yes, at long last. Thought we were never going to get rid of her. You know she's going to be married? Or perhaps you don't?'

This was the culmination of all confusion.

'No. No, I – I didn't know,' she murmured.

He was walking beside her, leading her to his car, taking it for granted that she would accept his offer of a lift, for taxis were not easily obtainable for the ten-mile journey.

He was glad to be able to seize on a topic that was far removed from the embarrassment of anything personal to her.

'She's dithered about long enough, in all conscience,' he said cheerfully. 'Had some sort of a row with him, which is why she's stayed here all this time, but now they've made it up. My mother will be no end pleased about it.'

'Who – who is she going to marry?'

'Kurton Blay, *Sir* Kurton Blay. Man who's been in the papers a lot lately in connection with these take-over bids. You must have read about him? Millionaire probably. Can't think what he sees in Jane,' with brotherly candour, 'but he's crazy about her. Came down last week and settled it with her, and now she's wearing a diamond as big as a saucer and they're all lovey-dovey,' and he opened the car door for her and put her in.

Poor Felix, she thought. Had he really cared for Jane, or was it only that he had been as lonely as she?

A tiny sprig of hope began to grow within her. Might it not be possible for them to re-make their lives, since everything was in such confusion?

She had made no response to Toby's pleasant chatter, had not even listened to it, but suddenly, as they approached the road that led to the house, she stopped him.

'Would you mind putting me down here, Toby? I'd rather walk the rest of the way,' and he was glad enough to do so.

245

It was a queer business, returning like that and without luggage or anything, and he had not been relishing the prospect of probably having to go into the house and meeting Felix at such a moment.

But when the car had gone on, she felt reluctant to go on to the house. She did not know how Felix would receive her, and she needed more time in which to think of the possibilities of the future now that Jane was no longer a factor.

Would it be possible to start again? She knew that it was what she wanted beyond all things, that she still loved Felix and would never be happy away from him. Perhaps he would be willing to make some sort of life with her, or to try it at any rate.

She walked on, taking the familiar way to the cottage without realising she was doing so, until she stopped short. His battered old car was standing in the lane. She understood now why she had never been able to persuade him to part with it, though she had had a smart little coupé of her own.

Softly, her heart thudding, her feet making no sound on the path still muddy from recent rain, she unlatched the gate and walked up the sad-looking garden path between empty flower-beds that had once been Granfer's pride and joy.

The door stood ajar, and she pushed it open. It made a squeaking sound of rusty hinges, but the man sitting with his back to it had not even heard it. He sat in an attitude of profound dejection, his hands on the arms of the chair, his head bent.

She had never seen him like that before. He had a despairing, defeated look. Felix defeated!

A sound like a sob rose in her throat. He heard it when he had not heard the opening of the door, and wheeled round, stared at her as if he had conjured her up out of his thoughts, and then rose unsteadily to his feet.

'Eve,' he said, and then '*Eve?*' as the fact of her physical presence penetrated his mind.

For an instant it seemed to her that his hands had made a gesture towards her, but in the next they had fallen to his sides again.

'I'm sorry,' he said, the impenetrable mask on his face again, his eyes cold and expressionless. 'I didn't know you were coming or I would have been at the house to meet you.'

'I haven't been to the house yet.'

Her throat felt dry. Her body was rigid. If she had let it relax, she knew it would be shaking.

He looked away from her.

'You must not stay here. It's too cold. How did you get here?'

Trivialities were all they could find to talk about yet.

'Toby brought me. I met him at the station. He took me almost to the house and then I walked.'

'How did you know I was here?'

'I didn't know.'

He moved for the first time since he had sprung up out of the chair.

'I'll take you to the house,' he said.

'No, Felix. Not yet. I – I'm sorry about Jane.'

His brows knitted in surprise and perplexity.

'Jane? What about her?'

He's pretending he doesn't care, she thought. Or perhaps he doesn't even know?

'Toby told me. She's gone back to London. She's going to marry Sir Kurton Blay.'

His expression did not change, except to grow more puzzled.

'What of it? What has Jane's marriage to do with us?' he asked, and she knew how idiotic she had been, and that there had been nothing, *nothing*, between him and Jane. The tiny sprig of hope grew in her heart, but his face and his manner did nothing to encourage it. His eyes were as hard as stones, his mouth opening and shutting like a trap merely to let the words out. If it were not Jane, it was certainly not Eve; perhaps not anyone at all. What hope lay in that?

'Has anyone been talking to you about my friendship with Jane Millen-Hayes? This place is a hotbed of gossip but I didn't know it would reach you or that you hadn't more sense. Jane was my tennis partner. Nothing more. And I was doing

247

my best to mend things between her and Blay. That surely isn't what you came to talk about?' with supreme contempt.

Had she ever really believed it, any more than she had believed the story about Ellice Grant? Had she not rather caught at anything which would bolster up her injured pride because when she had come back to him, he had not wanted her nor made any attempt to get her back?

'No,' she murmured faintly. 'I – there were other things—'

'Well, whatever you have to say to me might as well be said here and now, so I'll light a fire,' and she watched him in silence whilst he brought paper and wood and in his efficient way soon had a good fire blazing.

'You may as well sit down,' he flung at her over his shoulder and she sat meekly in a chair.

Had she and this cold-eyed, hard-faced man ever been lovers? Ever known those starry nights of a happiness which would, it seemed, last for ever? Could it have been all make-believe on his part or had he ever loved her? Yet he had made no attempt to win her back when she had been under the same roof, and his, she knew now, for the asking. Proud and resentful she had been, but how easily he could have broken down that pride and resentment!

'I've seen Pawnsford,' he said when he had washed his hands at the kitchen sink and come back to her, not sitting down but leaning against the table. 'I understand that you want me to divorce you. May I know the name of the man?'

'There isn't – I mean—' she said in a low, shamed voice, unable to look at him.

His next question, made her jerk up her head and stare at him.

'Why were you ever engaged to Lewis Belamie?'

'You – you can't believe that this has anything to do with him?' she asked incredulously.

He shrugged his shoulders.

'How am I to know what to believe since you've never told me anything?'

'He lent me money to pretend to be engaged to him, a hundred pounds. I've paid it back, of course. I was in a mess.

I'd never been without money before and hadn't any idea how to manage. I owed money to Marcia and the shops. I'd lost my job and didn't know how to get another and when Lewis offered me this hundred pounds for what I thought was just to be a sort of holiday – well, probably you don't understand. I don't myself now. I must have been mad and then everything turned out so differently. I got to know Mrs Belamie – and – and you, Felix.'

Her voice broke and failed her. She could not look at him or she would have seen that his face had changed and his eyes had softened.

So that was it? His mind flashed back to the time when she had first come to Weir House and he had seen her as she was then, high-spirited, careless, embarked on that idiotic scheme out of which had come the complications, the tragedy which had made her grow up and brought her to this.

Before he could decide what to say, she started to speak again, all her defences down and stark truth between them at last.

'There isn't any other man. There never has been. I love you and always have but as you don't love me, I thought it was the only way I could set you free. Oh – Felix—' and before he could stop her or guess her intention, she had sprung from the chair and run out of the house and down the path, reached his car and flung herself into it.

He had left the keys in it, and though he was after her like a flash, it was too late. The car leaped forward, driven at furious speed down the lane, steering a crazy course. He ran wildly after it, calling to her, but if she heard him she did not stop and the next moment, failing to take the corner, the car crashed into a low stone wall, hung there for an instant and then turned over.

A man working nearby reached the wreckage at the same time as Felix, and between them they dragged her out just before the car burst into flames.

'She's still alive, thank God,' said Felix between white lips. 'Go to the cottage and telephone for a doctor and then help me with her,' and as the man ran off, he gathered her unconscious body into his arms and held her.

'Oh, Eve, my darling, my darling, why did you do it? Why didn't you wait? Why didn't I stop you? My love, my love – open your eyes. Speak to me!'

And as he agonised over her, slowly her eyes opened.

'Felix,' she murmured. 'Felix.'

'Oh, my darling, thank God! Thank God! Don't move. Don't try to say anything,' but she had slipped back into unconsciousness again.

A fencing of hurdles enclosing some sheep stood near. He laid her down with the utmost gentleness and had wrenched one from the ground and when the man came back, they put her on it and carried her back to the cottage and laid her on the floor, his coat folded under her head.

'You got the doctor?' asked Felix, feeling powerless to do any more for her.

'Yes, sir. He'd just come in and he said he would pick up Miss Ford on the way.'

It was no more than ten minutes before he heard the doctor's car, but they were the longest ten minutes of his life. Little moaning sounds came from the injured girl but she was still unconscious and they told him she was alive, and when the doctor had made a cursory examination, they carried her up the stairs and left Emma to get her into the hastily made bed.

'I think she's suffering from no more than shock,' the doctor told them. 'There don't appear to be any broken bones, but I'll have another look at her when you've put her to bed. Do you want any help, Nurse?'

'Help? Me? I'll soon have her comfortable, but the place is very cold, isn't it? I'll have all the hot water bottles you can muster, beer bottles will do, as I don't suppose you've got the real thing here! And as soon as possible, she ought to be got up to the house. You'd better go downstairs again and get a stiff whisky or something, Felix. You look even worse than the patient.'

She showed no surprise at Eve's presence, but she had been greatly exercised in her mind about her long absence and thought that it was high time that she returned to her husband

and her duty. Something had obviously gone wrong again between these two beloved but difficult people, but now that they were thrown together again, whatever the reason or cause, it was to be hoped that they would show a little sense. She meant to keep Eve here as long as she could, for ever if possible.

Whilst she was undressing her carefully, Eve recovered consciousness but looked about her uncertainly.

'Emma? You here? What happened?' she asked faintly. 'Where am I?'

'Where you ought to be, in your husband's home, or one of them. You had an accident with the car, Felix's car, but by a miracle and the mercy of heaven, you don't seem to be much damaged. Can you lift your legs to get into these pyjamas? They belong to Felix. I found them in a drawer and they'll have to do until we can get you home and into something of your own. No pain?'

'No, I don't think so but I feel bruised all over. Emma – where is Felix?' her voice still faint and uncertain.

'Downstairs having, I hope, a strong whisky. He looked as if he needed it.'

Eve lay still and silent as Emma tucked her into Felix's bed.

Was she remembering, or only imagining, his words that had come vaguely through her semi-consciousness?

'My darling,' he had called her, and 'my love, my love'. Had that really been Felix?

She closed her eyes again and did not open them when he came into the room.

'Is she conscious?' he asked in an agonised whisper.

'Yes. You'd better come in. She's asking for you,' and Emma went out of the room and closed the door firmly, a hand on the doctor's arm.

'Leave her for the moment,' she said. 'I fancy her husband is going to be the best doctor.'

Felix came to the bed and went down on his knees beside it and laid his face against Eve's hand.

'My darling,' he said in a shaken whisper.

'Is it really you? Did you say that?'

She still could not believe that it was not just a figment of her imagination, a beautiful dream that would vanish if she opened her eyes.

'Oh, Eve – my love – my little love,' he whispered, and when his lips came to meet hers gently, she knew that it was true.